Sight

A novel by

T.R. Braxton

MONTEBELLO BOOKS

This book is dedicated to Jack Brax, also known as Besowitz Bashoyntin, still my best friend, strongest supporter, and truest critic. Here's looking at you, Jack!

Sight

Book I- Innocence

1

Childe Nathan and the Northward Flight

I.

They came at night, as was their murderous custom. A burning cross illuminated the sinister darkness. Spook hats revealed a cadre of hateful eyes.

They dragged their victim from his house, intent on hauling him to a horrible reckoning. He kicked and screamed curses, bidding his family to turn away. His pride did not allow him to beg.

His pride could not save him.

He spat at his assailants as they marched him off, the gesture expressing his hatred for them and all that they embodied. The butt of a shotgun dislodged three of his teeth, knocking him to the ground.

Hard soled boots launched a vicious assault on his ribs. Two of the curved bones fractured before hateful hands yanked him to his feet.

"I ought to blow your head clean off, nigger," the man whom had struck him with the shotgun snarled.

"Naw you don't, boy," a booming voice disagreed. "This coon don't deserve a quick death. Gonna make him suffer for all the trouble he's been causin'."

Held fast, the black man offered no resistance as he was swept away. Instead, he focused his energy on not crying out during the eminent torture and lynching. No matter how much they hurt him, he wouldn't give the bastards the satisfaction of hearing him cry out.

"There's a tree waitin' for you, nigger," the man with the booming voice taunted. "A tree an' a rope." A hateful chuckle passed his lips. "But first you'll suffer. Gonna make you suffer somethin' awful."

II.

The boy leapt from his sleep, his strange eyes bulging in terror. Seven years on earth had been more than enough time for him to learn that his dreams often forecast an approaching reality. He streaked into the quarters where his Papa and stepmother slept.

No sooner had he entered than Papa sprang up like a man-sized Jack In a Box.

"What is it, boy?" the man grunted, striking the bedside lantern alight.

The trembling boy flew into his father's arms with a force that nearly toppled them both. His stepmother moaned something unintelligible, turning over and claiming more of the cotton blanket for herself.

"What is it, Nathan?" Papa asked again. "Tell me what it is, son."

"They're coming, Pa," Nathan gasped into his father's sinewy shoulders. "They're coming soon."

The man stood the boy up as he got to his own feet. He grasped his son's face as he leaned over so that they were at eye level. The boy's irises shone an ethereal light, as they always did when the sight was working in him.

"Who's coming, Nathan? Who?"

"The sp-spooks," Nathan stammered. "The spooks with the burning cross. They're coming for you, Papa."

James Walker knew then that the night riders had marked him, just as he knew that some poor Colored had identified him as the organizer of meetings among homesteaders. He didn't doubt that the fellow had the secret beaten out of him.

James knew that word was bound to get out, sooner or later. He'd figured on being picked up by the local authorities and thrown into jail as a rabble rouser.

He hadn't figured that the night riders would come for him. He had no idea that the Klan was poised to ride again. The original spooks in sheets had been suppressed by the government when he was but a small boy. He had no clear memories of its actions, only terrifying accounts that his father had shared with him as a youth. James's father wanted him to be able to instantly recognize if such a threat ever arose again. Well, now it seemed to have done so.

If it wasn't for Nathan, James wouldn't have known until it was too late. Once again, the power within his young son both amazed and scared him. But the boy's ability was not nearly as terrifying as the prospect of falling prey to the new night riders. The legacy of their forebears preceded them, leaving no doubt about what they were capable of.

"When are they coming, son?"

Nathan's visage twisted in deep concentration. He closed his eyes, placing a small brown hand on his forehead. He swooned before managing to steady himself. His eyes popped open.

"Tomorrow night, Papa," he gasped. "They're coming for you tomorrow night."

III.

It was a cold January night in 1902, at least cold by Alabama standards. A young Negro woman writhed in a rickety bed, using every bit of strength she had to push her child into the world.

A midwife leaned over her, dutifully applying a cold compress to her fevered forehead. The woman's husband waited outside the birthing room, feeling helpless against her tortured screams. His murmured prayers belied his sense of hopelessness.

The roar of an approaching motor and the sight of automobile lights interrupted his pleas to the Lord. He rushed to the door of the small farmhouse.

The man who exited the beast of a vehicle carried a huge, weathered satchel. There was a regal air to his walk.

"In here, Doctor Woodson," James Walker said to the graying, bespectacled man whom he hoped to be the salvation of his wife and soon to be child.

Woodson was the only white doctor in the county known to treat Negroes, even if they did have to come through the back door of his office at irregular hours. James had never forgotten their first encounter, when Helen was just a few months along in her pregnancy.

"I'm hardly a champion of the Negro cause," Doctor Woodson had remarked. "I just realize that whether it passes from a white hand or brown, money's just as green."

James's mind crashed back to the urgent present as he hurried Dr. Woodson to the birthing room. "Helen's bad," he said. "You have to help her."

"I'll do the best I can," Dr. Woodson's tone was solemn as they reached the parlor that had been transformed into a makeshift birthing area. "You'd best wait out on the porch."

It was the second time that James had been made to wait elsewhere since his wife's labor began.

The midwife had earlier instructed him to wait in the hall on account of his presence only helping to overexcite his wife. Now, Dr. Woodson wanted him outside of the house altogether.

"I won't leave my home while you cut on my wife," James argued.

"You will leave, because I am her doctor and I am telling you what's best for her," Woodson growled. "It's also what's best for you!"

Against his own desire, James exited to the porch. As he sat in his big chair, he realized how bitterly cold the night air had become. That detail would burn itself into his memory, never to be forgotten.

IV.

James did not bother to be gentle or polite as he shook his second wife awake.

"What is it?" she grumbled, rubbing her eyes.

"Damn, woman. You could sleep through a Texas Twister. Couldn't you?" He frowned. "Well you have to get up, now."

"What for, James? It's the middle of the night?"

"No time to explain, woman! We have to pack."

"Pack for what?" Naomi sat up beneath the bed covers, noticing Nathan for the first time.

"What are you doing in here, Nathan?" she grimaced.

"He saw something. He came in here to warn us," James answered. "Now when I say we have to pack- we have to pack!"

V.

A sea of blood coated Dr. Woodson's garments.

"Worst breeched birth I've ever seen," he spoke solemnly, placing a hand on James's shoulder as he stepped onto the porch. "I had to do a caesarian. I'm sorry, James. These things don't usually end in death. But your dear Helen's body just couldn't stand the ordeal."

James gasped and fisted his hands before placing his right hand over his left breast. He headed inside, on a beeline for his liquor cabinet. He eviscerated a tall glass of brandy in two long swallows.

Nightmares of this very scene had besieged James for months, nightmares that were no false harbingers. Helen had been sick for most of her pregnancy. James had spent hours beyond number hoping that she would come through the birth intact, but he wasn't at all surprised that she didn't.

Surprise or not, the pain was still bitter. The sense of loss was acute, final.

A second glass of brandy insured James's composure. He'd allow himself to weep for his lost wife later. His newborn child awaited him.

"I want to see my child." He headed for the birthing room, stirred by the wailing sounds of new life.

Doctor Woodson stepped in front of him. If he had been Colored, James would have moved him aside, but even his misery did not stop him from remembering not to touch a white man.

"I want to see my child," he repeated in a listless tone.

"Not with your lost wife in there," Dr. Woodson urged. "It will be too much for you, James."

"I want to see my wife, too," James sighed. "I want to kiss her goodbye."

"Very well." The doctor stepped aside, grabbing James's arm as the widower opened the door. "But first, there's something about the child that bears warning."

VI.

The April sun yawned, opening its' eyes after a restful sleep. James Walker and his wife finished loading their bedroll onto his carriage. His young son helped with the smaller items.

James soon guided a pair of young horses from his seat behind them. The muscled legs of the steeds were due to transport the family on a number of stops this day.

Their first stop was in the cornfields on their own property. James brought the carriage to a stop and stepped down. "Hezekiah!" he yelled into the yellow and green sea. "Hezekiah?"

A sweating, well-muscled man soon emerged from among the stalks. He wore a straw hat. "How are you, boss?" the man asked.

James laughed. "How many times do I need to tell you, Zeke? I'm not your boss. You're an independent agriculturist operating on my land."

Hezekiah grinned. "I'm a sharecropper," he said. "A sharecropper on your land. I reckon iss a sight better than bein' on some peckerwood's land, though."

"Ain't it the truth?" James extended his hand, enjoying an uncharacteristic slip into improper English. "Listen up, Zeke. I have a proposition for you."

VII.

The discarded caul was membranous and slick, the texture of a wet snake skin. The veil, as superstitious people referred to it, was not what mortified James. The Deep South teemed with tales of such a birth portending clairvoyance and other types of fantastic powers. But James was an educated man, his father having been one of the first Negroes to own land in Butler County. Four years at Tuskegee College had forged a man of reason, so James didn't keep with such backward superstitions.

He knew that the presence of a caul on a newborn's head was a natural, if rare occurrence of childbirth. What mortified him was what the veil covered.

He resolved to kiss his dear Helen goodbye before granting his full attention to the strange newborn. She lay still on the pallet, a beatific smile fixed on her face. Her still eyes stared toward heaven.

James did not doubt that heaven had claimed his beloved wife. Nor did he doubt that she'd gone willingly, pleased that her earthly work was done. He took the child they had created together from the young midwife, knowing that his earthly work had just begun.

VIII.

Having settled matters with Hezekiah, James next exited the carriage outside of a rustic two-story home. He marched to the front door, pounding on it as if trying to force it in. To his surprise, a plump, grim-faced woman answered. "What do you want?" she asked, placing her hands on her hips.

"Good day to you, Emma Jean." James smiled, trying his hand at charm in the face of this unexpected circumstance.

"I said whatchu want, James?" Emma Jean hissed. "Oh, I know! You want to see Julius. Don't you? Well, that won't be happenin' seein's how he's locked up at the county jail."

"The county jail?" James's eyes bulged. "What for?"

"On account a rabble rousin an' bein a public disturbance." Emma Jean's bronze face turned a deep crimson. Her neck bobbed back and forth like a chicken's. "On account a havin' meetins with the likes of you. Now, git the hell off my porch."

Emma Jean stalked into her house and slammed the door shut.

James realized that Julius would have been out of jail if he had given James up. He supposed he owed old Julius an apology if he ever saw him again. The man had more steel than he'd thought.

But if not Julius- then whom? Twenty two homesteaders had met with him in the old barn, seven of them Colored. James didn't think the authorities would dare to violate a white Anglo-Saxon's right to peaceful assembly by brutalizing him. That left six others to choose from, at least one of whom had given him up.

James wanted to face his betrayer before he left Alabama for good. He wanted the bastard to know that his weakness might have cost James his life.

IX.

Once the caul was removed, thick folds of skin that engulfed the newborn's eyes were exposed.

"I've never seen anything like it," Doctor Woodson spoke in a reverent tone. "I've heard of such occurrences, but in twenty seven years of medical practice, I've never seen it for myself."

"Can anything be done?" James clutched the now silent baby to his breast.

"There must be an operation, of course," Doctor Woodson said. "I will not be the one to perform it. I will have an esteemed colleague visit you from the hospital staff in Greenville. He is at the vanguard of modern opthalmology."

"Do you think that the surgery might harm him?"

The doctor shook his head. "Either he'll be blind or he will see. That is not much of a risk, for he is already blind."

X.

James found the man whom had betrayed him at his fourth stop.

Sitting in his parlor, John Avery looked worse for wear. His right eye was badly bruised and swollen almost completely shut. His bottom lip was purple and looked fit to burst. There were splints on the pinky and index finger of his left hand.

Despite the brutal treatment his erstwhile ally had received, James couldn't help thinking that John looked a lot better than James would look if he remained in Butler County come nightfall. John's wife treated James to a hostile glare before leaving her husband alone with him.

James fought back a chuckle, amused by his newfound popularity with his friend's wives. "Sheriff Allen do that to you?"

John nodded. "Him an' his deputies." He picked up a washcloth lined with ice and pressed it to the swelling over his eye. "They rounded us all up. All the Coloreds't attended that meetin'."

"They got no legal right to do that."

John grimaced. "Yeah? Try tellin''em that when they come for you."

James furrowed his brow, staring daggers at the beaten man. "What makes you think they're coming for me?"

John bowed his head, letting the hand that held the washrag rest on the table before him.

"I....," he stammered. "I- I jus' figgad they'd round up everybody who was at that meetin'. I jus' figgad that."

"You jus' figgad that?" James snarled, voice barely above a whisper. "You jus' figgad that or you know? You know because you gave everyone up." He pointed an angry finger. "And you named me as the ringleader!"

John looked up. "What was I supposed to do? Stay in that jail? Take more beatin's?"

James bellowed, pounding the table with both hands. "I would've gotten you a lawyer when I got wind of it! I would've gotten you out."

" 'N when would that a been? After two or three more days a me gittin' beat on 'n starved? After two or three more days a me not even bein' given nothin' ta scrub the filth off maself wit'?"

James took a deep breath, flattening his palms on the table. "It would've been good for the cause in the end."

"What cause? Ownin' land free 'n clear in Butler County? I got news for you, most Colored ain't fortunate enough to be born into land ownership. Most Coloreds are lucky if they inherit a chicken an' a decent pair of britches."

"You think I don't know that?" James shouted, leaping to his feet. "You think I don't know how damned fortunate I am? That's why I try to help my fellow homesteaders win the same privilege I have. But I guess you and I aren't fellows after all."

John grunted as he got to his own feet. A defiant expression emerged on his battered face. "No, sir. I guess we ain't. We ain't fellows. An' you kin shove your cause directly up your hindquarters."

John's wife reappeared, placing caring hands on her husband's shoulders as she helped him back into his seat. She fixed James with accusing eyes.

"My husband cain't take too much excitement in his condition, Mr. Walker."

James picked his hat up off the table and straightened it on his head.

"Not to worry, Mrs. Avery," he matched her formal speech. "I'm going now."

He stepped past his grudging hosts and exited the parlor. He paused on the sliver of floor just before the living room and spoke without turning.

"Just so you know, John. They weren't going to arrest me. They were coming to kill me, tonight. They were coming to kill me because they know that without me around the rest of you Coloreds will never put up the fight you need to put up to gain what's rightfully yours. I hope your injuries heal up nicely."

James didn't wait for a response. After all, he had another very important stop to make.

XI.

Doctor Gabriel Addison was the most renowned opthalmologist in the small pool of Alabama surgeons. James could tell that the esteemed gentleman viewed the impending operation on Nathan as a grand opportunity.

James saw the operation as a no lose circumstance for the Doctor. If the procedure proved unsuccessful, the man's profession would hardly strike a black mark against him. After all, harming a Negro baby was nowhere near as upsetting as harming a white child.

On the other hand, the successful completion of such an operation would surely bring Addison international renown in his field. A feat of such magnitude would render the patient's ethnicity moot and validate the performance of future procedures on white patients.

Baby Nathan was only a month old when the operation date was set. He had spent that time in unrelenting darkness. Silence and stillness were his arms, embracing the black void that surrounded him.

Nathan's activity was so minimal that at times it seemed as if he didn't realize he had left the fluidic cave of the womb. He only complained when he was hungry. Even then, he managed only low-pitched sobs. Infantile giggling was rare, as was the playful movement of his tiny limbs.

James's gratitude for Nathan's survival was tempered by the acute sense of loss he felt for his departed wife. He wasn't confident that the coming surgery could help Nathan, but he agreed to the procedure because he did not want his child to live a life of darkness. James felt certain that his beloved Helen would have shared that sentiment.

Everything James had ever strived for and all that he believed about right and wrong paled in comparison to his desire for his son to see. He decided that if the

Good Lord would grant him the boon of Nathan's sight, he wouldn't ask for anything else as long as he lived.

XII.

"What do you mean only 700 dollars is available?" James said, scowling. "I have 1100 dollars invested in this bank! I earned every red cent of that money. Why is the entire amount not available?"

Sweat dappled the brow of the Colored clerk who faced James's ire. He was a small man, with close cropped hair and immense spectacles. ""I'm very sorry, Mr. Walker. I can assure you that the entire amount will be available in a few days."

"I don't have a few days!" James banged on the square desk that separated them. "I leave town today!"

"We could wire the remaining balance to your destination," the clerk suggested, his voice shaky. "That's the best that can be done on short notice."

James exploded into laughter. He slapped his knees and nearly fell from his seat. "I do apologize," he straightened up, voice and mannerisms aping an embarrassed southern belle. "I suppose I should have given you advance notice so that you could have all of my money ready for my use. After all, this is a Colored bank. I most certainly should have known better."

The clerk's cheeks flushed as he lowered his eyes. "It's the best we can do, sir."

James returned to his own voice, managing to keep it low and even. "I suppose it will have to do. Only do me one favor."

"Sir?"

"Look me in the eyes when you're causing me one of the worst inconveniences of all my days on God's green Earth!"

Minutes later, James left the bank with seven hundred dollars in hand. He wasn't pleased about waiting for the rest of the money to be wired to his destination, but he couldn't stay until it become available. Four hundred dollars was a large sum of money, but a dead man could not spend it.

XIII.

James didn't care that the cost of Nathan's surgery and aftercare had devoured a large slice of his savings. Nor did he care about being herded into the Colored entrance of the hospital, like some thief in the night. He only cared that Dr. Addison proved as skilled as advertised. He only cared that his boy could see.

Baby Nathan had the strangest eyes. The tiny pupils were green, which was unique enough in itself. Still, the irises outdid the pupils. They were hazel save for the outer edge, which formed a thin green ring. James couldn't help thinking that they were as ethereal as a cat's eyes at nighttime. As strange as his son's eyes were, he did not consider for a moment that they signified anything mystical or supernatural.

Naomi, the young midwife whom James decided to keep on as a nanny, once made a passing reference to such a possibility.

James's response was as deliberate as it was harsh. "As someone who is quite skilled at what she does and has had an intimate bond with my child and late wife, I would enjoy continuing to employ you, Naomi. But I'm not certain that will be possible if you insist on speaking of such nonsense."

Naomi hastily agreed to keep any future notions of the like to herself. She didn't know that James lacked even the slightest inclination to make good on his warning since he didn't see how he could get along without her.

Business was James's strong suit, not caring for a newborn. He was a merchant and something of a farmer, although he rented out most of his generous acreage to Colored sharecroppers. He was also something of a crusader for increased opportunities among the Colored in his home county. He raised and donated money to keep the schoolhouse for local Negro children open, among other endeavors.

James's time with the boy would come when he grew bigger. For now, he would defer to Naomi in any child nurturing matters that didn't involve silly superstitions. For a better than customary wage, she cared for the baby, fed and bathed him. She also cleaned house and cooked good food.

Having Naomi around freed James to concentrate on a man's duties. In many ways, having Naomi around was almost like having a wife. Not that anyone could replace Helen. The pain of Helen's loss was a tireless hound on James's trail. Holding the baby they created in his arms was the only thing that truly brought James peace.

He'd kiss Nathan and murmur to him. "Your mother gave her life to create something so beautiful. Yes, she did. Your mother gave her life for you, you beautiful boy."

Nathan always laughed when James kissed him, regarding his father with those beautiful, mysterious eyes. The crystalline wells of those eyes always left James content.

XIV.

The persistent locomotive chugged along its track, causing the only slice of earth Nathan had ever known to shrink further and further from view. He, James, and Naomi were the only passengers in the Colored car.

While Nathan marveled as a child enjoying his first train ride should, James grumbled at the spare quarters he and his young family were confined to. Jim Crow is a rotten son of a bitch, he thought.

The Colored Car was the rearmost car of the train and the mobile equivalent of a dank cellar. Its musty smell offended James's nose. He felt bilious resentment of the knowledge that the Colored porters were sure to tend to the dining needs of he and his family last. James longed for the days when Jim Crow would lose its stranglehold on the Colored community. He believed that longing without action was senseless, so he took action often.

His boldest maneuver in pursuit of social change had been mobilizing the twenty-two homesteaders whom had met at his home two nights ago. He had felt encouraged by the fact that fifteen of the attendees were whites of low station. James believed that a white man without his own land was almost as bad off as a Negro. He also believed that if such white man were smart, they would stand with Negroes in pursuit of bettering themselves.

Each of the gathered homesteaders faced staunch opposition from the government and banks of Butler County. Under the Homestead Act of 1862, the terms of land acquisition were quite clear. A man could move in on unclaimed acreage, improve upon it for the overall good of the local jurisdiction, and submit a completed application for ownership of that land. There was no provision in the act to exclude Negroes or families whom lacked community standing. Yet, the county bigwigs up in Greenville actively blocked the approval of homestead claims for such men.

It didn't take Sherlock Holmes to figure out why. The politicians and bankers were in bed together. They wanted to snatch land away from would be homesteaders so they'd be free to sell it to the federal government or develop some cash cow of an investment, such as more gambling houses.

James had inherited his own land from a father who'd been gifted by his former master after Emancipation. James was relentless in galvanizing the struggling homesteaders, wanting to see others gain what had been his birthright. During the meeting, they all agreed to pool their resources to hire legal counsel.

That was before the sheriff and town magistrate cooked up bogus charges of public disturbance and arrested all of the Negroes who'd attended (save for James). Other than that Judas John Avery, James expected the rest of the arrested to be released today. The plan seemed to be to have them out just in time to see what became of men like James. Well, all they would see now was the dust from his proverbial tracks. James hoped to be wrong in his belief that the sharecroppers lacked the steel to see the fight through without him around.

James believed that many of the men whom intended to string him up come nightfall were county officials by day. The sheriff and his deputies probably had spook hats in their closets as well.

After all, the original incarnation of the Klan had been birthed by such leaders. James's father had told him that, just as he'd told him that the pastime of such men was hateful violence.

James wished that he could have stayed in his home on the outskirts of Greenville, but he knew that was no longer possible once Nathan described his vision of the night riders. James had come to know long ago that young Nathan's sight rarely erred.

XV.

"I do appreciate all your help around here," James said, smiling at Naomi.

"It's my pleasure, Mr. Walker." Naomi flashed two rows of pearls back at him. It took James a while to notice, but he now realized just how pretty she was.

She reached to clear his finished dishes from the dinner table. James sprung from his seat and seized them from her. "No, let me get those."

"You gon' to do my job for me, now, Mr. Walker?" Naomi asked, looking concerned.

"Your job this evening is to accept a humble demonstration of my appreciation," James spoke over his shoulder, clanging the dishes into the sink. He turned and motioned toward the table. "I want you to have a seat, Naomi."

The young woman's eyes shifted into surprised circles. "Mr. Walker, I cain't...."

James furrowed his brow. "You're still working for me, correct?"

Naomi nodded.

"Very well, then. Your last duty for this evening is to sit and allow me to serve you some of the delicious food you have prepared. Surely you don't intend to be insubordinate to your employer?"

"No, Mr. Walker." Naomi smiled, bemused. "I don't intend to be insubordinate."

She settled into a seat at the large dining table. James heaped a plate of tasty vittles and sat it before her. He poured her a tall glass of sweet tea before seating himself across from her.

"I know you must be hungry, as hard as you work around here." He looked into her eyes. "I know you have a time with my boy."

Naomi blushed. "He's no bother, Mr. Walker," she said, pushing at the food with her fork. "I'm awfully sweet on him, to tell the truth."

"Yes." James smiled. "He's quite the boy. I'm so glad he's turned out healthy. You know with the way he was born...."

"I know," Naomi interrupted him. "It's a blessing. He's a blessing."

James stood up and poured himself another glass of tea. He cast a long glance at Naomi as he returned to his seat. Her eyelids fluttered as her pupils fled to the table.

"Why do you look at me that way?" she asked.

"I look at you that way because I'm seeing you for the first time."

Naomi laughed. "I do believe somethin's gittin' into you tonight, Mr. Walker."

James shrugged. "I do believe you're right." He smiled. "Is that bad?"

Naomi's pupils ceased their flight and met his. "It doesn't seem bad, I guess. I just don't know if it's proper."

James shifted in his seat. "Don't be alarmed, Naomi. I'm just a lonely widower, in need of some conversation. Would you be kind enough to indulge me with some?"

"Alright." Naomi sat her fork down. Her hands formed a brown tent in front of her untouched plate.

"Damn, girl. You don't eat and talk at the same time?"

"Not on this occasion, I don't."

James laughed and slapped the tabletop. "Alright, then." He cleared his throat. "So tell me a little about yourself."

She shrugged. "There ain't much to tell."

He cocked an eyebrow. "Surely there must be volumes."

Naomi took a deep breath and leaned back in her seat. "Okay, well – I been reared to midwife from a young age. I learned from my mother and aunt. They learned from my grandmother. They say she got free around 1850. Passed down midwifing as a skill that will always be needed."

James sighed. "I should've figured it was a family skill," he said. "You were so good to my wife. You're so good to my child."

"Thank you." Naomi unleashed a smile that could guide ships to shore. "You know I'm going to school next year? Been savin' up for it. Gon' be licensed. Then I might really be able to make a decent living at it. White women and Colored gon' line up for my services. That's what I hope for, anyway."

"Hot damn, Naomi," James exulted. "I love to hear a Colored person with a plan. I think that's the only way for the Negro race to progress. Through plan and action. You know, I feel almost embarrassed that we haven't talked like this before. Here you've been kind enough to stay on a year after my son's birth. You've looked after him expertly, cooked and cleaned like an angel– and I've never really talked with you."

"Well, I don't know how kind it is, Mr. Walker." Naomi held her palms out in front of her. "You do pay me well, after all."

"I guess I do." James tapped the tabletop. "Still, I appreciate everything you do. And it's nice to talk with you." He stood up. "I think I've kept you from your dinner long enough. I'm going to look in on, Nathan."

He began to walk away before stopping in his tracks. "Oh- and Naomi?"

"Yes, Mr. Walker?"

A broad smile engulfed James's features. "I hope we can talk again some time."

Naomi's face flushed as she grew a smile of equal measure. "That would be fine by me, Mr. Walker."

XVI.

"Papa." Nathan tugged at his father's arm. "Do we have far to go now?"

James rubbed the boy's coarse crop of hair. "We don't have far to go on this train, Nathan. We're maybe an hour from Atlanta. That's a bigger city than you've ever seen. We don't have time to sight see, though. We're just going to change trains to one that's heading North."

"We're going to Baltimore. Right, Papa?" Nathan whispered. "We won't have to worry about spooks in sheets there."

James nodded. "That's right, boy. I'm going to strike it big in business there. There are far more opportunities for Colored men further north. Who knows, in a few years we might do well enough to move on to New York."

Nathan closed his eyes and leaned back in his seat. "We won't need to go to New York, Papa," he said, opening his eyes a few moments later. "Baltimore will be just fine."

James clouted his son upside the head. "What have I told you about abusing your talent, boy? I told you, it's wrong to get an unfair advantage in life."

"James," Naomi complained, diverting her attention from the landscape passing in the Colored car's single window.

James leaned toward her and whispered in her ear. "Don't challenge me on this, woman. I don't want him misusing what he was blessed with."

She responded with her own whisper. "You don't want him misusing it or you don't want him using it at all? Just remember that without his blessing, this might have been your last night on earth."

James fell silent, trumped by the simple truth that had passed his wife's lips. Still, he didn't want to encourage the boy to summon his sight at random.

Nathan had lost the only person who might've taught him proper use of his gift before he was old enough to reap the full benefits of the tutelage. Now it was left to his father and stepmother to mold him. But how could the ordinary mold the extraordinary?

Just moments ago, the boy predicted that they would do just fine in Baltimore. James closed his eyes and said a silent prayer for his son's unbidden forecast to prove correct.

XVII.

"What's the matter?" James asked.

Naomi sighed. "I think I've gone and made a big mistake," she said.

James placed a sinewy arm around her, pulling her naked torso into a spooning position.

"You call what we just shared a mistake? That doesn't do much for my ego."

"It's a mistake if I expect to be courted," Naomi muttered into her pillow.

"Well, now. I guess that's true. Thing is, I don't intend to court you."

"I knew it." Naomi pushed his arm away, revealing a furious visage when she turned to face him. "Listen- I'm no strumpet! I'm not here for a cheap thrill."

James smiled then. It was a kind smile, bereft of guile. As much as she wanted to, Naomi could detect no cruelness in it. If she had, if would have been easier for her to storm off in a huff and retain what little dignity she had left.

"I know you're no strumpet, Naomi." James dared a quick peck of her lips. "I could tell you haven't traveled that road too many times before."

Her face plummeted, embarrassed. "S-so you didn't enjoy it?"

James responded in the most earnest voice he could summon. "Hell yes I enjoyed it, Naomi. I felt like you were sharing something very precious with me. And you can't be a strumpet, because I'm far too smart to fall in love with that sort."

Naomi gasped, placing her right hand over her left breast. She cast a prolonged stare into his eyes. She did not glean even a tiny hint of deception in his returned gaze.

"Don't toy with me," she warned.

"I don't mean to toy with you, Naomi." James accomplished the uncanny feat of flashing a broader and kinder smile than he had before. "And I don't mean to court you. Why waste time with formalities when we could hurry and get married? That is- if you'll marry me. Will you marry me, Naomi?"

Naomi jumped out of bed and stood stock still, in naked, nubile glory. Her hands covered her face as if she were a child afraid of the dark.

James took two slow steps toward her, removing her hands from her face and pulling her into a tender embrace. "Please say yes, Naomi. Please say yes."

"Yes," she sobbed into his chest. "Yes!"

They danced around the bedroom, hand in hand, naked as newborns. They were married two months later.

XVIII.

James breathed a sigh of relief while boarding the train in Atlanta. Naomi squeezed his arm, no doubt sharing the same unvoiced sentiment.

Hezekiah had driven them the fifty miles from Greenville to Montgomery to board the previous train. The married couple had been worried that the authorities of Alabama would apprehend them at the Bessemer or Birmingham stop- that James wasn't safe from the trumped up charges which had landed the homesteaders in stir. James could have stomached cooling his heels in jail for a worthy cause, but he was certain that his fate would be much worse than an arrest if his adversaries got their hands on him.

James felt much safer as the train from Atlanta headed north. In five hours, they'd change to another train in Columbia, S.C. He hoped to sleep as that one chugged through the night, ending its long route in Baltimore.

James couldn't wait to arrive. Maryland might technically be a southern state, but it wasn't the Deep South. It was far different from Dixie.

James's cousin Virgil had told him as much years ago, when he'd first tried to convince James to come north through written correspondence.

"You ought to sell off that old farmland and come up to Baltimore," Virgil wrote. "You could do better in business up here, for sure. And you wouldn't have to worry about no peckerwood trumping up a reason to throw you in jail or swing you from a tree."

James had passed up his cousin's invitations for years, choosing to pursue change in the Deep South. Though he was aware of how unsafe his immediate surroundings could be for Negroes, he never truly feared being lynched or wrongfully incarcerated. He felt entitled to a kinder fate- especially considering that the cost of his land inheritance had been losing his parents as a young man.

James had always figured that if he fought for right the right way, things would eventually work out as he wished. In the wake of Helen's death, he became more and more determined to further the cause of Colored folks. He became obsessed with it.

He had lost Helen in childbirth only a few years after losing both parents to tuberculosis. The twin tragedies served him as a cruel lesson about the frailness and temporary nature of life. Those who are here today could be gone tomorrow. With that harsh lesson stained into his soul, he decided that he ought to have more than what the racist structure of American society deemed his privilege. Perhaps his strongest belief in life was that other Coloreds and whomever else society deemed to keep trampled underfoot should also have more.

James now knew that his incessant pursuit of such beliefs would have led to a violent death, had it not been for the boy. What a boy he was. Watching the fruit of his loins stare out the window from his train seat, James ached with love for him. James wished it hadn't been necessary to chide Nathan during the previous train ride, but he didn't want his son turning into some sort of sideshow who called on his abilities all the time. There was nothing to be done about the occasions when the sight just seized hold of the boy, but he didn't want Nathan abusing something no science or scripture could explain.

James smiled in bittersweet fashion, allowing himself some overdue relaxation. He scooted over to his son, sharing a view of the big window. He mused that this train's Colored car was much less shabby than that of the previous one. Perhaps a dozen other Negroes shared its space. James surprised himself with the ability to share Nathan's undiluted amazement while digesting the rapidly passing landscape. Scenes of towering, verdant forest and fantastical wetland passed before them. Nature's wonder was only slightly intruded upon by the smoke stacks of industrialization. America was a beautiful country.

A great swell of excitement swept James's dread aside. He felt full with the certainty that he would still have all the opportunity he craved- just not in the state of his birth. Baltimore awaited him.

If Virgil spoke true, Baltimore was a place where James could pursue his ambition without the worry of being dragged off by hateful spooks in the dead of night. James had never known Virgil to be a liar.

XIX.

Nathan was just a few months past his second birthday when he first showed signs of the sight.

"Horse hurt, Papa," he spoke during breakfast, nibbling on a piece of sausage that Naomi had cut small for him. The pleasant spring sun shone through the kitchen window, giving an ethereal glint to his already fantastical eyes.

"What are you talking about, boy?" James smiled, scooting his own chair closer to Nathan's wooden high chair.

Nathan swallowed the sausage before lifting his drinking cup to his lips. He sucked at its nipple with pleasure before setting it down. "Horse hurt, Papa," he repeated. "Horse hurt, today. The big horse."

James's smile twisted into a frown. "I don't like that, Nathan. That's not a good joke."

Nathan looked across the table at Naomi. It seemed to her that his eyes betrayed a depth of awareness that was impossible in such a tiny child. She had never dismissed the circumstances of his birth as mere physical anomaly. Unlike her husband, she didn't think that education precluded superstition.

"Horse hurt, Mama. Horse hurt."

"Yes, baby," she responded.

"Yes, baby?" James bellowed. "Surely you're not going to encourage such behavior, Naomi."

He stood up and pushed his chair in. "Nathan, I know you're little more than a baby, but you are an exceptionally smart boy and it's never too early to learn that although we may think certain things are funny, they just aren't acceptable. After you finish breakfast, I want you to go to your playpen. Without toys, of course. You are to remain there for one hour."

Nathan waited in his assigned location while Naomi approached James in the corridor between the living room and the kitchen.

"I wonder about you sometimes," she whispered.

"What would you have me do?" James matched her volume, peeking at Nathan over her shoulder. The still tot stared at the floor. "He has to learn that that sort of thing is not acceptable."

"Acceptable?" Naomi somehow managed to maintain her whisper and yell in the same breath, her whisper voice quaking with frustration. "James, you speak as if he was a young man already."

James whisper-shouted right back. "And you speak as if everything he does is a ray of sunshine."

"Isn't it?" Naomi smirked, her voice rising. "Has it even occurred to you- Mr. Walker - that your son might truly believe that one of the horses will be hurt today? Have you even considered that?"

The headstrong expression on James's face departed. An embarrassed smile crept into its place after a few moments of silence. "As a matter of fact, I hadn't," he confessed, grasping his beautiful wife by her shoulders. "I'm sorry. I guess you must be pretty sore with me."

Naomi's face remained stern. "Now, what on Earth makes you say that?"

James grinned. "The fact that you called me Mr. Walker. Like you always do when you're angry with me. Do you think he may have dreamed about the horses?"

Naomi nodded, allowing herself a small smile. She turned and looked at Nathan. The boy grinned and clapped his hands.

James brushed a hand against his wife's. She grasped it, intertwining her fingers with his. He marveled at the strength in her grip.

James pulled free, bringing the moment to a reluctant end. "I guess I'd better make it right with him," he said, still grinning.

Naomi grabbed rough hold of her husband, whispering into his ear. "You're damn right, you'd better. Then later you can make it right with me."

"Love to," James chuckled, making his way to Nathan. He bent at the waist and hoisted the tot from his temporary prison. James wrapped his son in a tight hug, ruffling the miniature bird's nest of his coif.

"Sorry, I was stern with you, Nathan," James said. "Thought you were trying to put one over on your Papa."

He extended his arms to hold his son in front of him. "I guess you were just trying to tell us about your dream. I guess it's hard for someone barely two years old to relate a dream. Tell you what. I'll give you an extra piece of candy to make up for it later. That okay with you?"

Nathan smiled and nodded his head.

"Good! We're square, then." James set the boy down. "One happy little family again. Well, Papa's got to head into town, now."

He thought for a moment, resting his chin on the knuckles of his right hand. He dropped to his knees in front of Nathan.

"Don't you worry, Nathan." He squeezed the baby fat around the toddler's cheeks, eliciting a squeal of laughter. "Junie will be just fine." He spoke of his chestnut mare, the largest of the four horses he owned. "She'll finish the day just as she began it. In tip-top shape."

A haunted expression deposed the smile that had decorated Nathan's face. It was an expression that should visit no toddler in a just world. He bit his lip and hung his head. "No," he moaned. "Junie hurt. Big horse hurt, Papa."

James felt no anger this time, only concern for his son. He kissed Nathan on his forehead before straightening up and turning to his wife.

"Poor boy's really frazzled," he said. "See if you can't comfort him, Nay. I'll return just as soon as I can."

"Of course." Naomi swept the boy she'd come to love and accept as her own into her arms. "He'll be alright, James. You just be careful heading into town."

Even in such curious circumstances, it gave James satisfaction to hear her clearly pronounce the "g" at the end of "heading". It would have been "headin'" before he'd started stressing the importance of proper speech. He was glad to have such positive influence over the woman he loved.

"Don't get spooked, Nay." He smiled. "You know I'm an excellent driver."

"Yes, you are." Naomi leaned past the child she embraced to plant a kiss on her husband's lips. "Still, I cain-can't help being a little nervous. I guess the boy's worry is catching this morning."

A few minutes later, James piloted Junie and Lulu Bell as they pulled his carriage up the coach road. He meant to conduct his business and immediately return home.

He sensed that his young family needed his composure on this day. That boy, God love him as his father did, could be downright strange. For her part, Naomi could be downright skittish.

James attributed that quality to Naomi's youth. She had just celebrated her twenty first birthday, nine fewer birthdays than he had known. She was extremely intelligent, hard working, resourceful, and adaptable. Still, she bore the skittishness of youth, the tendency to overreact.

James hadn't noticed it before he married her. He'd been too busy being swept along by her physical beauty, effervescent spirit and stunning devotion to his son.

Though he'd come to recognize Naomi's skittishness, James didn't feel any less fond of her. If anything, being able to detect flaws in his beloved provided strange comfort. He mused that he had his own fair share of them.

James's train of thought was disrupted when the carriage made careened to the left and came to a clumsy halt, coming close to upending. Junie brayed an alarm that soon gave way to pained whinnying. James righted himself in his perch and climbed down.

"Easy girl." He approached the big horse with care, placing a comforting hand on her heaving, heavily muscled side. "Easy. Let Papa see what's wrong."

He stood by her ear, murmuring comfort until the heaving of her torso decreased. He began checking for her affliction once she grew still.

A large rock had become lodged within her front left horseshoe.

Whispering and calming the big steed all along, James slowly and carefully removed the offending object. Moments later, he steered the carriage towards home, keeping it at a slow crawl so as not to further damage Junie's hoof before a vet could examine it. He spoke soothing words to her the entire way.

The rational portion of James's mind argued that what happened had been pure coincidence. The small part of his mind given to fancy held a different opinion.

XX.

"Hot damn, it's good to see you, boy," a stout, bear of a man declared as he embraced James.

James returned the embrace with equal enthusiasm. He couldn't decide which was more exciting- seeing his cousin Virgil for the first time since he was 14 or arriving in a place that offered far more opportunity than the Deep South.

Nathan and Naomi completed the quartet that stood outside of Baltimore's Mount Royal train station. James's smile cast a pleasant glare as he made the proper introductions.

"Virgil." He made a small flourish with his arm, as if he introducing the President of the United States himself. "This is my lovely wife, Naomi. I know you're probably wondering how I ever hitched myself to such a peach of a woman. Rest assured, I haven't figured that one yet, myself."

"Nice to meet you, ma'am." Virgil bent to kiss the hand that Naomi demurely offered. "You're quite the lady, if James letters tell the truth."

Naomi laughed. "If his letters say that he can't get along without me, then they should be taken as Gospel. I see now that flattery runs in the family."

Virgil chortled, his ample midsection and chest heaving. "An' I see that you're a firecracker, too. I cain't wait to introduce you to my wife, Alma. You an' her gon' git along just swell."

Still smiling, James nudged Nathan towards his much older cousin. "This of course…."

"Is your handsome son, Nathan!" Virgil exclaimed, bending to the boy's eye level and extending a broad paw. "Nice to meet you, Nathan."

Nathan's small fingers disappeared inside Virgil's mitt. "Your hands are soft," he said.

Virgil cackled like an excited coyote. "As a matter of fact, they are, little cousin. See your big cousin's got to keep these big ole hands gentle. That's because I'm an artist. I know I might not look the part, but I got the talent, boy."

Nathan smiled. "Could you draw me a picture sometime?"

"Sure thing, little cousin. But first things first. I got to git you folks to your lodgings."

A few minutes later, they all boarded a crowded streetcar. It was a new experience for James and his young family. Though he had seen such conveyances during his few trips to Birmingham, James had no occasion to set foot on one before now.

He drank his new city in, watching streets of cobble stone pass in the streetcar's wake. Baltimore seemed much grander than Birmingham, the largest city James had ever been to. There were no farmhouses here, only brick buildings and storefronts, many far taller than even the tallest buildings in Greenville. In fact, Greenville would struggle to fill Baltimore's boot. Scores of brick rowhomes sprung from the ground like spring flowers. Immaculate marble steps lay at their feet. Further along, brick tenements pulsed with activity and screamed of overcrowding.

The difference in architecture, roads and methods of transportation portended a new world of possibilities for James. He would become part of the growing industry in this city. Through hard work and business acumen, he would soon claim one of these brick buildings as his own.

Once he managed that, he would see if he couldn't become a galvanizing force among the Colored in this burgeoning city. Things might be a lot different here than in tiny, rural, Greenville, Alabama, but he could already tell they weren't different enough.

The fact that all of the Negroes were crowded into the back of the streetcar served as prime evidence of second class citizenship. James wouldn't raise a fuss just yet, but he didn't think that a seat in the back was acceptable for any Negro or other person of color. In time, he would find out how many Negro citizens of Baltimore he could influence to share his viewpoint.

2

Undeniable Proof and Reunited Cousins

I.

Naomi chose not to press her husband about the horseshoe incident, knowing him well enough to foresee that he'd bristle at the notion of Nathan having a clairvoyant moment. She knew that if she was right about the boy, sooner or later James would be confronted with evidence too strong to deny

She'd been watching and waiting the boy's entire short life, patiently expecting his capabilities to emerge. The incident with the horse was but a taste of what she anticipated.

Naomi had no doubt believed that being born with a veil portended clairvoyant power. The growths that had been removed from Nathan's eyes meant that he had born with three veils.

Naomi might not have gone to Tuskegee like her husband, but she knew about a lot more than caring for children and pregnant women. She knew that James's commitment to education and modernity prevented him from considering any truth that couldn't be explained by science, even if that truth seized him by the collar and screamed into his face. She also knew that what happened with the big horse had been no coincidence.

Nathan predicted that Junie would be hurt and indeed she was. If that wasn't evidence that the boy had the sight, then what was?

A skeptic might have argued that Nathan's premonition concerned a fairly insignificant event. Naomi chose to focus on the fact that Nathan had managed such a prediction as a mere toddler.

Naomi speculated that Nathan's powers would prove to be incredible as he grew. No, speculate wasn't the right word. She hypothesized. James would have liked that word.

Naomi had been bed side when the boy's mother died after pushing him forth into the world. Helen kissed the newborn once before asking Dr. Woodson to hold him while she spoke to Naomi. Dread and wonder filled Naomi as Helen's dying hands squeezed her. Those hands possessed a strength that should not have been possible in one whose body was so ravaged. Naomi looked into Helen's eyes as the light within them flickered, listening to her last urgent words.

"Take care of my boy," Helen said, nearly crushing the bones of Naomi's hands with her fevered grip. "Promise me you'll take good care of him."

Naomi nodded hard enough to bring her chin to her chest. A single tear dropped from her face onto Helen's struggling bosom. "I promise."

"Thank you," Helen said. Naomi would never forget the serenity in those final words.

The dying mother birthed a peaceful smile as she breathed her last. That smile was the smile of one whom had accomplished something greater than herself, of one gone unburdened to meet the heavenly father.

Naomi believed that God had shown Helen all that her son was capable of before he took her. That was why she requested that Naomi safeguard him.

When she promised Helen that she would care for the boy, Naomi had no inkling that she would come to love and marry his father. Yet, she had. Perhaps it was God's plan.

As much as she loved and honored James, Naomi loved Nathan more. Nathan was one of God's chosen- blessed with what Naomi knew would prove to be tremendous powers.

She was just as certain of Nathan's awesome power as she was of the eventuality of James coming to recognize that power for the supernatural blessing that it was.

II.

After exiting the streetcar, Virgil led James, Naomi, and Nathan on a four block walk to his humble brick rowhouse in Old West Baltimore. Along the way, he explained that the section of town they entered was populated by a great majority of Colored folks.

"We're livin' good here, y'all." He smiled. "I know you never went anywhere in Alabama an' saw mostly Colored faces. I'm telling you, y'all are gon' love it here." As if conspiring to lend veracity to Virgil's statement, a number of Colored travelers passed them on the street, heading to and fro.

James thought that the passers by carried themselves with a bit more pride than Negroes back in Greenville. It seemed that just about every man of color back there moved in a permanent defensive posture. Such body language communicated that they only wished to conduct their business and return home without suffering some sort of humiliation or victimization. The Negroes in this part of Baltimore seemed much more at ease.

James enjoyed the full tour of his cousin's home soon after arriving and being introduced to Alma and Virgil's young sons, David, and Eli.

Virgil proved prescient about his wife and Naomi becoming fast friends. The two women lost no time falling into chatter with each other, as if they were long lost sisters. Alma was a lovely and charming woman, though a bit large for James's liking. Not that any woman could hold a candle to Naomi in his book, anyway. The only one who could have was Helen.

Virgil's place was far more roomy than it appeared from outside. The first and second floors had cavernous corridors with high ceilings. The sparsely decorated living room gave way to a spacious kitchen that housed a modern stove and sink.

Virgil showed off the running water in the sink as if encountering it for the first time. He waited patiently as it ran a brief brown before giving way to a clear stream.

"Runnin' water ain't no rare thang around here, James," he chuckled. "Ever'body I know has it on account o this fancy sewer system they have in Baltimore. Like I told you in my letters, I ain't had to truck wit' well water in years. The boys hardly ever seen it. Ain't got no outhouses, neither. Got a toilet in the bathroom. Lots of folks got 'em. Hear tell the well off folks got two or three in they house. Ain't city life grand? You could get used to this, couldn't you?"

James nodded. "I suppose I could." He thought of hauling water and venturing to the outhouse back at the farm. Not having to do either was a welcome change.

"You suppose you could?" Virgil laughed, clapping his cousin on the shoulder. "You always was a cool one, cousin! Even the last time I saw you when you were what- thirteen? Fourteen? Damn, I'm glad to have you here, boy!"

He stepped back so that he could look into James's eyes. "So what you think about my home so far? Nice, ain't it?"

"It's very nice, cousin," James said, nodding his approval. "I'm glad to see you've done well for yourself."

Upstairs held three spacious bedrooms and a bathroom. Virgil showed James the room he and Naomi would share, explaining that he had been using it as a home art studio. "Not to worry, though," he said. "I'm glad to give it up for family. I'll work out of the attic now. Got a trapdoor on the second floor leads right to it. Iss big enough for a person to room in, even."

Once James and his family's belongings were settled into their rooms, Virgil invited his cousin down to the basement. The spacious area was separated into distinct halves. One side housed a large wash basin and sink. The area that he and James occupied was set up parlor style. They sat at a large table that faced a towering mahogany cabinet shelved with dinner plates and glasses. A phonograph sat immediately to their left, on a much smaller table.

James nursed a glass of lemonade as he half-listened to Virgil prattle on about the minutiae of his daily life. The pleased host explained that the good finery was kept in the basement and that his sons were forbidden from coming down there.

"I ketch 'em nosin' around down here, I wup 'em good." Virgil smiled as he talked. "They break enough stuff as it is. A woman never birthed more destructive a pair. They don't mean nothin' by it, just awkward I guess. Still, I ketch 'em 'round here, I tan there hides good. Don't know how I'd replace this good stuff down here if it got broke up. Ever since photography caught on 'round here, I'm losin' a good portion of my business. Folks would rather have a photograph of themselves than a painting. Even if it was painted by these magic hands." Virgil held his hands up, twirling them around for show.

James's eyes widened. "Still, you support your family solely through art work?"

"Mostly," Virgil said, nodding. "I do odd jobs every now an' then. Mostly house painting, signage an' such. But mostly, yeah, through my art work. That's somethin'- ain't it?"

"It certainly is. I mean, you always could draw and paint amazingly well. But a Colored man supporting his family only through art? And outside of New York City? I know we're nearly a decade into the twentieth century, but that's a rare thing."

A mischievous glint emerged in Virgil's eyes. "Not if my most well to do patrons don't even know I'm Colored."

James leaned toward Virgil, his curiosity piqued. "Whatever do you mean by that?"

He sat captivated as Virgil gave a detailed explanation of how he came to straddle two very different artistic worlds. One world was the Colored world that was largely isolated from Baltimore's white world, only coming into contact with it for employment or landlord-tenant purposes. Virgil was well known throughout this small but proud world for his exquisitely rendered portrait work, which depicted everything from group scenes to family pets. As he'd already told James, in recent years he made less and less money from Colored people. The exploding popularity of photography greatly decreased the demand for such work. When he did get commissions, it was for significantly less than the going rate for skilled photographic portraits.

"I aim to git into photography myself," he said. "Soon's I kin git some equipment an' a place to set up a darkroom. I'm sure I kin take some damn good pictures. Cain't beat 'em, might as well join' 'em. Right? Supply an' demand is the way of the world."

Virgil digressed, explaining how he came to maintain profitability in that other Baltimore Art World- the one that consisted of upper middle class and wealthy white art patrons. He told of how he'd come to know Charles Thurmont. He'd set up a drawing pad on his portable easel outside of Lexington Market some time back (as was his custom on Saturdays and some weekdays). On the edge of the easel sat a sign that had the words Dime Drawings scrawled on it. With his ability to produce a masterful pencil drawing within minutes, Virgil had become accustomed to making a dollar or more on a good day. Though he had no permit, the cops who walked the beat usually didn't bother him because they admired his talent. From time to time, they requested free drawings.

Virgil obliged with a smile, never hesitating to play the part of the humble aw shucks Colored boy. During this repeated enterprise, Virgil encountered many whites who treated him like an idiot savant or trained monkey. "They act like s' a miracle that a Colored man could be so skilled," he chuckled. "That's good for me, though. The more miraculous they think it is, the more likely they are to throw me some silver. You know?"

James sensed bitterness beneath Virgil's laughter. Hell, he was bitter for his cousin. He doubted that Virgil would have to hustle for dimes in the street if he were a white artist.

"Anyway," Virgil continued, "one day this white fellow comes up to me, asks for a drawing of him and his friends. So I git real pickaninny-like for 'im, show my choppers an' say, 'It'd be my pleasure, suh'. He frowns an' tells me I oughtn't call 'im suh, that he's just a college kid, that I had to be older 'en he was."

Virgil chuckled, amused by the memory as he retold it. "So I says, 'Yes, suh. Anything you like, suh.' He rolls his eyes, takes a sigh an' says he'd like for me to make 'im a damn good picture. I smile an' tell 'im that's my business. So him and his two friends stand off to the side, on the cobblestone path they got down there and I make a real nice picture for 'em. I git the background an' all. I'm tellin' you, James. It was one of the best pencil drawings I ever done."

"So did he like it?" James asked.

"Hell, yes he liked it!" Virgil's voice sang with pride. "That picture about knocked that old boy's socks off. Him an' his fancy college friends raised a big fuss over it. Then he tells me he'd feel like he was takin' advantage by only payin' me a dime. I says, 'A dime's fine with me, Mister. A dime's my stated price.' I pointed to the sign. He frowns, says maybe my stated price should be a good bit higher. I says maybe nobody would buy any if it was higher. He says the right people would, people wit' a good moral center."

Virgil chuckled again. "I asked how much he thought I should charge, as a person wit' a good moral center. He reached down in his pockets and handed me two shiny half dollars. I tell you cousin, my eyes nearly popped out of my big ole head. Nearly flew off into the great blue sky, they did. His friends seemed to be surprised like I was. Maybe they didn't have as good a moral center as he did. Anyway after I damn near kneeled before him like he was the second comin', he scolded me something awful, tellin' me that I was far too humble."

Virgil threw his voice, trying to sound like a wealthy white person. "Undue humility can be a hindrance to the tremendously talented. That's what he said."

Virgil laughed again. "He used two dollar words like that all the time. Come to think of it, he kind of talks like you. I found out later that he went to the big local college. Johns Hopkins, they call it. I guess the fancy words is part a bein' college learned. They'da never let your Colored behind through those doors, though. Even if you are plenty smart. I hear even regular white folk cain't get into that school."

James impatiently motioned for Virgil to go on.

"Oh, right," Virgil said, chuckling. "I'm gittin' off the subject, again. You know once I git to talkin', the conversation's subject to go off to the four corners of the Earth."

James nodded and smiled. "Same as when we were kids."

"Amen to that," Virgil said. "Anyway, he takes his drawin' and starts to walk away. Then he hands one of his friends the pitcher and comes back over to me. I swallow hard, hope there ain't no trouble brewin', but he just asks for my name. He reaches his hand out after I tell 'im. I stare at it a second 'fore I realize he means to shake wit' me."

Virgil's eyes widened as if the surprise had just occurred. "That white boy actually shook my hand! A good firm handshake, too. Didn't wipe his hands off on his clothes or make a face like he was on the toilet after he was done, neither. Tells me his name is Charles Thurmont III, tells me he's from a well to do family. Tells me he never seen such a good drawing, that a man of my talent oughtn't have to peddle his work on the street. I tells 'im I ain't mind. He says that he damn well minds even if I don't. Asks me if I got a studio. I tell 'im I work out of my home. He asked me where home was and I told him Old West Baltimore, of course. I don't know where else he expected a Colored man to live in this city. Then he asked if he could come by my place some time!"

Thurmont did just that, showing up in the wee hours one night. He and Virgil faced each other across the kitchen table as Thurmont revealed a bold scheme. Virgil agreed to produce works that Thurmont would present as his own, claiming to the local art world that a latent talent had bloomed within him. All profit would be split down the middle. The caveat was that Virgil would produce works different in style from his figural and portrait work. That way, no one could ever connect the two men.

"That was a small trick for me," Virgil said, grinning. "I can make any kind a pitcher come alive. Watercolors, landscapes, city scapes- you name it –I can do it. Do it with style like nobody else. Anyway, I might be getting less work from other Coloreds, but the money I bring in from the arrangement with Thurmont never lets me down. It done me good enough to git' this house an' keep some nice thangs. Ain't a bad hustle. Is it?"

James's face twisted into a scowl. "How could you be such a damn fool?" he hissed.

Virgil's jaw plunged toward the table. "What?"

"You heard me!" James banged the table. "You've been a damn fool. Allowing some pale bastard to take such advantage of you."

Virgil sat stunned for a few moments before managing, "Thurmont's not taking advantage of me. Thurmont's helped me to have a better life."

James shook his head, exasperated. "It is the white man's boon that so many Negroes are so short sighted. I had hoped you were different."

A vein pulsed on Virgil's forehead. His voice became a low growl. "Now, you see here, James Walker. Cousin or not, no man disrespects me in my own house."

James took a deep breath, a weak smile replacing his scowl. "I mean no disrespect. And this is a nice house. You might have had much more, however."

"An' how you figure that?" Virgil demanded. "How you figure I might've had much more?"

"Forget it," James said. "It's obvious that we'll never see eye to eye on the matter."

"No, I will not forget it." Virgil pointed a large finger at his cousin. "You brought it up, now I want to hear it. How might I have had much more?"

James sighed. "You might have had much more if you hadn't allowed that scheming white vulture to take credit for all that you created with your God given talent. You might have done more than manage. You might have become quite rich."

"Rich?" Virgil sprang apoplectic from his seat. "Ha! Sure I might a became rich. I also might not a done better'n I was already doin'. I might never've gotten what I do have for myself an' my family. I might a gone on sharing a room with seven other Joes down in Slump's Alley, scrapin' just enough for meal money. I wasn't left property like you, James. I had to make a sure choice."

"How do you know that white boy's even giving you as much as was agreed upon?" James asked.

Virgil held his arms out in a wide arc, palms up. "Maybe he ain't givin' me half, cousin. Maybe he ain't givin' me a quarter. If so, I don't give a damn! Iss still more than I'da gotten on my own. You think them chinchy white people would put some nigger's art in their houses and museums?"

James sighed and shook his head. "We're not niggers. We're people, just as good as any of them."

"Think I don't know that? Try tellin' it to them."

James rose slowly from his seat prior to staring into his cousin's inflamed eyes. They stood that way, silent, pupils dueling for a long time.

"Oh, I aim to tell them," James said, a defiant smile spreading across his face. "I aim to show them. If I have anything to do with it, conditions will become much improved for Coloreds around here."

Virgil laughed and shook his head. "I might a known the first thang you'd try to do was stir thangs up. You were always so full of big ideas, even when we were young. First started talking over my head when you were but 10 and I was 14, I guess. Suppose nothin's ever gon' be simple for you, nothin's ever gon' be enough. You couldn't just accept the fact that although iss still a white world, Baltimore is a hell of a lot better than where you jus' come from. You fresh off the train an' you already talkin' 'bout how you gon' make things better. Well cousin, things already are better. You jus' need to take the time to smell the damn roses!"

James considered his cousin's argument and nodded. "Maybe things are better. But they're far from satisfying." He gesticulated with both hands as his emotions got the better of him. "Not when Coloreds are still second class. Not when a man as talented as yourself feels he has to pass his work off as someone else's to make money, not when a cracker who probably can't draw a stick figure gets to take all of the credit and at least half of the profit for the beautiful work you create. They might not make a pastime of lynching Negroes up here, but they're oppressing us just the same."

Virgil laughed without humor. "You ought to climb on a soapbox, sound a bullhorn maybe."

"Perhaps I will," James said.

Virgil furrowed his brow. "Perhaps you'll be kind enough to wait until you've secured your own lodgin' before you start any rabble rousin'. I don't want to be lumped in with any such nonsense. Why'd you pick now to come here, anyway? I been tryna git you to come North for years. I have to say, I'm startin' to regret it, already. Why'd you choose to come now?"

James's face tightened. "That's not your concern," he growled.

Virgil laughed and clapped his hands. His eyes danced as if he were a detective whom had just solved a crime. "Piss off the wrong folks, I bet. Still you're fool enough to try an' make waves here?" He shook his head. "I guess some folks are too smart to ever learn anythang."

Virgil backed up and turned toward the basement stairs. "Whatever the case, I mean what I said. Don't you git me involved in none a your foolishness. Unlike you, I think a carin' for my family 'fore I think of tryna be some big man. Keep your damn ideas to yourself until you move out a my place. Otherwise, I'll have to throw you out. You will not bring trouble to my house."

Virgil started up the stairs, stopped and looked at his cousin. "I think the world of you cousin, but you got to stop bein' so greedy. Thangs are good for Coloreds here. You ought to give yourself a chance to appreciate that. You'll be a much happier man."

James did not reply, knowing that doing so would be futile. Virgil had his narrow minded view of the world; James had his broad, ambitious one. He would respect Virgil's wishes of not stirring anything up until he'd obtained his own lodgings. But once he was settled on his own, he intended to accomplish things that most Coloreds weren't capable of envisioning in their fondest fantasies.

III.

Two uneventful weeks passed between the incident with the horse and the picnic that James and his young family enjoyed in an inviting meadow just beyond their fields.

Thick, greasy ham sandwiches slathered with mustard and all the trimmings, a layered chocolate cake, two dozen deviled eggs, and a lidded pitcher of country lemonade (all prepared by Naomi) were packed into a large red picnic basket. Husband, wife, and young son sprawled on a large red and white striped blanket, letting the mid-May sun warm them.

James slipped into brief reminiscence of similar picnics he'd shared with Helen. Those fine days had often culminated with lovemaking on a blanket like the one he now lay on. He banished the thought, thinking that this time with Naomi and the boy should be held in at least equal esteem. He felt guilty about thinking of Helen while he was with Naomi.

He didn't suppose he could avoid it, what with how he'd lost her. Still, his love for Naomi was powerful. Every day he felt grateful that God or whatever greater power had seen fit to bless him with a second beloved.

"Open up," Naomi said, an adoring smile on her face as she held a deviled egg in front of his mouth.

James matched her smile and obliged, allowing her to drop the egg into his mouth. He chewed it slowly, savoring its zesty flavor before swallowing.

"You always were something with deviled eggs, Nay."

"I thought I was some kind of cook, period," she said, feigning offense.

James sat up and wiped his mouth. "You let me be the one to toot your horn-you hear me, gal?"

Naomi smiled. "Well, you need to toot it a little louder."

James's eyes toured her pleasing figure. "I'll toot it plenty tonight, darling. Don't you worry."

Her beige face flushed as she giggled. "Will you now?"

"Damn straight." James grasped her shoulders and planted a loud smack on her full lips. He then turned his attention to Nathan. The boy had already finished eating. He now occupied himself with his wooden spelling blocks.

"What are you spelling there, Nathan?" James asked.

Instead of answering, Nathan began to move the blocks with urgent focus. His intense focus on the activity made it seem like something far more significant than child's play.

"Let's have a look," James said, moving closer.

Nathan had a total of thirteen blocks. Each displayed one letter of the alphabet on one side and another when flipped.

The toddler moved with preternatural quickness, flipping two blocks so that they spelled M-A. He picked them up and set them down again to represent repetition of the pairing.

"Mama?" James beamed, full of pride. He rubbed Nathan's short crop of hair. "Damn, son- you're learning how to spell quite early."

He turned to Naomi, whom had drawn as close as he had. She pointed toward Nathan, calling James's attention to the next spelling that the boy sped through. L-O-V-E. Nathan flipped aside the first two blocks in the word without pause, placing an M in front of the E.

"Yes, she does, son." James nodded, still all smiles. "Just like I do."

Nathan continued without pause, hands moving with the kind of quickness and dexterity that would be exemplary for a professional card sharp, let alone a two year old boy. Not once did he look up from the blocks. James could have sworn that the boy's hazel and green eyes were glowing.

I-K-N-O-W S-H-E transitioned into another L-O-V-E, which metamorphosed into another M-E.

James clapped his hands. "You ought to know, boy…" Naomi shushed her husband, gripping his bicep to indicate that he should be still and silent.

James complied, although he couldn't understand why his young wife wanted him to be quiet on a triumphant occasion like this. He always knew Nathan was bright, but doing something like this meant he might prove to be a genius.

Nathan's next spelling derailed James's train of thought.

B-U-T N-A-O-M-I flowed into N-O-T.

For the first time since Nathan began, James did not feel good about what his son was doing. Nor did he feel good about the fact that the boy's eyes were definitely glowing.

The next set of words caused James's blood to run cold.

M-Y-R-E-A-L morphed into M-O-T-H-E-R.

James just registered Naomi drawing in a shocked breath. He took no notice of his own shallow breathing.

Nathan continued to work the blocks without pausing or looking up. Never once did his hands mishandle his tools.

M-O-T-H-E-R became M-Y-R-E-A-L, which gave birth to M-O-T-H-E-R once more. James didn't bother wiping away the sweat that beaded on his forehead.

I-S- D-E-A-D was next, quickly giving way to I-S-A-W- I-T.

Naomi's fingers scrambled for James's right hand. He accepted her grip, matching her urgent squeezing of his palm.

I-N-M-Y-D-R-E-A-M gave way to L-A-S-T N-I-G-H-T, which begat I-K-N-O-W, which became I-T-T-R-U-E.

A frigid spirit danced along James's spine.

Nathan continued, still not pausing or looking up. James thought he heard the boy's breathing growing labored, but perhaps it was Naomi's or his own.

I-S-A-D- B-U-T progressed into I-H-A-P-P-Y. M-A-M-A H-E-L-E-N delivered D-I-E H-A-P-P-Y. D-I-E H-A-P-P-Y shifted back into M-A-M-A H-E-L-E-N, which lost no time in becoming D-I-E F-O-R- M-E.

James's felt as if he were trapped in some drug induced hallucination as he continued to watch the letters reveal truths Nathan had no earthly means of knowing.

M-A-M-A H-E-L-E-N appeared again, giving way to H-A-P-P-Y. H-A-P-P-Y birthed I-N- T-H-A-T P-L-A-C-E. I-N- T-H-A-T P-L-A-C-E birthed T-H-A-T G-O-O-D, which morphed once more into P-L-A-C-E.

James drew a breath so deep that his exhale sounded like a tiny steam whistle. Naomi squeezed his hand hard enough to cause pain.

P-L-A-C-E changed into I-S-E-E-I-T, which gave way to T-H-A-T G-O-O-D P-L-A-C-E. I-D-R-E-A-M-I-T was spelled next, followed by T-H-A-T P-L-A-C-E again.

Enraptured by his son's incredible display, James was just cognizant of Naomi's soft weeping.

T-H-A-T P-L-A-C-E fled, leaving S-H-E T-H-A-N-K Y-O-U. N-A-O-M-I was next, returning to S-H-E T-H-A-N-K Y-O-U. That phrase was followed by T-O-C-A-R-E F-O-R M-E.

Naomi released James's hand and pitched over, sprawling across his lap. Her sobs grew much louder as she hugged her own shoulders.

Nathan swept all of the blocks aside and yawned, placing a tiny hand over his mouth. He rubbed tired eyes that no longer glowed.

"Mama Naomi sad?" he inquired, gazing at his stepmother.

"N-no," Naomi said, straightening up. She wiped her face and forced a smile at the same time. "No, baby. I'm not sad."

Nathan frowned. "You sad, Mama. Grownups sad."

James nodded in agreement with that inarguable truth. Nathan was not yet three years old, but he knew that grownups got sad, no matter how they tried to fool him.

They'd tried to spare the child the burden of Helen's death by allowing him to believe that Naomi was his mother. It had not worked because Nathan had seen the truth. He'd had a vision, one that he spelled out in his toy blocks. It now seemed possible that he'd communicated with his dead mother.

James could not dismiss the fantastic events that had just occurred as coincidence. He considered himself a believer of science. As such, he knew that evidence proved theory. All of the evidence at James's disposal pointed to his son having supernatural powers.

"Its' okay, Mama and Papa." Nathan positioned himself in the nook between them, hugging each adult with one short arm. "Everything okay."

James hoisted the boy into his lap before searching his wife's eyes with a silent question. Within seconds, Nathan was sound asleep. His spelling activity had worn him out.

"What will we do?" James spoke in a tremulous whisper. "What can we do?"

Naomi sighed and shook her head. "I don't know." Her eyes were as red as they were wide. "But I know of someone who might."

IV.

Try as they might in the days following their argument, James and Virgil could not restore their once easy camaraderie. Unease and resentment lurked just beneath a polite façade.

James wondered if he would have done better by keeping his opinion of Virgil's arrangement with Thurmont to himself. He'd always had a hard time accepting how slow the average Colored was to stir. The still long shadow of slavery and the even longer shadow of Jim Crow left many of his brethren content with whatever crumbs the white man tossed them.

The belief that the Negro had both accomplished and suffered too much to be relegated to second class citizen was James's greatest conviction. He knew that there were others out there whom felt the same way, brilliant men like W.E.B. Dubois who argued for racial reform.

Still, he felt as if he'd been too harsh with Virgil. Once he took time to reflect, he realized how proud Virgil had been of the scheme he'd cooked up with Thurmont. The big guy's chest had been all puffed up. He'd been glad to be able to provide comfort for his family.

James had forced Virgil to confront the truth of his exploitation in severe fashion. He hadn't meant to hurt Virgil's pride, but the shock of such injustice had caused his disparaging words to issue forth like a geyser.

James now reasoned that he should have saved his injurious words for the true culprit- Thurmont. That predatory Caucasian and others like him thought nothing of exploiting Negroes. They rigged the game of life from start to finish before reveling in tainted victory. What men like him did to Coloreds was akin to bullfighters squaring off against bulls that had already been bled for several pints before being released into the arena. Poor Virgil was only trying to provide for his family. He had nothing to be ashamed of in the context of the situation.

James decided to apologize to his cousin after Sunday dinner.

The two families went to church beforehand, an activity that James didn't exactly jump for joy about. Though he believed in God or some form of higher being, James could take church or leave it.

He just couldn't disregard the origin of the black church enough to fully immerse himself in the experience. He never lost sight of the fact that for generations, white Christians had twisted the message of biblical passages to brainwash people of color into believing that bondage was their preordained lot in life. The knowledge that the Negro often used Christianity for inspiration and to great advantage was not enough for James to forgive the fact that it had been forced upon his people. He was fully aware that many slaves had used coded messages in freedom songs masked as spirituals to plot escapes into free lands. He also knew that countless numbers of his people had used the Christian faith to sustain themselves in the face of miserable living conditions. Still, he couldn't help thinking of Christianity as much more than a bitter pill that whites had forced Negroes to swallow.

James only went to church because Naomi wouldn't accept otherwise. His choices were to attend church with her on Sunday or deal with a nasty attitude all week. The matter of church was one issue in which she never deferred to him.

Christian faith was just one of the similarities that Naomi shared with James's departed Helen. The women became fast friends once Naomi came to care for Helen during her pregnancy. James supposed that it was only natural for two such kindred spirits to become so fond of each other.

It was Naomi's faith that kept her from being distressed about having borne no child of her own. "I think the Lord means for me to reserve all my mothering for Nathan," she once said. James didn't think that idea held any water- that more likely there was a problem with her ovaries- but he didn't dare argue against her means of comforting itself.

Virgil and Alma had informed their guests that they attended Bethel AME Church, on the lower east side of the city. "It's the first Colored church in Baltimore," Virgil said, a cat that just ate the canary grin plastered on his face. "Got a big ole congregation. An' Pastor Freeman sure kin preach. That's a preachin' Colored man."

After a breakfast of bacon, eggs, and grits, the three adults and three boys headed out in their Sunday finery. James thought that Alma looked mighty pretty in her shimmering church dress and fancy hat. Still, she had nothing on his Naomi.

Maybe he only felt that Naomi was the most beautiful woman around because he was so smitten with her. If so, James hoped that he would never love her any less.

The second Mrs. Walker took her Mister's arm just as Alma took her husband's. As they all walked to the streetcar stop, the three boys milled about ahead of them, passing the occasional lick. Virgil chided them to walk straight and stop playing on the way to church. After they fell in line, he mused, "Boys will be boys."

"Yes, they will," James agreed, reaching out to rest a hand on his cousin's strong shoulder. He couldn't wait to smooth things out with Virgil after supper.

Fifteen minutes later, they all exited the streetcar on Caroline Street. "There weren't any whites on that streetcar," James observed.

Virgil shrugged. "I guess they don't take too kindly to ridin' wit' our kind on the Lord's Day."

James chuckled. "Perhaps they don't want to soil their own houses of worship with our residue."

Alma rolled her eyes and turned to Naomi. "I do believe these men oughtn't talk that way while approaching the house of the Lord. Would you agree, Naomi?"

"I wholeheartedly agree," Naomi said, staring at James and applying pressure to the arm she held.

James chuckled. "I believe we'd better hold our tongues, cousin."

"Either that or have them cut out," Virgil said, smiling while holding his hands before his face as if cowering in fear.

The church was a wondrous sight to behold. The few churches James had attended in Alabama resembled shacks or clapboard houses. Once inside such shabby structures, he invariably found himself packed in with dozens of other

Coloreds, unable to move any better than a canned sardine. To make matters worse, such churches never failed to have dirt floors. He'd sit through two hours of preaching, singing, and testifying, while sweating through his clothes and getting clouds of dirt on them.

James often mused about whether conditions were much worse for his ancestors during the Middle Passage. He had seen his share of large, beautifully constructed churches from the outside, but none that Coloreds were allowed into. Bethel AME was the first exception to the rule that he'd laid eyes upon.

The colossus of architecture dwarfed the smaller surrounding buildings on Caroline Street. It was all Byzantine arches and huge windows. A ten foot tall cross adorned its' massive roof.

A huge sign enclosed in glass stood in the left center of the lush lawn that bisected the path to the double-door front entrance. It read, "Welcome to Bethel AME Church, Brothers and Sisters in Christ."

Helen and Naomi pulled the three boys closer as they all fell in step with the throng of nattily dressed Negroes approaching the entrance. James seemed to exchange a pleasant greeting with each step he took.

Once inside, they were all directed to their seats by a kindly old usher. James marveled at the glorious interior.

If it had not been a church, Bethel might have made a splendid theatre, what with its' impossibly tall ceiling and massive balcony section. A sea of pews stretched across the floor level. The preacher stood before a huge oaken pedestal, at the head of a massive stage. His powerful voice boomed through the house of God, welcoming all whom had come to hear the Lord's message on this beautiful day.

James surprised himself by being swept along the tide of worship. Hymns were sung with fervor- at least 500 beautiful Colored people sounding their voices in unified joy.

Soon, the preacher began the day's sermon, a message of perseverance. Charismatic and commanding, Pastor Freeman made repeated references to the story of Job, using it as a metaphor for the experience of Coloreds in America. Screams of "Yes, Lawd," and "Thank you, Jesus," exploded at frequent intervals, as if some of the congregation were set to timers.

Large women grew wild with excitement and fanned themselves with paper fans. Individuals possessed by the Holy Ghost rushed into the aisle at frequent intervals, flopping about like fishes out of water. Virgil, Alma, and Naomi clapped their hands and swayed their arms as Pastor Freeman's words invigorated their spirits. Virgil and Naomi's boys smiled as they clapped along. Nathan joined in a few times, though his clapping lacked fluidity.

James remained as outwardly reserved as his son, but he left feeling better than he ever had following a church service. He was still miles from becoming a bible thumper, but he found the preacher's words to be reaffirming. He would persevere as Job did, as did the Israelites and others who suffered great tribulation in the bible. There would be no quit in him, not until things got better for him and his kind.

James realized that just being in Baltimore meant that things were a little better for him. Colored folks might be second class here as well as in Alabama, but it was a much better second than he'd been used to. Negroes would never have been able to build such a beautiful church in the Deep South. Negroes would never have been able to build anything so grand.

James's pleasant mood accompanied him home and stayed for the delicious dinner Naomi and Alma cooked. James and Virgil shared a number of jokes and childhood reminiscences during the meal. James felt the veil of tension between them slowly lift.

3

Burned Land, Old Ruth

I.

Virgil invited James back to the basement after dinner. They sat at the same table where they'd argued.

"Have a drink?" Virgil asked. "We ain't shared a proper one since you first got here."

"Sure the Lord would approve?" James said, smiling. "It being his day and all."

Virgil chuckled. "The Lord don't mind a man sharin' a nip with his houseguest every now an' then. Ever'thang in moderation- right?"

"The Church says amen to that."

"Amen, cousin. Amen."

James stopped laughed and shifted in his seat. ""Listen, Virgil. About the argument we had…"

Virgil slapped the table before popping to his feet. 'We'll talk about it after I come back wit' our drinks." A grin stretched across his face. "Got some brandy ever' bit as good as what they got down in Dixie, cousin. Only break it out on special occasions. Cain't think of nothin' more special than hostin' my cousin, who's my guest after some twenty years of separation. You hold tight."

Virgil trotted up the stairs with a quickness that belied his stocky build. James felt relieved that his cousin seemed certain to accept his apology.

The house telephone rang as he waited for Virgil to return. The startling and reverberating sound was rare in Virgil's home. James wondered who the caller was, doubting that anyone would call about artwork on a Sunday.

"James." Virgil called from the top of the basement steps, surprising his cousin.

"Y-yes, cousin?"

"You got a phone call from Greenville. It's urgent."

The hairs on James's neck stood at attention. He didn't need Nathan's clairvoyance to feel a sense of foreboding.

"You hear me, cousin?" Virgil called again.

"Yes. I'm coming." Anxiety filled James as he hurried up the stairs. Virgil handed the u-shaped receiver to him when he reached the living room.

"Hello?" he spoke over the crackling line.

"Boss?"

"Zeke."

"Yeah, Boss. Iss me. Listen, I got terrible news for you."

James's body knotted into a ball of tension.

"They burned your land, Boss. All of it."

James remained silent as the disastrous words sunk in. He was vaguely aware of Virgil watching him.

"You hear me, Boss?"

James cleared his throat before responding in a near whisper. "This is not one of your better jokes, Hezekiah."

"I cain't hear you, Boss," Hezekiah's voice crackled on the line. "You'll have to speak up."

James bellowed, "This is not one of your better jokes, Hezekiah! I didn't think you capable of jesting in such poor taste!"

There was a pause on the other end of the line. James heard the sound of throat-clearing amidst the continued crackling.

"I know iss a shock to hear it, Boss," Hezekiah spoke in a slow, measured fashion. "But believe me, I'd never kid about somethin' like that. You know me better than that." Another pause. "I'm real sorry, boss."

James was aware of the women of the house joining Virgil in watching him. He didn't care if the whole world watched.

"How did this happen?" he screamed. "When did this happen?"

"They came the same night you left," Hezekiah answered in a mournful tone. "In the middle of the night. Set all your fields ablaze. Time I woke up to the smell reachin' my little plot, she was already burnin' something awful. Then I had to make sure there weren't none of 'em who done it around. I reckon they wouldn't a been too kind to any witnesses. I did manage to git your horses out. Bu that was all I could save." He choked on his next words. "I'm so sorry, James."

James's lips trembled as he dug his free hand into his own thigh. He squeezed the muscle with all his strength, needing the physical pain to fight back his anguish. The land his father had fought for- that his tragically deceased parents had left him as an inheritance. The power of land ownership. It was all gone.

Although James thought he had left Alabama for good, he'd had plenty of plans for the family homestead. By James's design, Hezekiah and the other sharecroppers were to continue working the land, each sending him a generous monthly tribute. Hezekiah was to be in charge- he was a man who could be trusted. There wasn't a dishonest bone in his body. The tribute money- which would have been James's free and clear- was to supplement James's endeavors in Baltimore.

Now that plan was shot to hell. No doubt by the same men who would've killed James if he'd stayed. He hadn't imagined that they would exact their vengeance on the land if they couldn't get their hands on his flesh and bone.

Daggers of hate stabbed at James's stomach and chest. Sweat beaded his forehead. He slammed a fist into his own ribs to stave off an anxiety attack. His wife and cousin started toward him, only to retreat from the wild look in his eyes.

Virgil went to the liquor chest and poured a glass of the brandy he'd offered earlier.

"Boss?" Hezekiah spoke over more crackling.

James seized the drink with his free hand, causing some of it to splash to the floor.

"Just a second, Zeke," he answered, amazed by how calm his voice sounded.

He drained the brandy in one draught, his chest burning before his taste buds had enough time to make a decision. His stomach warmed as those same taste buds determined that the drink was quality stuff. James handed the glass back to Virgil, who lost no time in pouring another.

"Why'd you take so long to call me? That was three nights ago."

"I know it, Boss. But you know we got no long distance booths in the sticks. Had to wait 'til I could travel into town. Plus I was worried that them who done it might have eyes on me."

James nodded, although he knew Hezekiah couldn't see him. He waved Virgil off when he offered the second drink. "I guess that's about right. I'm sorry my problems came back on you."

"You ain't the one burned your own property, Boss. Least I did git to the horses. They damn near trampled me when I let 'em out the barn. If this ole boy wasn't so light on his feet, I'd be laid up right now."

James chuckled. "You always were a swift one. How are they doing?"

"Alright now, I suppose. Still a bit skittish. Had a hell of a time trackin 'em down once I set 'em loose. Seemed like they might flee clear to the Gulf itself."

"I want you to sell them."

"What? Boss …."

"You heard me, now. I want you to sell those horses. Send me two-thirds of the profits as soon as you're able. Keep the rest for yourself. Can you handle that, Zeke?"

"You know I kin boss. An' that's mighty kind of you - to throw me some of the profits. I'm sure sorry 'bout your land. Terrible thing, watchin' it all go up in flames like that."

James took a deep breath and cleared his throat. "No use crying over spilled milk, my good man. Just have to figure out how to go on, that's all. What do you plan to do for yourself?"

Static reverberated through the phone connection as Hezekiah chuckled. "Hell after what happened, me and the missus got to talking. Figured we don't want to stay around here much longer. We're gon' tie some loose ends, then head north like you did. Don't reckon we'll come to Baltimore, though. Got family in Cleveland and Detroit. Gonna git on the train, head to one a those places. Figure at least in the North Coloreds shouldn't have to worry 'bout their homes bein' burned or bein' dragged off in the middle of the night. We ain't the only ones talkin' 'bout leavin', either. In light of what happened, lots of Coloreds figure they done had their fill of what Dixie got to offer."

James sighed. "Can't say I blame a single one of you," he said. "You see I've already gone."

"A good thing you did, at that. Hate to think of how it might have been if you were here when they came."

"I hate to think of that, too," James agreed, not letting on that he knew exactly what would have happened if he had been present that night.

"How you like it up there in Baltimore?"

"I can't say Coloreds get a fair shake here, but its' a sight better than what us 'darkies' get down in Dixie."

Hezekiah laughed. "Amen to that. You take kere now, James. You hear? I'll be gittin' that money to you soon as I sell them horses, alright?"

"I know you will. You take care yourself, Zeke."

James set the receiver back onto its cradle before accepting the second glass of brandy from Virgil. He drained it as quickly as he had the first.

"A word alone with my wife, please." His voice was somber, tiny.

Virgil and Alma adjourned to the kitchen.

James sat the glass down and collapsed onto Naomi's shoulder. "They burned it all down, baby," he whimpered. "Those crackers burned it all down."

Later that night, he lay in bed, Naomi held tight to his breast. Thoughts of white men destroying his family's property danced a hateful jig through his head. A single, unchecked blaze had desecrated all of his acreage. Crops that supported both he and the sharecroppers that he'd shared the land with had been charred beyond any use.

The vile bigots responsible for the destruction would face no consequences from the authorities. James felt convinced that a good number of those whom had come to burn his birthright were the "authorities". He had no difficulty visualizing that old peckerwood sheriff in the finest of spook hats, gleefully torching his family's land.

James considered heading back to file a proper insurance claim. He knew that the company holding his policy would wish to determine whether or not he had torched the property himself before they issued any payout. While he was there, he would file a civil suit against the town of Greenville. Perhaps he could discover the identities of some of the desecrators.

James knew that he'd left there a wanted man, but now he wanted retribution. The likelihood that the perpetrators would have no consequence other than many a laugh into their beer turned his stomach.

The sound of the bedroom door creaking inward startled James from his bitter thoughts. Nathan appeared in the archway, clad in his pajamas. The boy's strange eyes shone like a lantern. He seemed to glide across the room, arriving at James's bedside without a single creak of a floorboard.

Nathan stared into his father's eyes, his voice low and soft. "They'll kill you if you go back."

James rolled Naomi off of him. She groaned and pulled the cover over herself, too far into the land of sleep to register Nathan's presence.

James sat up. "What are you talking about, son?" he grunted.

"I know what happened," Nathan said. "I know you're mad, but you can't go back. They'll kill you if you go back, Papa. I saw it."

James sprang from the bed and seized the boy by his arms. "Did you now? You're good for seeing things- aren't you? Well, answer me this, Mr. I See Everything. Why didn't you see that they would do it? Why didn't you see that?"

"I did." Nathan accepted the pressure on his puny limbs without grimace or cry. "But I didn't tell you. It was you or the land. Your life is more important than land, Papa."

James released the boy, falling to his knees and covering his face as he surrendered to the tears that had been fighting to overwhelm him for hours.

"I'm so sorry, son," he gasped, pulling the boy into an embrace. "I'm so sorry."

"I'm sorry too, Papa." Nathan wrapped his small arms around his father. "I'm sorry, too."

James wept without restraint, perishing thoughts of the awesome burden of having abilities like Nathan's. That was something to consider on another occasion. For the time being, he only wanted to be comforted, just as the special little boy in his arms only wanted to comfort him.

II.

James halted the carriage at the end of a narrow dirt road, about twenty yards to the left of a small, dilapidated cabin.

He and his family were now at the far southern tip of Alabama, only a few miles from the Gulf of Mexico. The summer heat here felt even more severe than in sizzling Greenville, despite the forest that surrounded them.

A hungry mosquito nipped James's elbow as he looked at the cabin. He sighed before steering Junie and Angel up the dirt patch that served as a poor facsimile of a front yard. Angel tensed and brayed her resistance before submitting to Junie's superior strength and determined obedience.

James felt glad to arrive at just past noon, since the ethereal nature of his surroundings put him in mind of an Edgar Allen Poe tale. They would be nowhere near this strange outpost come sundown. He stepped down from the driver's seat and helped his family from the carriage.

"So this is the place, huh?" he asked Naomi. "I hope things turn out as you say." He didn't offer that his bowie knife lay strapped within his left boot, in case any danger should arise.

"She not bad," Nathan squeaked as only small children and mice can. "The lady not bad."

James shivered. He could never get used to having his mind read, or whatever it was that Nathan did. He loved his son more than anything in the world, but that didn't prevent his skin from crawling in the face of the boy's strange talents.

"I'm certainly not, sweetheart," a voice full of gravel yet still feminine wafted from the doorway of the cabin. Angel whinnied and jerked her head, causing Junie to nuzzle the younger horse for reassurance.

A weathered old woman stood where the voice had come from, wearing a shawl over a simple brown dress that appeared to be homemade. Her stature was that of a child. A mane of wild white hair streamed from her head. Wrinkles as gnarled as an old tree trunk covered her bare arms and feet. Her gray toenails might have been fashioned from dust. James thought that she had to be the oldest woman he'd ever seen.

A guttural laugh escaped the jumble of dry, withered flesh that served as the woman's mouth, sending her shawl flapping. "You can trust your son in such things, Mr. Walker. I am most certainly not 'bad'." Her approximation of a reassuring smile was all gums, save for the few nubs that served as teeth.

James struggled to keep a calm demeanor, thinking that if he were not a man of firm scientific beliefs, he might accept the woman as inarguable proof of the living dead.

"I can assure you that I am not dead, Mr. Walker," the unsettling voice came again, the sound of someone sharpening blade against stone. "Nor am I dying. I am merely very old, no doubt ancient in your eyes. I am the one you all seek. Come into my humble cabin so that I may acquaint myself with the boy."

James watched Nathan as he smiled at the old woman. The old woman returned Nathan's smile. Naomi smiled, too, her eyes dancing with excitement. James wondered just what the hell his second wife had roped him into.

"Well," the old woman said, motioning behind herself. "Are you all going to come in or not?"

The family followed her in seating themselves on the earthen floor of the cabin, in front of a huge stone fireplace. A wicker chair that had seen better days was the only piece of furniture within. A great black stove that called to mind a witch's cauldron sat in the left corner of the floorless room. James found himself thinking of the old woman who intended to eat Hansel and Gretel.

"She nice lady, Papa." Nathan placed a tiny, reassuring hand on James's knee. "She nice lady."

"Yes I am, boy." The bony witch grinned, her gray pupils becoming the eyes of a ghost in the light that shone through the open window. "I am a nice lady. And a friend."

Nathan returned her grin, arousing a small cloud of dirt as he scuttled closer.

"Nathan," James said, instinctively reaching for his son only to have Naomi pull his arm back to his side.

"She is a friend, honey," Naomi whispered.

"Yes, I am." The old woman nodded, rubbing Nathan's head with the bony relics that served as her fingers. "Young Nathan senses it. Haven't you seen enough to trust him in such matters...James David Walker? Or shall I call you JD?"

James bit his bottom lip to stop it from quivering. "You can call me Mr. Walker! Only my father called me JD."

The woman tossed her head back and unleashed another of her guttural laughs. James's eyes pleaded with Naomi, who smiled and squeezed his hand. Meanwhile, Nathan settled himself into the hag's lap.

"Nice lady, Papa," Nathan said, still smiling. "Nice lady."

James felt as if he were trapped within a house of horrors. He felt angry at Naomi for convincing him to come to such a place. He felt furious with himself for having been convinced. Beyond those emotions was fear for his strange, wonderful, terrible child.

"My apologies, Mr. Walker," the old woman said. "I thought that perhaps using your childhood nickname would help you feel more comfortable. Judging by your reaction, it did not have the desired effect. But then, though my sight is strong, I am not a reader of minds. I can sense things, though."

She rubbed Nathan's head again. "I sense that this one already has powers to rival my mine. It shines from him, like a bright light amidst the blackest darkness. It pulses through his body, like lightning trapped within a bottle. As he grows older, it will resist all attempts at containment; all attempts at suppression. Young Nathan must be taught to manage his abilities- to wield them only for good. If not, his abilities will surely manage him. That could result in much harm. To himself and others."

"And you know that just from being around him?" James asked

The old woman's gray pupils flashed black- for a split second appearing as burning coals. Her weathered face twisted into a sneer that James found monstrous. "No! You know that just from being around him! " she howled.

At that moment, young Nathan looked up at his father. James could have sworn that his son wore an expression of paternal patience. The notion that a toddler was capable of such chilled him far more than the old woman's howl.

"Don't be scared, Papa." Nathan walked over to James and rubbed his back with a tiny hand. "She our friend. Ruth is our friend."

"Ruth?"

"Yes, Papa. Her name Ruth."

James gulped hard, wiping emerging beads of sweat from his forehead. "Is," he managed, "Her name is Ruth. What have I told you about that?"

"Sorry," Nathan said. "Her name is Ruth."

"That's a good boy." James swept Nathan onto his lap, kissing him on the forehead. "You'll learn proper speech yet."

"Well, I believe he does very well for a child less than three years old," Naomi grumbled one of her oft-repeated assertions.

"I have no argument with that, Nay," James said, trying to disarm his wife with a grin. "Still, one is never too young to improve."

"James Walker," Naomi chortled, "would you keep your mind on the subject at hand?"

"What subject is that, dear?"

"That subject, Mr. Walker," the old woman interjected, "is your son's education. He's going to need a different one from the stout book learning you will obviously provide him with. He's going to need to learn to manage his abilities."

"And I suppose you intend to teach him?"

"That is my aim," the old woman said, nodding with enough vigor to shake her cotton mane. James wondered that birds did not fly from it. "But he is not ready yet. Two and a half years old is far too young, even for someone as powerful as Nathan."

"Powerful?"

"Oh, yes. The power within your young son is far too great to ignore. It must be cultivated- watered like a garden. But unlike a garden it will not wilt and die if it is not tended to. Instead, it will rage like a wildfire."

James's eyes bulged. "You're trying to tell me that..."

"I am telling you that which you already know but hope to deceive yourself about."

James started to respond, but then stopped himself. He nodded as he squeezed the terrible treasure he had sired to his breast. "You say he is too young?"

"Yes. At his age, it is still difficult to tell between imagination and reality," Ruth explained. "Such is the case even for a boy as bright and intuitive as Nathan. To try and teach him now would only serve to confuse him."

"Then when?"

"Bring him to me after his fifth birthday. He should be ready to begin then."

James nodded his assent.

"Do not worry, Mr. Walker. I know that when you look at me you see an old and ghastly woman and perhaps what you see is true. But this old and ghastly woman has dedicated her looongg life to helping others. And I will surely help your son when he is ready. I believe that his 'education' is the last earthly task the good Lord has seen fit to charge me with. I will take good care of your young Nathan. That is a solemn promise."

She hauled her creaky bones to their feet, her smile once more betraying her dearth of teeth. "Now that we are agreed, it's best you take your young family and go home. I will see you all again at the appointed time."

Nathan must have waved a dozen goodbyes to the old hag as he was lifted into the carriage upon his family's exit. "Nice lady," he chirped as his father led the horses back onto the narrow wooded road. "Ms. Ruth is a nice lady."

James couldn't decide who he found more unsettling as he navigated the long trip home- the old hag or his young son.

4

Leaving Nathan and Opportunity

I.

James enjoyed a hearty breakfast before bidding goodbye to his wife and son and stepping out into Old West Baltimore on a balmy Saturday morning. Virgil joined him on the street in short order, having also kissed his wife and children goodbye.

This early June day was an occasion for business, not women and children. Neither James nor Virgil said much as they began the nine block trek to their destination.

James watched his new Baltimore neighborhood spring to life as he walked. Women and children used soapy buckets and rags to clean marble steps to a fine sheen. The jolly red-haired mailman Mr. Coleridge whistled and greeted folks with an easy manner as he walked his route. Other folks walked their dogs or ambled to their own destinations.

James had no idea where the people he passed were going, but his destination was of utmost importance. Just a few days ago, he'd seen an ad in the classified section of the *Baltimore Evening Sun*. The ad told of a storefront and housing rental in the heart of Pennsylvania Avenue. Its' asking price was 42 dollars per month. Even better, the last two words of the ad were "Coloreds Welcome."

There was no doubt that James was Colored, just as there was no question that he could raise 42 dollars a month. Hell, now that the damn Colored bank in Greenville had managed to wire him the rest of his savings, he had over a thousand dollars. It took a month, but the bastards made good.

Depositing his money in a Colored bank was a mistake James didn't intend to repeat now that he lived in Baltimore. For the time being, he kept his money hidden under his mattress. It didn't draw interest that way, but at least he could get to it when he needed to.

Virgil lost a struggle to contain himself as they walked. "Hot damn," he yelped halfway to the destination, slapping James on the back. "You really 'bout to do it, cousin! You really 'bout to have your own business! Ain't many Colored men kin claim that."

"I'm not going to count my chickens before they hatch, Virgil," James responded. "A deal's not a deal until all parties involved put their John Hancock on the paper."

Virgil shrugged. "I guess you right. Still, I think ever'thang'll work out fine. These Baltimore crackers ain't as hateful as the ones down South. Least they not stupid enough to let black skin keep them from making green money."

The brisk pace they kept brought them to the storefront within twenty minutes. The prize James desired sat at the bottom of a brick building that looked sturdy enough to withstand artillery fire. Judging by the number of second floor windows, James assumed that there were three bedrooms within. A pristine new Ford Model-T sat unattended across the street.

The storefront's shades were drawn, giving it a deserted appearance. James knocked anyway, expecting the owner to be inside.

A tall, pasty fellow with reddish brown-hair opened the door. The man wore a dark pin striped suit and dark dress shoes. He cocked his head like a curious cat, sizing James up before extending his right hand. "James Walker- I presume."

"Yes, sir," James said, smiling and taking firm hold of the hand that had been offered. "You are Mr. Breslin?" His eyes performed a delicate dance, maintaining enough contact with Mr. Breslin's eyes as was customary during an exchange of business, yet not staring. There could be trouble if a white man thought that a black man was staring at him. James didn't need to be told that such held true even outside of the Deep South. The difference was that in Baltimore, lynching wasn't a guaranteed consequence.

James didn't give a damn about offending whites on most occasions. But for the sake of furthering his own agenda, he was determined not to anger the one before him.

"Yes, I am." Breslin motioned for James to enter. "Let's have a look."

Virgil started to follow James, only to be stopped by the alarmed expression that emerged on Breslin's face. "You are?"

James chuckled. "That's just my cousin, Virgil. He escorted me here. As I said during our phone conversation, I'm new to Baltimore. I needed him to show me the way. You'll have to forgive Virgil. He isn't much of a businessman. Otherwise, he would've known he was expected to wait outside."

James didn't need to observe his cousin's facial expression to know he was offended. Well, that was Virgil's own fault. He should have known better. James would smooth things out with him later. Right now, I'm not letting anything prevent me from leaving this meeting without a lease, James thought as he closed the door.

The interior of the structure was very large, with a trio of man height ice boxes and a sandwich counter situated near the left rear of its expanse. A sink and large stove-topped oven sat behind the sandwich counter.

James decided right then to devote one of the ice boxes to storing ice cream. He could churn and sell the cold, sweet treat, set up a soda fountain to accompany it, sell dairy and meat out of the remaining ice boxes, stock the store's ample shelves with cereal, chips, and the like. The place was perfect. He'd make wise use of the money he'd saved and have it hopping in no time. He meant to turn it into one hell of a convenience store, just for starters.

Excitement coursed through James, but he feigned calm as his potential landlord tooted the property's horn. Once they completed the tour of the store space, Breslin led James through the door at its rear. They climbed the staircase beyond, leading them to the living space. There was only one bathroom on the upper floor, but it was quite large. A round tub lay within, fit to stretch out and rest one's bones in.

The hardwood floors of the upstairs space were immaculate. James decided right then that he would make it Nathan's responsibility to keep them clean. The boy was now big enough to handle such a task.

There were three bedrooms, just as James expected. The rearmost one was the largest. Even the smaller ones were significantly larger than the room he'd slept in at the old farmhouse.

James intended to use the third bedroom as his office. Yes, this setup was just what he needed to provide a financial backbone for the activism he planned to throw himself into. He followed Breslin back down to the store, keeping up his nonplussed façade.

James had come to this meeting with the idea of securing a lease for rental, but he couldn't resist the more ambitious idea that screamed inside his head. Figuring that Breslin had inherited the store but didn't want to be bothered with running it, he decided to see if the white man wanted to cut all ties with it.

"If you don't mind me asking, Mr. Breslin," James measured his words, "How much would you be willing to sell this property for?"

Breslin's placid veneer shifted into a smirk. He snorted- an unsubtle show of disgust. "Well, if I meant to sell it- I'd let it go for about 3000 dollars. Those who can afford that price aren't looking to own property in this neighborhood."

James had no problem reading the subtext of that statement. Virgil had informed him that a lot of Germans and Irish had left Old West Baltimore as Negroes flocked toward it, preferring to live in areas where they saw only people of their own complexion. Most of the remaining whites in the area were Jews. To hear Virgil tell it, they'd soon be pulling up stakes as well. James didn't agree with that prediction by his cousin, figuring that at the very least, area businesses would be dominated by whites, so long as commerce was good.

It was clear that Breslin was incapable of entertaining the notion that a Negro would have as much money as he'd just mentioned. It was just as clear that he was not looking to sell. Still, pride wouldn't allow James to choke back his next statement.

"3000 dollars?" He said, thinking of his handsome savings. "I could raise a third of that as a down payment. If you would like, we could reconvene after you draft a deed of sale. I would very much like to own this place."

"Would you, now?" Breslin sneered, resembling a dog bearing its teeth. "I bet you would. Thing is, I don't wish to sell. I only wish to rent. That is why I listed the property in the newspaper as a 'rental'."

James nodded, realizing he'd made a big mistake. A man like Breslin had no qualms making money off Coloreds, but he had a big problem with them having real power. Property ownership was the key to power in this country. If James had been white, Breslin would have jumped at his offer. Instead, James would be lucky if he could conclude this encounter by accomplishing his original goal.

"That's fine, then." James cast his eyes downward, trying to assume the role of the humble Negro to save his original plan. He felt disgusted with himself, but far more disgusted with Breslin. "I'd still love to rent the place."

"Alright, then." Breslin's smile became that of a predator as he produced some folded papers from his suit pocket. He unfolded them on the vacant sandwich counter. James settled in next to him, on one of the round stools that jutted from the floor.

Breslin slid the lease papers over to him. James read them with care, finding the terms to be standard to his knowledge of leases.

"The terms are acceptable to me," he said, trying to sound meek.

"Excellent," Breslin chortled. "126 dollars will make our agreement official."

"126 dollars?" James struggled to keep his voice neutral, hoping to seem surprised rather than outraged. Outraged Colored men had a habit of finding their way to jail, or worse. "When we spoke on the phone you said you required first month's rent and security deposit. That's 84 dollars."

"Your math is perfect!" Breslin's kind smile and vocal pitch reeked of condescension. He seemed shocked that a Negro could multiply forty-two by two. "But to be perfectly forthright with you, now that I've met you I feel the need for further safeguard in this venture. You seem like the sort of man who'll have this place swarming with activity. I'm worried that there could be repair damages I haven't anticipated."

James heard the real message contained within that façade of caution, loud and clear. He was being extorted because he had overreached himself, been too prideful. Breslin meant to make James feel small, to show him that a white man would always be in control, even if a Negro happened to have enough money to purchase property within a large city like Baltimore. James decided to devour the huge slice of humble pie placed before him, thinking of doing so as a worthwhile means to a noble end.

Once he opened for business, he'd show himself to be the equal of Breslin and every other white businessman in town. That would be soon enough.

Breslin sighed. "Of course, If you find that unfair I can continue running the ad."

"No, no, Mr. Breslin. If that's what you require to ease your mind, I'm willing to pay."

The shark's grin resurfaced. "Actually, 168 dollars would put me perfectly at ease."

James nodded his assent as he fantasized about beating the rotten bastard to a pulp.

James watched as Mr. Breslin strutted from the store like a king rooster a few minutes later. The man's chest stuck out so far that it threatened to pop free of his ribcage and fly off, leaving his cold heart exposed.

James shrugged off the gloating. He had suffered heavy casualties, but as far as he was concerned he had won the battle. Once the dough started rolling in, he intended to win many more.

James devoted a few moments to drinking in the promising interior of his business to be before using his new keys to lock up. Virgil stood where James had left him. He didn't seem the least bit graced by his cousin's presence.

"How was it?" he grumbled.

James shrugged. "Good and bad," he said, watching Breslin put his Model-T in motion. The Cheshire grinning bastard had the poor taste to honk his horn and wave as he drove off.

"He gave me a hard way to go." James held out his copy of the lease and pointed to Breslin's signature. "Bottom line is - I got the John Hancock. Won't be long until I'm in business now."

"Congratulations."

"Thank you." James placed a hand on one of Virgil's meaty shoulders. The shoulder stood high and tense, just as James expected. "Listen, Virgil. I'm sorry about what I said earlier. I was just trying to make the bastard feel comfortable. I owe you a lot, cousin."

"Don't mention it," Virgil said, allowing himself a smile. The tension slowly left his shoulders as they eased into a relaxed position. "I should a known better than that. White men don't want to be alone with one Colored, let alone two." He laughed. "You see his face when I started for the door? Bastard looked like he was about to soil his trousers. I jus' bet he thought we might rob him or somethin'."

James let out a great whoop of a laugh, slapping his hands against his thighs. He leaned back against his new rental property, surrendering to the hilarity that engulfed him. "Could be," he managed between guffaws, "but he must've gotten over that fear real fast, because he ended up robbing me."

II.

Nathan climbed into the carriage without any adult assistance, his five year old movements as fluid as those of a trained athlete.

The climate was typical of a January day in Alabama, windy and hovering in the vicinity of fifty degrees. Way down near the Gulf of Mexico, the occupant of a lonely cabin waited for James and his family to make their journey. As he settled into the driver's seat and led his faithful horses into the road, James reflected on the time that had passed since their first visit with the old woman.

Two and a half years had sprinted by. Nathan had grown leaps and bounds in height and awareness during that fleeting time, shedding the squat awkwardness of a toddler. His limbs and torso had gained significant ground on his head. He was graceful and lean in his improved proportions, having lost much of his baby fat.

Nathan's eyes remained gray-green spheres of light. The magnificent orbs never failed to give his father pause. James often caught his son in deep contemplation, eyes seeming to seek out a realm beyond his surroundings. At times, Nathan's eyes lit up like candles.

James always managed to laugh off his own concerns. What do you think he's doing? He'd admonish himself. Communing with the spirits? That's a bunch of hogwash.

Still, James knew that Nathan's capacity for the spectacular defied all logic and science. The boy presented too much evidence of his special ability for James to build a sturdy barrier of denial.

One such incident occurred when they returned from dinner at a neighbor's home. Nathan's eyes bulged in terror as they exited the carriage. "Snake," he croaked. "On the porch. Copperhead."

Sure enough, a huge brown viper lay curled by the front door. James circled around the back of the farmhouse, grabbed his shotgun from the shed and blasted its' poisonous head off. As blood splattered the porch and the snake's ruined body jerked its' final death throes, James tried and failed to convince himself that the boy had simply seen it with his eyes.

On another occasion, Nathan awakened his father in the middle of the night, rambling about thieves getting into John Lawrence's onion patch. Lawrence was a white homesteader, the lone white man James counted as more than a speaking friend. He owned a small plot of land about three miles up the road. James called

Lawrence the morning after Nathan's rambling. He warned his friend to keep a careful watch over his fields, saying that he heard there was a band of thieves about.

When two days went by without any confirmation from Lawrence, James breathed a sigh of relief. He wanted to mark the outcome as proof that perhaps Nathan wasn't clairvoyant after all. What seemed to be supernatural might merely be advanced powers of perception. James reasoned to himself that an extremely perceptive person might seem clairvoyant at times.

That notion was dashed when Lawrence rang his phone the next evening. "I'll be a sonofabitch, James," Lawrence drawled. "You were right about there bein' thieves about. Caught two young colored boys in the patch just after sundown. Turned my shotgun on 'em. Felt sorry for the ole boys, though. They looked so damn hungry. Hell, me and Mable invited 'em up to the house for dinner. Seems the ole boys are on hard times, harder even than most. Had a nice dinner, ended up hirin' 'em on. I warned 'em, though. Any more shenanigans an' I'll turn 'em in to the 'thorities. Say, how'd you know?"

James invented a quick lie. "You know how it is out in the country, John. Folks talk. Sometimes you hear things."

John laughed. "Can't argue that. Well, next time you hear somethin', let me know. I won't question your ears again."

That last statement was a powerful argument for James not questioning Nathan's ability again. Still, he couldn't help himself. He burned with desire for Nathan to just be a normal kid.

But Nathan just kept providing examples of his ability, leaving his father with no alternative but to own up to what he was. Though the prospect of supernatural clashed with his rational beliefs, ignoring implacable evidence of the truth was even more contrary to James's way of thinking.

Once James accepted his son's uncanny ability, he made no bones about keeping it a secret among their small family.

"Other people might not understand you," James said during their first conversation about the matter. "And people are usually scared of what they don't understand."

As so often happened, the childish glint of Nathan's dichromatic eyes seemed to brighten and darken in the same moment, deepening into something sinister and beautiful, foreboding, and majestic. James shivered, feeling that the then four-year old was looking into his very soul.

"Like you get scared of me," Nathan said, his voice somber.

"No." A single tear escaped James as he swept the boy into his arms. "I could never be scared of you, Nathan. Never! You're my pride and joy, son. I just get scared of what you can do."

Nathan sobbed into his father's shoulder. "I get scared of what I can do, too."

"So you see, then. Don't you boy?" James squeezed tighter, looking out at his land from the porch chair on which he sat. "If you and I get scared, what might other people think? That's why we can't let anyone know."

"Because they might try to hurt me," Nathan verbalized his father's fears.

"I will never, ever let anyone hurt you," James swore, a flood of tears bursting forth. "Never."

"I won't let anyone hurt you either, Papa." Nathan squeezed with all the strength his little body could muster. "Never."

Nathan grew fastidious about keeping his powers under wrap, never revealing them when he had occasion to play with other children. He, James, and Naomi agreed that if he ever "saw" anything that seemed important, he would only tell them about it. If his little "glimpses" didn't seem important, he'd keep them to himself.

"Doing any differently hardly seems fair," Naomi told Nathan. "No sense cheating your way through life. That cheapens what God blessed you with."

Nathan nodded at those words, seeming to possess complete understanding of what his stepmother was getting at. It was a wonder that such a young boy could understand such high moral concepts, but Nathan absorbed them with no problem.

He governed himself well, managing to seem a precocious and perhaps genius young boy to those not in the know- not a supernatural freak worthy of fear.

The train of such thoughts chugged through James's head until the carriage pulled close to the family's destination. The winter sun stood at its' zenith when they arrived. Bright rays penetrated the woods that surrounded Ruth's cabin.

The ancient woman stood in the doorway of the worn structure, looking even more like walking death than she had during their first encounter. Her face was even more gaunt and wrinkled. Her neck was thin and prominent with bone, as was the rest of her withered body.

When Ruth smiled, James felt as if he were looking at one of the model skeletons that had been in his biology classroom at Tuskegee. The difference was that those skeletons held more than the three corroded teeth that were attached to the hag's ghoulish gums.

"Yes, I have aged even more, Mr. Walker." Ruth's cavernous grin widened as she addressed his unvoiced thoughts. Her voice had grown even more dry and brittle. "Though I may look like a cadaver, there's life in me, yet."

She held her arms out for Nathan to run into them. "Certainly enough life left for me to teach a certain little boy."

Nathan giggled as he leapt into her embrace. James could have sworn he heard the sounds of bones crunching as they collided.

Soon, they were all inside, once again sitting on the earthen floor of the cabin, a huge quilt spread beneath them. Ruth served the family of three a cold, dark tea. James eyed it with undisguised skepticism.

The old woman emitted another ghoulish laugh. "No worries, Mr. Walker. It is merely tea, from tea leaves. No eye of newt nor wing of bat in the recipe."

"She's a nice lady, Papa," Nathan assured his father. "She's not a witch or ghost."

Naomi's annoyance with James was obvious in her glare. James shrugged, thinking, It's not as if I said anything aloud. He wished his wife was able to read his thoughts as well, just for that one second.

He felt obligated to drink from his cup after Naomi and Nathan drank from theirs. He felt relieved to find that the beverage didn't taste like some sort of cow feces. Nor was there a worm crawling within. It could have used sweetening, but it was tea, alright.

He lapped the substance down in an effort to still the nervous energy that permeated his body. No, dread was a more apt description.

As he had two and a half years earlier, James's son attempted to comfort him, placing a small hand on his wrist. James looked at the boy. The boy nodded and smiled, speaking with the certainty of the converted. "She's going to help me, Papa."

Naomi also turned her attention to James, grinning as she squeezed his cheek. He chuckled as he always did when she did so, managing to smile and relax a little. He'd stay the course, not make waves. If Nathan felt so confident that the old ha-old woman would help, then so it would be. He'd never known the boy to be wrong about such matters.

"It is good that you have decided to trust me," Ruth said, staring into James's eyes. For the first time, he realized that her gray eyes were two-toned as Nathan's hazel ones were. Instead of green at the outer third of her irises, there was midnight blackness.

"The strange eyes are the mark of a seer," the old woman said. "It is the only physical indicator- other than the veil that is removed following birth. I did not want to reveal this before, but according to legend, those with double-veiled birth are the most powerful of seers. I was born with two veils." She paused to allow the gravity of her words to sink in.

"Nathan, however," She deliberated over her words, not wanting to alarm her guests. "Young Nathan…."

"Was born with three veils," Naomi finished the statement.

"No, he was…" James retreated toward his well-practiced veil of denial, before realization thrust it aside. "Oh, my God. The flaps over his eyes."

"Yes, the flaps over his eyes," the old woman said.

"But that means…."

"That he will be far more powerful than even I."

An overwhelmed feeling flooded James, bringing him just short of swooning. He looked to his right, at Naomi. She appeared solemn, determined to face whatever uncomfortable truth this encounter revealed.

He looked to his left, at Nathan. The boy sat rapt, spectral eyes pulsating, frozen upon Ruth. He was an open sponge, ready to receive all that his soon to be teacher offered.

"You can trust me, Mr.Walker," Ruth said. "You will have to trust me. I am the only one who has a prayer of helping Nathan to harness his awesome powers. In my thorough knowledge of the sight, it most often manifests itself during adolescence. The bearers of the rare double veil, such as myself, sees their abilities manifest a few years before that epoch. I was nine when I first saw signs of mine. Nathan, however…Nathan…."

Naomi finished another statement. "Has been using his powers since he was two years old."

"At least," Ruth's tone grew grave in agreement.

James suppressed an anxious laugh. Grave tones from someone who looks as if she were just removed from a grave, he thought, having no doubt that stress was making him loopy.

"He may have manifested as an infant, but had no capacity to communicate it," Ruth said.

James realized the great likelihood that old Ruth was correct in that assertion. There were many occasions when Nathan grew wide-eyed and spastic during infancy. James had interpreted such instances as normal infant excitability. Now he realized it might have been something more.

Damn, James thought. This is a lot for a rational man, a believer of science to absorb at one time. I thought I had an understanding of what Nathan was, only to learn that what I thought I understood may only have been the smallest inkling.

"His power will be awe-inspiring, at times terrifying," Ruth continued. "I must begin to teach him to harness it right away. You have done well in teaching him to conceal it from others, but as he grows older, that will prove far more difficult to do. Particularly once he reaches the pangs of adolescence."

She stood up then, her strange eyes glowing like lit coals. "You will have to leave him here. It is the only way."

"What?" James sprang up, stirring up a small cloud of dirt. "Old woman you must be insane if you think I'm leaving my son in the middle of the woods with you." He towered over her child sized frame.

Nathan stood and tugged at his father's sleeve. James turned and looked down into the boy's glowing, ethereal eyes.

"You have to trust her, Papa," Nathan urged. "She'll take good care of me. I have to learn."

"Yes, I must teach him," Ruth agreed. "And it is not safe for folks lacking the sight to be around when a seer is being taught. I could not begin to explain why, but let's just say there would be too much interference." She chuckled, holding her arms palms out to her sides to draw attention to the narrow confines of the cabin. "Besides, this place could hardly accommodate all of you."

"And I suppose it can accommodate Nathan?"

"Oh, yes." Ruth's horrible smile emerged again. "Nathan will be just fine."

"What will he eat?" James asked, as Naomi wrapped a comforting arm around his slim waist.

"Food will not be a problem," Ruth said. "I have my own garden out back. And I am quite the hunter and fisher. Let's just say I always know where my catch will be."

James stood silent, hand resting on his chin for countless beats. He broke the silence by asking how long Ruth intended to keep Nathan.

"For a few weeks to start with. After that, you may bring him to me every other weekend. That's the way things need to be. I know I am asking a great thing. I know it is difficult for you to trust me with your child, but trust me, you must."

James fell into silent contemplation once more. This time he broke the silence by asking if there was a post office near.

"In Lewiston. About three miles south, right at the lip of the Gulf."

"You ever leave these woods?"

"Believe or not, I do, Mr. Walker. I'm not a complete recluse. And yes, I will be happy to assist Nathan in writing two letters home per week while he stays here."

"I wish you wouldn't do that!" James barked. "It really spooks me!"

"My apologies, Mr. Walker. It is a very old and difficult habit to break."

James and Naomi bid an emotional goodbye to their son a short time later. As was so often the case, Nathan comforted them instead of vice versa.

"Everything will be okay, Papa. Everything will be okay, Mama," he said, embracing them at waist level. James knew that few things meant as much to his second wife as being called "Mama" by their special child. Not "Mama Naomi", making a distinction between her and the departed Helen. Just Mama.

He and Naomi managed to tear themselves away after a prolonged goodbye, leaving with a promise from Nathan to write and be well behaved. That promise was accompanied by a solemn swear from the old woman to take excellent care of him.

Naomi eschewed the carriage during the return trip to the homestead, climbing up front with James.

"You know, societal conventions say that it's not proper for a lady to ride out front like this," James said, attempting a little levity.

"I don't give a damn about societal conventions. And I don't give a damn about it being a bumpier ride up front. I just want to be close to my husband."

They bunched as close as possible as James drove. The sun shrunk from the sky as the tiny, snaking forest road gave way to more civil passages. Night had just emerged when the horses stopped in front of their home.

They bedded down for the evening a short time later. Naomi drifted into untroubled sleep, as if she were confident that everything would be alright. James wished that he could manage the same, but tossed and turned instead. He felt incomplete and downright miserable without the wondrous fruit of his loins nearby. He also felt wracked with worry. He already burned for Nathan's return, even though they had just parted.

III.

"What will you have, sir?" Nathan asked the burly customer on the stool, a charming smile plastered on his face.

"Give me one scoop of chocolate and one scoop of vanilla, on one of them sugar cones," came the gruff answer.

"Vanilla on top?"

"That's right, son," the customer said, a wry grin spreading across his features. "Hey, James," he said, turning on his stool and yelling towards the shelves that James stocked. "Your boy here is one hell of a worker."

Pride coursed through James as he nodded. Nathan was one hell of a worker. He showed a maturity and focus that belied his nine years of age and four and a half feet of height.

Over the past two years, the family business had blossomed in a whirlwind of activity that Nathan played an important role in. Besides beating the sun out of bed each day to help his father shelve just delivered merchandise, he helped to keep the kitchen and restrooms clean. But his most important job was serving soda pop along with the ice cream and cones that Naomi toiled to make.

Walker's did huge business in those confections, James having opened the first such Negro owned parlor in Old West Baltimore.

Every day after school and all day during the summer, Nathan served cones, floats, sundaes, and soda with a pleasant smile and courteous manner. His knack for service made him something of a neighborhood celebrity. Customers dubbed him "Young Soda Pop", besieging him with orders for their favorite confections.

Young Soda Pop evolved into Little Pop-the name that stuck. With the help of Little Pop, the store brought in much more money than James's regular earnings from the acreage he once possessed in Alabama.

James gave his son an allowance for working in the store, but *Walker's* customers paid the child much better. It wasn't unusual for Nathan to earn more than two dollars worth of tips in a week. He often made double that amount when he worked the longer summer hours. Thinking of the boy's future, James and Naomi decreed that Nathan was allowed to spend one dollar each week, setting the rest of his earning aside for savings.

They wanted Nathan to begin adulthood with a nice monetary cushion. If the boy went to college as they hoped, he should have plenty of funds towards those expenses. If he surprised them by choosing some other path, he was free to do with his savings as he pleased. After all, every dime would be money he had earned.

James combined ambition with business acumen, never accepting less than the best wholesale prices on the meat, dairy products, produce, nonperishable foods, and toiletries that the store sold. It wasn't long before *Walker's* sold just about everything a Negro could want, save alcohol and cigarettes. James had no desire to deal in such vices.

Within a few months of business, James had a grill and fryer installed so that Naomi could prepare hot food. Praise for her delicious burgers, sandwiches, and chicken flew through the neighborhood.

In little more than a year, James expanded the business by adding a small pharmacy. Through conversations with a recurring customer, Mr. Dennis, James found out that the man had a degree in Pharmacology. Mr. Dennis had spent eighteen years of his life working at white owned pharmacies. He'd worked at *Eckstein's* (a pharmacy a few blocks west on Pennsylvania Avenue) for the last eight of those eighteen years.

As Mr. Dennis enjoyed a cheeseburger and fries one afternoon, James asked him how much he made at *Eckstein's*. After Mr. Dennis answered, James offered two dollars more per week to work for him.

"You're serious?" Mr. Dennis asked, cheeseburger frozen in front of his mouth. "You aim to open a pharmacy here?"

James smiled. "Mr. Dennis, I never joke about matters of commerce."

Mr. Dennis agreed to take the job without hesitation.

It took four months and a bit of palm greasing for James to gain approval to add the pharmacy. He kept Mr. Dennis on during that time, paying him the promised salary although he hadn't performed any pharmaceutical duties yet.

James saw the workless pay as a necessary sacrifice. Having a licensed and experienced pharmacist already in his employ meant that the white folks down at the local Board of Commerce couldn't deny his endeavor for the reason of not having one. The Board's only recourse was to jack up his fees of declaration, something they would have done anyway.

That's how James's world turned. He just kept beating the white businessmen of West Baltimore at their own game, no matter how they tried to stop him.

Walker's soon grew enough for James to ask Virgil if he might hire his wife and eldest son David on.

Virgil agreed without reservation, although he was making pretty good money of his own. He had become the resident photographer at *Mrs. Laney's Lovely Pictures*, one of the few other Negro owned businesses on the Pennsylvania Avenue strip. Virgil was doing better than ever with the racket he still had going on with Thurmont supplemented by the money from his regular photography commissions.

Still, he didn't mind his wife and eldest son working at the store. Doing so meant that Alma needn't bother with scrubbing white folks' floors and doing their wash.

Alma performed the duties of her new job par excellence, showing herself to be as capable a cook as Naomi. Having interchangeable cooks meant that Walker's served quality food from open to close.

David backed Nathan up in everything save confectionary duties, showing a great deal of maturity for a normal 12 year old. He washed dishes, carried hot food to the quartet of tables James added beyond the lunch counter, and cleaned floors and bathrooms. He also kept an eye on his little brother when Virgil didn't take him along to the studio.

James managed the business with unerring acumen, leaving the pharmacy to the dependable Mr. Dennis. James was having the best times of his life, despite the occasional roadblock thrust in his path by the white world.

Walker's stayed busy from 8 am to 8 pm on weekdays and from 8 am to 4 pm on Saturdays.

Negroes took pride in the store, it being the first and only Negro owned business of its nature in Old West Baltimore. Walker's grew into much more than a place where folks could get good food, toiletries, groceries, and pharmaceutical items. It became a place where Negroes gathered to unwind and unburden their worldview among other Negroes.

Just as Virgil predicted, the already majority Colored Old West Baltimore became more Colored with each passing day. It seemed like damn near every Negro within the city limits with two dimes to rub together was housed in the area. The more Negroes moved in, the more Germans, Italians, and Jews moved out. It wasn't long before a white resident became a rare sighting.

White businesses remained, however. It seemed that whites didn't mind making money off of Coloreds, but they damn sure didn't want to live among them.

That was just fine with James. From what numerous conversations within his store revealed, that was fine with most Negroes.

Their quarrel with the separate but equal doctrine wasn't the separate part. It was that no part of segregated life stood within shouting distance of equal. How did equal amount to Negroes crowding into the back while riding public transportation or always entering from the rear? How did equal amount to Negroes having to use inferior restrooms and water fountains?

As a Negro business owner, James caught far more racial grief than his brethren whom followed what was accepted as the natural hierarchy by toiling for whites. Beat cops sometimes burst into his store. Their hateful eyes gleamed with the intent to strike fear into James and his patrons. They always uttered something to the effect of "I'm watching you, boy," as they departed.

That bastard Breslin proved a much sharper thorn than the cops when he informed James that he would be raising the rent from 42 to 50 dollars per month at the time of lease renewal. Breslin knew as well as James did that a nineteen percent increase was highly unethical- but what was James going to do? Lose his business? Lose his residence?

Instead of complaining or resisting the impending increase, James proposed that he pay 60 dollars per month. Breslin's blue eyes nearly popped free of his head at the astronomical offer. A skeptical expression replaced the landlord's look of amazement in the next instant, but James already knew he had his fish on the line. He knew that there was no way that Breslin would turn down the opportunity to be paid nearly one and two thirds times the going rate for a commercial rental in Old West Baltimore. The only caveat was that he draw up the new lease for a period of five years. So it was that each man came to position the other just where he wanted him.

James was a firm believer that money was power, perhaps even more so for Negroes than for whites. It was his thriving business (with its' central location) that placed him in position to pursue leading his Negro neighbors in future activism. He wasn't willing to give up that location, but he didn't want Breslin to be able to raise his rent by random and ridiculous sums every year. So he secured the exorbitant rate of 60 dollars a month for five years, figuring that Breslin would someday take the price far beyond that if he continued to settle for short leases.

James believed that Breslin and those like him would not always hold the upper hand in American society. If James had anything to do with it, Breslin and his like would lose their monopoly on prosperity during James's lifetime. Now that he had secured such a lengthy lease, James felt even more emboldened to pursue social and economic progress for the Negro in Baltimore.

5

The Apt Pupil and the School Bully

I.

Although Ruth appeared haggard and ghastly, Nathan felt quite at ease with her. He "knew" that she was full of kindness and desire to help him. His young mind recalled their first meeting with clarity, although he'd been a mere toddler at the time.

Nathan's mind was much more developed than a typical child his age, as it had been far more advanced than a typical toddler's. As intelligent as he was, he couldn't understand what the big commotion was about his powers.

His ability seemed commonplace to him. He hadn't known anything else. His sight felt as natural as walking.

Nathan obeyed his parents' wishes in not speaking of things that he saw whenever they encountered others. He rarely mentioned such occurrences around his father at all.

His behavior was different when only in his stepmother's presence. She often encouraged him to use his sight when they played little games together. One of her favorite games was setting up a scavenger hunt around the property.

Naomi always delighted at how quickly Nathan found the items she'd hidden, clapping her hands and making comments such as, "I swear boy. It's like you read your Mama's mind."

"Read your mind?" Nathan said, raising his small eyebrows the first time she made the comment.

She nodded, still smiling. "Yes. It's like you could see inside my brain, to know what I was thinking. That way you know where I put everything."

Nathan shook his head. "No, Mama. I can't see in your head. I swear."

She went to him then, kneeling to place an arm around his tiny shoulders.

"It's alright, baby. I'm not poking fun. It just makes me happy to see you do such wondrous things. You know I wouldn't poke fun- right?"

Nathan nodded.

The woman he knew as "Mama" pinched one of his cheeks. "Well, Young Mr. Walker. If you can't read my mind... then how do you always know where I hide things?"

Nathan thought hard, trying to think of the words to describe a kind of psychic magnetism that led him to the desired spots. All he had to do was visualize each item she called out to him to be pulled toward the proper location. It was as if each hidden item were a hunk of metal and the force guiding him was the world's most effective metal detector.

Lacking the vocabulary to provide such an explanation, he chose one much simpler. "Somethin' pulls me, somethin' pulls me toward what I want. It's like magic. But Papa says there's no magic."

"Does he now?" his mother said, smiling. "Well, between you and me, Nathan- your Papa doesn't know everything."

Are you ready to learn, Young Nathan? Ruth's voice sounded in Nathan's head, yanking him from his reverie. He and the old woman regarded each other as they sat on the earthen floor of her cabin. A bemused, nearly toothless smile stretched her wrinkled face. Nathan understood that she had thought the words at him, no sound leaving her lips at all.

That's right, boy. I can think right at you. Her coal colored pupils glinted in her gray eyes. What's a matter, boy? Cat got your tongue, so to speak? Or you just don't realize you can do it, too? Go on. Think at me, boy.

Nathan shifted in place and tried what she said. *Your eyes have two colors, just like mine,* he thought.

No, not just like yours, boy. Your eyes are like a cat's. Mine are like ash and night. But they are two colors, just the same. As I told your folks, the strange eyes are part of the deal for folks like us. Now, can't we discuss something that hasn't been talked about already?

"I think your eyes are..."

The ancient woman pursed her dry lips. *Don't you speak out loud, boy! I want you to think everything at me for the time being. Now, what about my eyes?*

I think your eyes are pretty.

A pleasant sensation coursed through Nathan's mind. His head filled with delight.

Is that how you think a laugh, Miss Ruth?

The sensation repeated itself. The old woman's dark eyes brightened to a high sheen. *I say. You are a quick study, child. Yes, I can laugh and smile on the inside, just as well as on the outside. Shoot, regular folks can do that. They just can't do it in somebody else's head. That's your first lesson, boy. Anything you can communicate outside of yourself, you can do it on the inside just as well. Especially when you're around one of your own kind. I do declare, boy. I'm going to have a fine time teaching you.*

They spent the rest of the evening thinking at each other. It didn't take long for the act to become second nature to Nathan.

A satisfied Ruth brought the lesson to a close, allowing her young charge to look on as she prepared dinner on her cauldron of a stove. She regarded him with cheer as they sat down to plates of roasted corn and charred rabbit before lantern light.

You've got the knack already, Nathan, she thought at him. *I expected to have to spend a few days teaching you about this, especially with you being so young and all. But you fooled me. You're a special one, alright. I've taught a number of seers since I came here, most of them having just reached adolescence before arriving. As I told your folks, that's when most of our kind realize their powers. It kind of lies quietly in them until then, not surfacing often enough or in a powerful enough way for them to suspect anything other than having an unexplainable premonition or two. Heck, some folks haven't come to me until they're adults. A lot of such folks never mastered mind talk at all, even if the sight was strong enough in them for them to do so. The ones who did suffered many failures and frustrations before gaining any knack for it. But you- you got it right straight off! At only five years old!*

Ruth clapped with exuberance, causing her withered palms to produce a sound akin to a lit firecracker. At the same time that he heard the sound, Nathan felt her giddiness in his mind. It pleased him that she was so pleased with him. He knew that his parents would be happy to learn he'd done well.

Yes, child. You're a special one all right. Maybe even more special than old Ruth, already. And I'm pretty special when it comes to mind powers. Shoot, I'm a living legend. Ain't I? The Woman of the Gulf Woods is what they call me. Some call me the Hag of the Gulf woods, which I could understand if it came from folks who had actually seen this bag of wrinkles and bones. Never mind that. I'm rambling on, boy. I got one more thing to teach you, tonight. But first I'll let you eat your dinner.

Having discovered that thinking at Miss Ruth was just as vigorous an activity as running and playing on the farm, Nathan lifted a rabbit leg to his mouth. He was all set to take the biggest bite his five year old mouth could manage when a thought disrupted him.

You're forgetting to say grace, boy! Lead us in grace.

Nathan bowed his head, thinking his prayer to Miss Ruth. *God is great, God is good. Let us thank you for our food. Amen.*

Amen, Ruth thought. "You ever had rabbit before, Nathan? You can speak out loud, if you like."

Nathan nodded. "Yes. Mama Nay- Mama made it before."

"Is that right? I bet it was good, too. Bet you never had it charred like mine, though." Ruth pointed at Nathan's plate. "Dig in, boy."

Nathan wolfed his vittles down, finding that the taste of the food suited the cook's confidence. *Thank you, Miss Ruth.*

You don't have to thank me. "It's my pleasure to feed such an angelic child."

A short time later, Nathan lay wrapped in an old blanket on the earthen floor, in front of the old woman's cracking fireplace. Not sleeping in a bed didn't bother him at all. The sounds of night creatures emanating from the woods now that the sun slept didn't bother him either. The only thing that did bother him was missing his Mama and Papa. Still, he was happy he was learning well, like they wanted him to. He couldn't wait until Miss Ruth helped him write a letter to them. It would be a wonderful day when he saw them again.

Miss Ruth squatted down next to Nathan, interrupting his thoughts just as they tightened their grip on him.

Got to tell you one more thing before I let you say your prayers and drift off, boy.

Yes, Ma'am?

Know how I showed you that you can think laughter and happiness at others?

102

Yes, Ma'am.

Well, you can also think anger and sadness at others. One as powerful as you can think all sorts of things at folks, some of them bad things, things you're too young to even feel yet. Most seers can only think at others like themselves- but the strongest ones- like me, can even think at regular folks. It might not come across as clearly as to another seer, but it comes across just the same. And If I can do it, you can surely do it.

An intense stare fell upon him. The glowing of her dark eyes seemed to join the fire in illuminating the cabin.

You'll want to stay out of regular folks' minds, Nathan- especially if you're feeling bad. One as powerful as you might do harm to folks like that. You don't want to do no harm. Do you?

No, Ma'am. Nathan's hazel and green eyes also glowed in the darkness. The green mirrored the finest jade as it was backlight by the fireplace. *I don't want to harm anyone.*

"Good." Ruth smiled and rubbed his head. *Just remember what I told you about staying out of regular folks' heads and just maybe, you'll manage not to.* "Don't worry, I'll keep reminding you." *You say your prayers and get to sleep, son. Maybe tomorrow, I'll start you on talking to animals.*

"Animals?" Nathan squealed in anticipation. He loved animals.

Ruth nodded. "That's right. I know you'll love that." She rubbed his head once more. *What boy wouldn't?*

II.

Nathan knew that his parents wouldn't like what he'd done. Now that it was over, he didn't much like it himself. He hadn't wanted anything like this to happen, but John Turner had left him no choice.

The big sixth grader had teased and roughed Nathan up at the grade school for weeks. The brute never failed to make his move whenever adult attention was elsewhere. A typical exchange consisted of John snatching Nathan up and shoving him behind the school house.

"Got ya now, cat eyes," the adolescent behemoth would growl. "Everyone thinks you're so special, but I think you're just a freak. Eyes like a cat an' all. Just ain't natural."

John would pin Nathan against the wall, leaving the smaller boy helpless before his heft. He always expressed his amusement with high, cackling laughter. "Hey, maybe you ain't even human. Maybe you turn into some creature at night- like in one a them monster books. Maybe I ought to mess you up bad, before you turn. You little freak!"

"Let me go!" Nathan would cry, mounting a vain struggle to break free.

"I'll let you go when I'm good and ready, you lil bastard."

"Mrs. Thompson will notice we're missing, soon."

John's face always twisted into a grimace of hatred and resentment at having his prey inform him that his fun had to come to an end. He always took steps to achieve utter domination before turning Nathan loose. That meant either a punch in the stomach or knee in the balls. He always promised worse if Nathan dared to tell the teacher. So it went, day after day.

Nathan had known the bullying would come before school even started. John lived nearby. His grandmother sometimes brought him into *Walker's* or gave him money to get his own treat.

John saw Nathan working in the store, receiving all sorts of praise and tips from older customers. He saw Nathan with a mother and father, living a happy family life.

Once school started, John saw how bright and well mannered Nathan was in class. The teachers and other students all liked Nathan.

It was all too much for the big boy to stomach. He made up his mind to humiliate Nathan as much as possible. Nathan was at first resigned to taking some punishment from the bully. After all, he had to "keep up appearances", as his parents repeated without end.

In addition to his parents, a certain old lady in a certain far away woods had spared no resources in making him aware of the consequences for allowing his special abilities to become common knowledge. So Nathan tolerated the bullying. He didn't mess with John's mind, didn't use his clairvoyance to predict what the bully's next actions might be. Doing so would've helped Nathan best the big boy in a fight, but Nathan didn't think it prudent.

Nathan had been skipped forward to sixth grade because of his brightness and maturity. John on the other hand, had started school a year late on account of slow development as a tyke.

John was two years older, about six inches taller and forty pounds heavier than Nathan. Nathan was smart enough to know that if he used his powers to best John, he would provoke a flood of attention. It would be far more attention than he was comfortable with. So he made up his mind to take whatever the big boy chose to dish out, unless John went too far.

John interrupted Nathan's walk home a few days before Nathan took action against him. The bully parked his big body in his target's path, smacking one meaty fist into the opposite palm, a wordless gesture that spoke volumes.

Nathan sighed and placing one reassuring arm on Eli's shoulder. He placed the other on the shoulder of Eli's classmate, Woody. Nathan always met his younger cousin outside of the fourth grade classroom and walked home with him and his friend.

"You already roughed me up once today, John," he complained.

John sneered. "Who says I only git to rough you up once a day?"

"Nobody," Nathan response was calm and unblinking. He wasn't really afraid of John, knowing that the big brute only bullied him because he allowed it. "I just thought you might show some mercy in front of my cousin and his little friend."

"I just though you might show me some mercy in front of my cousin and his little friend," John exaggerated Nathan's excellent diction, eyes burning with contempt.

"I hate the way you talk. You know that? Like your doo-doo don't stink as bad as the rest of the Negroes. If you think I care about how these little runts like me beatin' on you, you out of your fool head. Hell, it might make things more fun."

"So you've come to beat on me?" Nathan asked. He nudged the two smaller kids far off the walkway and into the grassy lot they had been standing alongside, not wanting them to get caught in the path of any fisticuffs. If John chose to fight, Nathan aimed to defend himself as best he could without using his powers. When John accosted him at school, he didn't resist because he knew it would only get so far. But this situation was far more dangerous than an encounter at school. Without any adults around to stop him, John might beat Nathan bloody. Nathan would have to fight back, though he would surely lose without resorting to using his powers.

John laughed, the malicious glint remaining in his eyes. "No, Dummy. Not today. I just stopped you to serve notice."

"Notice?"

"That's right." John smiled a shark's grin. "See, fifty cents a week just ain't enough anymore."

"Come again?"

"You heard, you rainbow eyed freak. Fifty cents a week ain't enough to keep me from takin' it easy on you no more. Ole John needs more than that, what with inflation an' all."

The only thing inflating is your greed. I've had almost as much as I can stand from you.

"Wha'd you say?"

Nathan wrestled control of himself. He hadn't meant to think at the big bully, but his anger had gotten the best of him. He'd been giving John fifty cents every week, money that he earned working in the family store, just to keep the bully from really hurting him. That was half of the earnings that Nathan's parents allowed him to spend as he wanted. Now the big bastard wanted more. Nathan had no intention of stomaching that.

"I didn't say anything, John."

"You sure about that?" John lunged forward and grabbed Nathan by the collar. The look in his eyes was almost feral. His nostrils flared and his color was high. "I could a sworn I heard you say something."

"No." Nathan dipped his head, hoping that a display of submissiveness would prevent the impending assault. "I swear I didn't say anything. How much do you want now?"

John released his grip on Nathan's collar, giving a powerful shove as soon as his hands were free. Nathan allowed himself to tumble to the ground, knowing it was what the big brute wanted to see.

Uproarious laughter escaped the bully. He slapped his meaty thighs with his meaty hands. "You mean to keep from rearrangin' your face, you little freak?"

Nathan nodded, picking himself up from the sidewalk. "Yes." He made a quick glance into John's mind, checking to see if the bully meant to attack him.

A quizzical expression briefly decorated John's face. His familiar contemptuous sneer soon replaced it. "A dollar a week'll do it."

"A dollar?" Nathan croaked.

"That's right. One dollar." John advanced, smacking his big fist into the opposite palm again. "Either that or one ass whuppin' a week."

Nathan started to say something before thinking better of it. He had no intention of giving John all of the spending money he was allowed each week. Giving away half of it to keep from stirring up trouble was one thing, but he worked too damn hard to give up all of it.

Nathan worked too hard to not get to enjoy any of his earnings. He had to complete his homework and work in the store every afternoon and all day on Saturdays. Why should John get every penny of his hard earned spending money? No, he just couldn't accept that.

Nathan decided that he had no choice but to stop John's bullying, although he kept his intentions to himself for the time being.

"No." He bowed his head again. He slumped his shoulders and threw in a lip quiver for good measure, knowing the big ape would get a kick out of that. "I have no problem with that."

"You have no problem with that?" John mocked. "Good." He jarred Nathan's shoulder with a heavy handed slap. "Good decision. I'll be expectin' the first payment on Friday."

John smacked his meaty fist into his meaty palm twice more, the intensity of his contempt continuing to smolder in his eyes. Then he turned and sauntered away. "Friday, you little freak," he called over his shoulder. Peals of laughter escaped him as he crossed the street.

Nathan took a few moments to compose himself before motioning for the smaller kids to join him.

"David would fight him for you," Eli said, coming as close to growling as his squeaky little voice would allow.

"Yeah," Nathan agreed. "He would. But the junior high is eight blocks away. He couldn't be around to keep John from taking payback on me. Plus John's so mean, I'm afraid he might try to hit one of you guys."

"We ain't afraid of that big monster!" Eli and Woody crowed in unison.

Nathan laughed and placed an arm around each of them. "I know you guys aren't. Not you two brawlers. You guys are bad news."

The following Friday seemed to arrive more quickly than any previous one. Sitting behind Nathan in Arithmetic class, John kicked his chair. Nathan waited for Mrs. Netterson to scrawl a problem on the chalkboard before turning to give the bully his attention.

Got my money? The brute mouthed.

I'll give it to you at lunch time, Nathan mouthed back.

You better.

"Is there something you'd like to share with the rest of the class, Misters Walker and Turner?"

"No, ma'am," they both chirped.

The bespectacled, gray-haired woman fixed her gaze on the larger of the two boys. "Perhaps you'd like to solve the next problem for us, Mr. Turner."

"No, ma'am," John responded in a timid voice. "I ain't sure how to solve it."

Mrs. Netterson scowled, placing her hands on her wide hips. "You ain't sure how to solve it? Well, then perhaps you'd better pay attention. How about you, Mr. Walker?"

It was a long division problem, child's play for Nathan. His usual approach was to decline such an opportunity, knowing that John would think of it as showing him up and try to retaliate later. But today, he wanted to goad the big boy. He would feel much better about what he planned to do if John were good and mad come recess time.

"Sure, Mrs. Netterson," Nathan chirped, springing from his seat to take the chalk from her hand. "I'd love to."

Recess could not come soon enough. Once it did, Nathan waited for John to motion him behind the school house. As soon as they reached the destination, the big brute shoved Nathan against the wall.

"What's the big idea in Arithmetic class?" he growled. "You tryin' ta make me look stupid."

As if you're not doing a fine job of that all by yourself. Nathan's thoughts were completely contrary to what escaped his lips. "No. I just wanted to get some credit in class."

"Well git some credit behind some other kid… you freak. Got it?"

"Got it."

"Good." John smiled. "Now, about that money."

"What money?"

John pinned Nathan harder against the wall, pressing his weight against the smaller child. "You tryin' to be funny, boy? The dollar you owe me for not beatin' your ass."

"I don't owe you anything," Nathan said, taunting his oppressor with a smile. "And I'm not giving you shit."

John's face twisted into a rictus of hatred. "Why, you little- ," he said, freeing his right hand and drawing it back in preparation for a punishing blow. His left forearm kept Nathan pinned to the wall.

You'd better leave me alone! Nathan thought hard at John, causing the big boy to release him. John clutched his pained ears, the hatred on his face now mixed with confusion.

Nathan smiled as he closed his eyes. He remained against the wall, thinking it was the perfect place to make his stand.

"What the hell?" John crouched into a boxer's stance, his meaty hands probing the air.

That's right, I did that. You bastard, Nathan thought. *I really am a freak like you thought. I can get in your head and do anything- ANYTHING I want. Now this is my last warning for you to LEAVE ME ALONE!*

John staggered backward before managing to right himself. The leer on his face became more hateful and savage than ever.

"I don't know how you're messing with my head, you little freak," he said, pressing forward. "But it won't stop me from whippin' your ass."

Have it your way, then, Nathan thought, before seizing complete control of John's faculties. *Punch yourself in the gut,* he shrieked inside John's head. *Punch yourself in the gut. Punch yourself in the gut hard! Hard I say!*

Nathan didn't need to open his eyes to know that he was being obeyed. Instead, he delighted in the miserable groaning that followed John's fists ramming into his own body.

Nathan sensed red anger give way to cold fear inside his erstwhile tormentor's mind. The victim turned aggressor wasn't yet satisfied. *Now, scratch yourself. I said scratch yourself- you big ape! Scratch yourself!*

A miserable whimper exited John as he raked his fingers across his own face.

Now choke yourself, Nathan commanded. A cruel grin parted his lips as pleas for mercy emanated from the bully's mind. *Mercy! Ha! Mercy like you showed me? No, I'm not done with you yet.*

"Please," John gasped.

Please what? Ha! I know… please choke yourself!

"Plea-."

I said choke yourself! Do it now! Choke your-selfff!!!

A round of gasps preceded a soft thump. The thump was followed by more gasping. Nathan opened his eyes to admire his handiwork and felt a rush of revulsion. John was on the ground, meaty hands pressed against his own windpipe, spit bubbling his lips and eyes wide like a dying fish.

Stop! Nathan commanded. *Stop choking yourself, now!*

As John's hands fell to his sides, Nathan realized that the bully would have continued until he passed out if Nathan hadn't stopped him. This was not the way he'd planned things at all.

His intention had been to scare John enough to stop the bullying. He had no designs on making the boy choke himself so hard that he bruised his own throat. Nor had he meant to make John rake his own face bloody. He didn't even remember issuing that command.

The fact that the big brute deserved some punishment was not debatable. Still, Nathan didn't like what came out of himself when he did the punishing.

Nathan knew that he needed to throw a final scare into John, to keep him from trying to tell what happened. He figured that the truth would achieve that purpose.

That's right, John. I did this all with my mind, he thought at his fallen adversary. *And I can do much worse. I can make you kill yourself if I want. Just make you grab a knife and stab it into your own guts so that you die. Or make you slit you wrists and force you to sit quietly until you bleed out. If you ever mess with me again or tell anyone what happened to you, I think that's just what I'll do. I'll kill you, John. And I'll get away with it, too, because I won't have to touch you to do it. Got it?*

"Got it," John croaked, throat raw from his own attack on it.

You'd better have it. Nathan walked away, feeling confident that John was now terrified of him. The big boy wouldn't tell anyone what happened and even if he did, no one would believe him.

As it turned out, John didn't need to tell anyone in order for Nathan to be brought to the principal's office.

Mrs. Netterson was shocked at John's bruised neck and puffy eyes when he returned from recess. "Oh, my," she said, placing a hand on her ample bosom, "Whatever has happened to you, John Turner?"

She wasted no time in accompanying the brutalized boy to the principal's office, sending the rest of the class across the hall to her colleague Mrs. Collins's classroom for safe keeping. When she returned without John, Nathan figured that there was a good chance that he might be summoned to the office at the end of the day. Nathan's sense of the inevitable was reinforced by several of his classmates being sent to the office as the day wore on.

Sure enough, Principal Trotter summoned Nathan just before the afternoon dismissal bell. John exited the austere suite just as Nathan entered.

"I swear I didn't tattle," the big boy grumbled, head hung low.

Principal Trotter's office was bereft of bright color or any other touches that might make a child feel comfortable. Various framed degrees and awards lined the wall behind his massive oak desk. Several framed photographs faced inward on its surface.

Principal Trotter motioned for Nathan to sit in one of three tiny chairs that faced the desk.

Instead of sitting on the large leather chair behind the desk, the dark skinned man sat on the edge of the oak structure itself. Doing so insured that he was only a few feet away from Nathan. Nathan knew that the manner in which Principal Trotter loomed over him was designed for intimidation.

Such antics were unnecessary, as Nathan was beyond mere intimidation. He felt terrified.

"Any idea why you've been called to my office, Nathan?"

"No sir," Nathan spat out a lie, knowing that Principal Trotter wouldn't believe him.

"Are you certain about that?" Principal Trotter asked, leaning toward his young charge. "It seems to me that you should have a pretty good idea."

"No, Principal Trotter. I don't know."

Principal Trotter smirked, a crease appearing in his broad forehead. "Alright. If that's how you want to play it, I'll tell you why you're here."

Principal Trotter straightened up, making a tent of his hands. He sighed and waited. He unfolded his hands and drummed his fingers on his knees. He waited and sighed. Nathan recognized all of those actions as more unnecessary intimidation. He wished the man would hurry whatever he intended along.

"Shortly after recess," Principal Trotter said. "Mrs. Netterson noticed that one of your classmates- John Turner- looked quite worse for wear. His neck was bruised and his eyes were quite puffy. I had a look at him myself. I'm no doctor, but I don't have to be one to assess that someone beat up on John. Beat him up and choked him as well."

Nathan widened his eyes in an approximation of surprise and confusion. He realized the importance of feigning innocence even if doing so couldn't possibly convince the principal.

Principal Trotter paused, furrowing his brow and fixing an unblinking stare upon Nathan.

Nathan struggled not to sweat from nervousness, knowing that to do so would make him appear guilty. He thought of Big Junie and the other horses back on his family farm. He'd always loved those horses.

"I questioned John at length," Principal Trotter said. "As did Mrs. Netterson. John claims he got beat up by some thug in the neighborhood this past evening. Claimed he was tossing bottle caps in the alley when some crazed vagrant set upon him, giving him a good beating. Quite a tale he told. Said the man seemed near ready to kill him- that he only escaped by kneeing him in his private area. Intelligent and logical man that I am, I couldn't help but recognize the huge perforations in his story. The biggest is that he didn't say anything to his grandmother about what supposedly happened. When I asked him the reason for that, he said that he was afraid that if he told her, she wouldn't let him go out on his own anymore. Next, I asked him why she hadn't noticed the bruising on her own. He told me that she had bad eyesight and that her glasses had recently been broken.

Of course, the entire story was hogwash. Would you like to know how I know this?"

Nathan nodded, sensing that it was what his interrogator wanted. Principal Trotter enjoyed showing off how smart he was.

Principal Trotter gave a smug smile. "First, there's the coloration of the bruises. As I said before, I'm no doctor. But I can differentiate fresh bruises like Mr. Turner's from day old ones. Also, Mrs. Netterson insisted that she did not notice a single mark on John before recess." Principal Trotter laughed, tossing his head back as if someone had just told him a side splitting joke.

"Forgive me." He placed a hand over the slight paunch of his stomach. "It's just that what young Mr. Turner next claimed is one of the most preposterous statements I've ever heard uttered, even from years of working with young boys, a population with a particular propensity for such preposterousness. Young Mr. Turner claimed that the bruises had been there all morning- that Mrs. Netterson had simply overlooked them." He dissolved into more laughter.

"At that point, I knew that there was no percentage in trying to get him to confess the truth. He is far too terrified to reveal the true culprit of his injuries." He fixed a stare upon Nathan once more, as if to say but I know it was you, Nathan.

"Before leaving, Mrs. Netterson confided that she could not account for John's whereabouts during the entirety of recess. She thought it quite possible that he and another student had snuck off and had an altercation. I asked her if he seemed to have any problems with other students in the class. She informed me that he can be quite the bully. I asked her if there were any classmates in particular whom he picked on."

Principal Trotter stood up before bending in front of Nathan, placing his hands on his knees. Their faces were so close that Nathan could smell hints of cigarettes and liquor. Those smells mixed with the failed camouflage of peppermint on the principal's breath.

Principal Trotter held his position for a long time, once more trying to intimidate his already terrified suspect.

Nathan hung his head, trying to show the submissiveness that Principal Trotter desired without seeming guilty. He was aware of Principal Trotter's awareness that he had assaulted John, though the principal would never dream of the extraordinary nature of the assault. He probably thought that Nathan had gone into a rage and done the deed with his own hands. Nathan didn't want to do anything to even strengthen the principal's belief in that off base assumption.

"Mrs. Netterson named a number of students she'd caught John picking on," the principal said. "You, my dear boy, were at the top of the list. She said that she's kept John after school for making mean spirited comments about you on a number of occasions. Said that he seemed jealous of you, that she could only imagine what tricks he might have played on you outside of adult supervision. So tell me, Nathan. Does John bully you?"

Nathan lifted his eyes to meet the adult's and nodded. "Not more than anyone else, though."

A bemused smile emerged on Principal Trotter's face as he straightened up. "And he won't do it again, at any rate. Will he?"

"I don't understand what you mean, sir," Nathan lied.

"The hell you don't," Principal Trotter spat, making an obvious attempt to shock Nathan with the uttered profanity.

"Honest, sir," Nathan said, bowing his head once more. "I don't understand."

Principal Trotter sat on the edge of his desk. His arms gesticulated wildly as his voice took on a staccato rhythm. "Do you mean to tell me, Nathan Walker, that

117

you did not assault John Turner at recess? That you did not beat him and choke

him? That you did not get so fed up with his bullying that you took leave of

yourself and let him have it? Is that what you mean to convince me of, Mr.

Walker?"

"Sir?"

"What is it, boy?"

Nathan gulped, clearing his throat. "How could I beat up someone as big and

strong as John? No one in our class can take him in a fight. That's why he's able to

pick on everyone."

Principal Trotter was undeterred. "I've thought of that myself, having plenty

of time to mull it over during the day. I can only conclude that your strength was

fueled by rage and bitterness, the type of rage and bitterness that can only come

from a person being tormented one too many times. I believe you went berserk for

just long enough to give John Turner one hell of a beating. I believe that you beat

him so severely that he's too scared to even tell on you. He much prefers

fabricating a ridiculous and implausible story."

He shrugged his shoulders. "Or maybe he's just too embarrassed to tell

anyone. After all, what bully would want to admit being bested by one of his

victims? Whether he admits it or not, several of your classmates stated that they

could not account for you and your erstwhile tormentor's whereabouts during the

entirety of recess. So at some point, the two of you were alone."

Principal Trotter leaned toward Nathan again. "Of course, I can't prove that

without John's confession. Not that that bothers me very much. Truth be told, I

don't mind hearing of a bully getting his just dessert. It's the bruises around his

throat that bother me. Choking is excessive, Nathan. Choking is not part of a fair

fight. That's why I'll have to let your parents know about this. As for John's grandmother- she does not possess a telephone. I'll have to stop by their residence this evening to see that she is at least aware of her grandson's condition. I won't say anything about you, though. Since he wants to hang on to that story about being attacked in the alley, perhaps he shouldn't be allowed to go outside on his own. Seems all he does is torment smaller kids when he does anyway."

Principal Trotter straightened up and walked behind his desk. He motioned for Nathan to approach, picking up the cradle of the phone that set on the desktop.

"Unlike John's grandmother, your folks have a telephone. It's high time I reach them on it."

Nathan's mother arrived at the school about 45 minutes later. Much to Nathan's relief, she did not confess to sharing Principal Trotter's belief in his guilt. She did promise that henceforth, Nathan would be sure to remain well within his teacher's eyesight during recess.

"That way," she said, "there will be no reason to suspect my son of any foul play."

Nathan waited for the admonishment that was sure to come as he and Naomi walked home together. They were a block away from the school when she started in.

"This family can't afford for you to get into trouble, Nathan James Walker." She only called him by his full name when she was cross with him.

"I know," the boy muttered.

"Because of you, Eli only had his little friend to walk home with today. Alma wasn't pleased about that. Nor will Virgil be when he finds out."

"I'm sorry. I didn't mean for that to happen."

She sighed. "How long has this boy been picking on you?"

"Since school started."

"Why didn't you tell your father or me about it?"

Nathan shrugged. "It wasn't so bad at first. And I didn't want to bother y'all, especially with how busy Daddy's been."

Naomi knew what her son meant. The wheel of James Walker's life turned on running his business and fighting to make things better for the Negro in Baltimore. He sermonized to anyone willing hear about how Negroes should fight to shed their second class status (and many who were unwilling). Of late, he had become involved with the NAACP and had even shook hands with W.E.B. Dubois himself. Helping her husband with his business and "organizing" left Naomi with very little idle time.

"You should have let us decide what's a bother." She gritted her teeth, turning to step in Nathan's path. She poked him in the chest. "You let us make the decisions. You hear?"

Nathan bowed his head. "Yes, Mama."

Naomi frowned and sighed before pulling him into a hug. "You used your powers on him, didn't you?"

"Yes, Mama." Nathan shrunk within her embrace, knowing that she wasn't pleased to learn this. He'd been warned time and time again about making such a display of himself. "I'm sorry," he continued. "He went too far. I didn't feel like I had another choice."

His mother released him then, nearly shoving him away. She turned and resumed walking at a furious pace.

"You had another choice besides half-killing someone." Her voice was low, but furious in tone. "How did you do it, anyway?"

"I got in his mind," Nathan grumbled.

"What? Speak up, boy."

"I got in his mind. Made him hit himself. Choke himself."

His mother stopped in her tracks, drew in a huge breath. Hand over her heart, she began whispering to herself. "Calm down, Naomi," she said. "Calm down. Lord, please give me the strength to remain calm."

She regained her composure and resumed walking, much slower this time. "How long have you known you could mess with folks' minds?"

Nathan grew frantic as he realized the implications of her question. "He's the only person I've ever done it to, Ma! Honest! And I only did it because I was trying to protect myself." Tears streaked down his face.

"Crying won't help it, boy. Does he know how you done it?"

Nathan nodded, wiping at his eyes.

"Use your tongue, son!"

"Yes. He knows I was messing with his head."

Naomi grabbed rough hold of her son's arm, marching him along the street. "Listen to me, son. You can never do something like that again. I know you got the sight… but using it that way just ain't right. It's like opening up Pandora's box. You remember that story I used to tell you?"

"Yes."

"Well, it didn't turn out too good for Pandora, did it? And just 'cause that boy wouldn't tell the truth about what happened at school doesn't mean things are over as far as he's concerned. Hell, he probably only held on to it because he figured no one would believe him. But if he ever could get someone to swallow it, we'd be in big trouble. It wasn't but a few hundred years ago that people were burned at the stake for witchcraft in this country. Things haven't progressed all that far from those days, Nathan."

"Yes, ma'am."

"Don't you 'Yes, ma'am', me. Your father would not be happy to find this out."

Nathan picked up on the phrasing of the latter statement right away. "Are you going to tell him?"

Naomi rolled her eyes. "Why? So I can see him practically throw a fit? No, this is one time your father won't get full disclosure from me." She quickened her pace. "That's why we'd better hustle back to open the store back up. Luckily, your father's at a meeting for that Colored Businessman's group he's involved with. So if he doesn't ask, I won't tell. Got it?"

"Got it." Nathan smiled, feeling a great weight depart.

"Don't smile at me, boy. I'm not doing it to keep you out of hot water. I'm doing it to spare your father. Now, you are not to do anything like that again- you hear?"

"Yes, Mama."

"I mean it, Nathan. You go doing something like that again... you could turn us all into outcasts. You don't want that – do you?"

"No, ma'am!"

"Alright, then. You be sure to mind what I said about it. I just hope that other boy's willing to let things lie now."

"He will. He's scared of me now."

Naomi seized Nathan in a fierce grip, turning him to face her. Her dark eyes bore into his spectral ones.

"Think that's good, do you? Well, its not. Son, sometimes when people fear something enough, they make up their mind to hurt it, maybe even kill it. I know that as special as you are you're still only ten years old, but you're not too young to learn that. And you'd better not ever forget it."

III.

"Ready to talk to the animals, boy?"

Nathan nodded and smiled as early morning light crawled through the window, massaging the cabin with its pleasant glow.

The boy and his teacher had just finished a breakfast of berries and dried apricots. It wasn't as good as the big breakfasts Nathan's mother cooked, but he liked it plenty.

"Well, come on." The old woman ventured outside, beckoning him to follow.

They walked down the dirt path in front of the cabin, birdsong serenading each step they took. They stopped at the edge of the narrow forest road.

"You see any critters?" Ruth asked.

Nathan's head swiveled as he scanned his surroundings. He saw nothing but trees and brush. "No, Ma'am."

Ruth laughed, her aged gums on full display. "You're looking with your outward eyes, boy. You need to be looking with the eyes inside you. Isn't that why you came here?"

Nathan closed his eyes, making a fruitless attempt to sense animals in the brush.

"I can't do it," he whined.

Ruth's strange eyes flashed hot as she pointed a bony, gnarled finger at him. "Don't you whimper like some cur dog, child! I won't have anyone with your abilities feeling sorry for himself - not even for one second. Now, try again."

Nathan did as she urged, but still accomplished nothing. "I'm sorry, Miss Ruth." He hunched his shoulders. "I don't know how."

She turned her back to him then, leaving only her white mane to look at.

All you have to do is clear your mind, boy, she thought at him. *Think of nothing but this forest and the brush before you. Let yourself be a sponge. Then you will come to sense them.*

Nathan did as told, emptying his mind with surprising ease. He soon sensed the presence of a small, simple-minded creature. The creature lived in constant anxiety, thinking only of food and watching for predators.

Nathan followed the tiny creature's anxious mind's eye as it roamed through the brush, ready to cut and run at a split second's notice.

Excellent.

Hearing Ruth's congratulatory thought startled Nathan, causing him to lose his connection with the creature. He felt the warm sensation of her laughing inside his head an instant later. *You'll have to hold your concentration better than that, young Nathan. Now seek that creature out again. Do not allow my presence to break your link with it.*

Nathan emptied his mind once more, entering the timid creature's consciousness with ease. The sensation of wild grasses greeted him. He felt as if he could taste the growth, though he had done no such thing.

A rabbit, Ruth thought at him. *Grazing. Along with squirrels, they are the most simple minded beasts in these here woods. How do you like the taste of grass?"*

Not much, Nathan thought. He was surprised to discover the ease with which he could keep his link with the rabbit and talk with Ruth at the same time.

She thought another laugh at him. *You shouldn't be surprised boy. I told you you're awful powerful. The only reason why you can't do everything I can do already is because you're young. Now, break your link with that critter. Be gentle about it.*

Nathan did as told, opening his eyes to look at the old woman. She turned to face him.

"What do you think about that creature?" she said.

"I thought it was very hungry and nervous."

Ruth nodded. "Not just nervous. Afraid. Rabbits spend most of their short lives in fear. With good cause, too. In these here woods, they're prey for foxes, snakes, owls, and hawks- just to name a few. Poor things hardly ever last two years. Course that's offset by how much they multiply. All they do is eat and make baby rabbits. If they didn't have so many natural enemies, they'd overrun these woods in no time."

She tilted her head, regarding her young student in the same manner that a curious cat might regard an unfamiliar object.

"You did real good for your first time linking with an animal. When I first did so, ages ago, I almost got caught up in what the animal was feeling. My first creature was an angry dog. Linking up with it, I almost went into a rage myself. And I was thirteen at the time. You have far better control than I did starting out - and at a far younger age."

She snickered. "Of course, I didn't have some old bag of bones to show me the ropes."

You're not a bag of bones, Miss Ruth, Nathan thought at her.

I most certainly am, boy, Ruth thought back at him. *No need to be kind for my sake. Let me show you another trick. I didn't think you'd be ready for it today. But you sure fooled me. You can watch this with your outside eyes.*

Within a few moments, a small brown rabbit came bounding out of the brush and across the narrow dirt road, stopping at the edge of Miss Ruth's plot of land.

"I called it here," she said, her withered lips parting into crescent moons.

The rabbit sniffed the air before hopping the remaining distance to the old woman. Bending over with ease that belied her age, Ruth stroked the space between the adorable creature's large brown eyes.

"I want you to link with it," she said. "Do it slowly."

Nathan obliged, clearing his mind and easing his way into the rabbit's consciousness.

You see, Ruth thought at him. *The little fellow's not afraid. Not even a little bit.*

I see, Ma'am, Nathan thought back. *But how?*

Not now, Nathan. Break the link.

After Nathan did as told, Miss Ruth stroked the furry creature a few seconds longer. "Goodbye," she sighed, rising to a standing position. The rabbit turned and scurried across the road.

"Now, you," she said, turning to her student. "You call one to you. Not the friend I just made either. Your mind's eye is like a net. I want you to cast it deeper into the brush. There are plenty of creatures inhabiting it. Especially rabbits."

Nathan cleared his mind and extended his consciousness. Soon, he found another rabbit.

Good, the old woman thought at him. *Now befriend it.*

How?

How do you make friends with anyone, child? Just do it.

Don't be afraid of me, little bunny, Nathan thought at the rabbit. *I mean you no harm. Please come to me.*

To Nathan's delight, a rabbit larger than the one Miss Ruth had interacted with came bounding out of the brush. It hopped across the road, not stopping until it reached his feet.

The smiling old woman's eyes twinkled in amazement. "With every feat, you show yourself to be more and more powerful," she said.

Nathan stooped to stroke the rabbit's furry head. Its' large eyes fixed on him without fear. *Thank you, my friend*, Nathan thought. *Thank you for coming to me.*

Alright now let him go, son, Ruth thought at Nathan. *That little rabbit needs to go on about rabbit business.*

Nathan rubbed the critter's head one last time. *Goodbye, friend.*

The unbound rabbit paused to observe its surroundings before bounding back across the road and disappearing into the brush. Nathan couldn't help smiling as he turned to his teacher.

"Enjoy that, did you?"

He nodded.

"Today, simple critters like rabbits. Soon, you'll be able to control noble beasts like horses without the need of a whip or reins."

Nathan's smile grew larger. "I think I'll like that, Miss Ruth."

She chuckled and nudged his shoulder. "Of course you will, son. What southern boy wouldn't?"

Her mirth shifted to seriousness an instant later. "Know how I told your folks you wouldn't go hungry on account of me being such a good hunter?"

Nathan nodded.

"Well, that wasn't exactly the gospel truth. See, I don't hunt at all. I kill critters with my mind."

"You do?" Nathan's eyes widened. His pupils flashed green for a moment.

Ruth nodded. "I'll save that lesson for a bit, son. It's too important to mix with anything else. We'll spend some more time linking with critters in the mean time. Maybe tomorrow you can try to work your way up to a fox. But, today we're headed to Lewiston. 'Bout time to send your folks a letter. Isn't it?"

Nathan jumped up and down in excitement. The wondrous things he'd just learned lost significance. "Yes, Miss Ruth. I'll be so happy to write to Mama and Papa!"

6

Rabble Rousing and Mastering Power

I.

Word that Nathan had bested John Turner spread like wildfire. His schoolmates thought that he had done it with his hands. Even his cousin David thought so.

"I didn't think you had it in you," he said as he clapped Nathan on the back. "I guess that big ox pushed you too far and made the devil come out. Bet he'll never mess with you again."

John never denied his peers' belief that Nathan had given him a fair beating. Nor did he muster the courage to look Nathan in the eyes again.

Once Nathan no longer had to worry about the big brute bothering him, sixth grade seemed to fly right by. The same could be said for the year 1912.

Old West Baltimore flourished with activity that year, much of which *Walker's* was the center of. The store became further entrenched as a gathering place for Negroes. A handful of new Negro owned businesses, such as *Honey's Hair Salon* and *Gus's Barber Shop*, joined it on the Pennsylvania Avenue corridor.

James wasted no time bringing the new businesses' owners into the fold of the Colored Businessman's Association he had founded. Nathan didn't understand much of what the CBA involved. He only knew that his father's involvement in it was another example of his constant quest to better things for his kind.

When the elder Walker wasn't busy with the CBA, he immersed himself in NAACP activities. He was always involved in some voting or food drive conducted by that organization. He also sold many copies of The Crisis, which he referred to as "The Seminal Literary Doctrine of the Struggles of the Negro in America."

Nathan didn't understand how his father could think Negroes were struggling, at least not in Baltimore. Alabama had been terrible, that was for sure. In Alabama, Black men lived with the constant possibility or being shot, thrown into jail, or lynched. Nathan remembered his vision of hooded men coming to murder his father. That sort of thing was an ordinary part of life in Alabama.

Things were much different in Baltimore. Negroes seemed to have their own little slice of the world here. The Walkers had luxuries they'd lacked down south, such as running water and electricity. In Baltimore, Nathan couldn't go outside without seeing another dark face. His family made plenty of money and was well respected within the community.

Still, Nathan's father ranted and raved about "white oppression" at regular intervals. He was always stirring things up, like when he assisted the NAACP in ginning up a rent strike against a landlord who allowed dozens of apartments in the neighborhood to fall into a state of disrepair.

"The great thing about the NAACP is that we're fighting for Colored people," James once said to Naomi, "but we have Jewish lawyers. You can't do better than Jewish lawyers."

The organization's lawyers convinced some of the tenants who were afraid to go along with the strike (due to fear of eviction) that no judge who saw the conditions of their living quarters would rule in favor of the slumlord (even though he was white and they were Negroes). In the end, the landlord caved and did the necessary repairs. "Seems his wallet couldn't bear the burden of a protracted battle," James gloated when he found out.

Nathan's mother once confided to him that his father couldn't be satisfied unless he was fighting "some cause."

"But that means he's never satisfied –right?" Nathan asked. "It seems like as soon as one fight is over he looks for another one."

Naomi chuckled as she stroked the hair atop her son's head. "That's right, Nathan."

"Why can't he just be happy with our family?"

"Oh, sweetheart." Naomi sighed as she hugged him. "There's a big difference between happiness and satisfaction."

"What's the difference?"

She sighed once more. "It's moments like this when I wish you were as simple minded as other ten year olds."

Nathan often wished the same thing, but he knew that doing so was pointless because there was no helping the way he was. His mother had a word for it - extraordinary. He hadn't minded being extraordinary when he was smaller- but now he wondered if being as ordinary as the next boy might be easier.

Once the initial clamor over him "whippin' the tar" out of John Turner subsided, Nathan managed to resume his role of the smartest, hardest-working, and most mature youngster in the neighborhood. He strained to shut his powers off (as if they were a mental faucet) so as to never threaten that role again.

He struggled with all his might against the occasional clairvoyance that attempted to visit him, using all of the power within him to block his own supernatural sight. He didn't imagine that resisting his gift would prevent him from foreseeing the most horrible tragedy of his young life.

II.

"Clear your mind, boy," Miss Ruth said. "Just like I showed you before."

Nathan closed his eyes, took a deep breath, and emptied all interfering thoughts, freeing his mind's eye to probe the forest surrounding the old woman's cottage. Just as he had the previous day, he sought a small creature to bring to his feet.

He soon encountered the consciousness of a creature close to frantic with nervous energy. He locked onto it and began thinking at it.

Come with me, small creature of the forest. Come with me. I will not harm you.

Nathan felt calm consume the creature's consciousness as it dashed out of the brush and across the forest road. It was a tiny brown mammal, spotted white with dark stripes and a bushy tail. Tail included, the critter was just longer than Nathan's hand.

"A chipmunk?" Miss Ruth asked, smiling her nearly toothless smile.

I thought you might try to hook something larger than a rabbit, she thought at him, *but I guess you choose to go the other way.*

Sorry.

Don't be sorry, boy. Let that little rodent go and try again.

"Yes, Miss Ruth." Nathan crouched and held his hand out for the chipmunk to sniff it. He couldn't resist stroking its' tiny head.

I said let the rodent go, not make it your boon companion.

"Yes, Ma'am." Nathan flushed, embarrassed. *You may go now, friend. You may go.*

The freed creature periscoped the area for predators before scurrying back from whence it came.

Now, try again, Ruth directed her charge.

Okay. Nathan took a deep breath, emptying himself out and sending his mind's eye out once more.

This time he sought out more clever beings instead of communing with the first consciousness he encountered. After an interminable amount of time, he broached the consciousness of a creature far more shrewd than the chipmunk.

Hello, forest creature, he thought at it. *I am Nathan Walker. Do not fear me. I have come to befriend you. Please come to me.*

Nathan read the creature's rudimentary thoughts as curious, but cautious. He sensed that it was surprised by his presence, but not afraid. It did not possess human intelligence, but this was no rodent, that would scurry to Nathan at the first urging.

Now you've latched on to a prize, Miss Ruth thought at him. A warm, tingling sensation accompanied her words. *That critter's kind won't come easily.*

What do I do?

No, no, son. You're better off figuring that for yourself.

As he maintained the mental link, Nathan wished he knew some of the creature's pleasures. He bet that if he had that information, he could entice it to come.

Although Miss Ruth had never mentioned any such thing, he wondered if he could probe the creature's thoughts. He decided to try, ceasing direct communication with it to explore its memory.

What he found was a collection of images, most of them concerned with foraging for food. He saw the creature as a cub- being shown how to dig for grubs and crack bird's eggs. He saw it gathering berries and insects from the forest floor. He saw it clasping food in its paws and washing that food in a stream before eating. He also saw the creature wrestling with members of its troop.

Thinking that he knew what he needed to do, Nathan made a slow withdrawal from the creature's mind. He headed into Miss Ruth's cabin and grabbed two sheaths of leaf-wrapped fruit.

The old woman smiled as Nathan returned to his previous spot on the dirt path. She watched as he unwrapped the berries and sent his consciousness back out. He seized upon the creature without delay, recognizing its' unique consciousness.

I return, he thought. *I return, my friend. I will not harm you. I offer you gifts if you will come to me.*

He sent the creature images of the raspberries and blueberries that the sheaths held. He assured it again and again that he meant no harm.

Nathan sensed the animal relaxing a bit more, deciding to head in for a closer look.

Soon, a large raccoon parted the brush and sauntered into the narrow road. It observed Nathan with keen eyes as it headed toward him, stopping about ten feet away, just off the edge of the road.

You're very careful, Nathan thought. *You're very smart. Okay, I'll set the food down for you.*

Nathan left the fruit for the raccoon's taking and backed up toward the cabin. Ruth remained where she had been standing, watching the encounter with great curiosity.

The raccoon glanced at the generous amount of fruit before glancing at Nathan. It looked at the fruit again and inched a little closer. It shot another quick glance at Nathan.

Nathan noticed that its' brown coat was streaked with white. Its eyes were deep wells of experience.

You don't get to be as old as me and Matilda there without being cautious, Ruth thought at him.

Matilda? You know her?

Concentrate, boy. You just might do a great thing, here.

"Sorry," Nathan spoke aloud, returning his thoughts to the wise raccoon. *It's okay, Matilda. These are gifts for you. I want to be your friend.*

A succession of surprising images flashed through Nathan's mind. Each one was of a raccoon of various size and age. Nathan realized that they were members of Matilda's troop.

Yes. He smiled with his lips and his mind. *Yes, your friends are welcome.*

A warm sensation emanated from Matilda's consciousness. She advanced a few steps closer to the food, before turning to face the brush and making a chattering sound with her teeth.

Six other raccoons emerged from the brush in short order. Two were full grown. The others were mid-sized cubs.

"You never cease to amaze me, boy," the old woman said as the furry clan settled into their feast. "You never cease to amaze me."

III.

James's landlord dropped in on him a few days after he had helped his neighbors defeat the slumlord. It was the first time James had seen Breslin in months and also the first time Breslin had come calling at the odd time of 7:30 AM.

"Good Morning, James," Breslin said after letting himself into the storefront.

"Good morning to you, Breslin," James replied, stifling both the urge to say that he'd prefer if the man knocked and the urge to ask him why in hell he had come unannounced.

"I prefer Mr. Breslin from those I conduct business with," the landlord said, face flashing a soft red.

"I'm aware of that," James said, standing behind the store's counter. "I only addressed you informally because that is the way you addressed me, sir. I believe it is proper manners to greet others as they greet you." He smiled. "So may I ask what brings you by? I know you received the rent payment."

Breslin nodded as he approached the counter. "Of course I have. You're always very good about paying promptly." He seated himself on a stool across from his tenant. "That should be expected since the rent you pay me seems a mere drop in the bucket of what you earn from this store."

James chuckled. "I wouldn't say 'a drop in the bucket' but I do alright, Mr. Breslin. I guess business is good for us both."

"I agree that as far as collecting payment from you each month, our business is good," Breslin said, "but some of your other actions threaten to negate that benefit for me."

James arched an eyebrow. "I don't understand what you mean by that, Mr. Breslin."

"I mean that your rabble rous- your activism is making me look bad with others I do business with," Breslin said. "Activism such as the rent strike against Mr. Myron Cole that you played a prominent role in."

"Mr. Myron Cole? Oh, you mean the slumlord who had dozens of Negro families living in shoddy and unsafe conditions? You mean that Mr. Myron Cole?"

"You know very well who I mean!" Breslin shouted, pounding on the counter top. "The actions you led against that man have caused quite an embarrassment for me within the circles I travel. I have no admiration for a slum lord, but I find suffering him much easier to suffer than having to consistently defend my renting property to a Negro Communist!"

"I am no Communist, sir," James said, struggling to keep his voice even. As inflammatory as his landlord's words were, he would not allow himself to seem aggressive while alone with a white man. Anything could happen if he did. He wasn't in Alabama anymore, but he could still end up jailed for assault without so much as touching this man. "I am only a man who likes to see his friends and neighbors treated with some facsimile of fairness. And I must say, perhaps you find your slum lord associate sufferable because you have never suffered living in one of his properties."

Breslin grew quiet for a few beats before responding. "Point taken, Mr. Walker. Now you must take my point. I can ill afford to be known as the white businessman who rents to a Negro troublemaker. People I associate with now have their eyes planted firmly on your actions. By extension, they now have their eyes planted firmly on me. I do not like that sort of attention, Mr. Walker."

James nodded. "What is it that you require of me, Mr. Breslin?"

"I do not require anything from you, Mr. Walker. I only request that you not use this store as a place to rabble rouse and spread propaganda. You might consider that radical political ideas rarely lead to monetary reward. As a businessman, even a Colored one, I expect you to understand that. You would agree that our current arrangement is profitable to us both?"

James nodded, fighting to keep the exasperation he felt from showing on his face.

"We're both making a nice profit. There's no denying that."

Breslin threw his head back in laughter. "Indeed, neither of us should deny that."

He stood to leave. "Profit is what a businessman should most be proud of, Mr. Walker. I would like for us both to continue to profit as a result of our landlord-tenant relationship. Ginning up controversy is not in the best interest of that. Do you get my meaning?"

"Oh, yes, Mr. Breslin," James said. "I get your meaning." And your 'meaning' doesn't mean a damned thing, he thought. Your meaning doesn't mean a damned thing to me.

IV.

James Walker status as one of the most successful Negro businessman in Baltimore only strengthened as 1913 unfolded. He lived very well, having even managed to buy his own Ford Model T. One of but a few legitimate Negro entrepreneurs able to afford such luxury, he motored the huge vehicle around town on the rare occasions when he had free time.

James found the automobile to be a clumsy conveyance and hoped that its' design would improve as more of them were made. Still, he took great joy in noticing the admiring eyes of those who watched him drive it. He felt much more esteemed driving than he did as a passenger on a streetcar or bus. As a pillar of the Negro community, he believed he had a certain image to uphold.

James took extreme pride in his role in transforming Old West Baltimore into something of a Mecca for Negro life. If he had anything to do with it, things would only continue to improve for the Negro in his adopted city.

James continued to devote most of his spare time to activity in the Colored Businessman's Association and the NAACP. Naomi often complained about him working so much, but she knew he wouldn't slow down. If making things better for his people meant less time for picnics and walks in the park, that was a sacrifice he'd have to make.

James was at an NAACP meeting when he learned about the likely passing of a housing segregation ordinance. The ordinance stipulated that the majority of Negroes be confined to living within Old West Baltimore, which consisted of 26 blocks of Pennsylvania Avenue and its' neighboring streets.

"Settle down folks! Please settle down!" the local chairwoman urged, banging her gavel to quell the uproar from those assembled in the lecture hall at Morgan College.

"We will not take this lying down," she promised, once the noise level of the attendees dropped to irritated murmurs. "It is one thing for Negroes to willingly congregate in one section of the city. It is another thing entirely for them to be forced there."

"You're damn right it is," James shouted, springing to his feet. "Colored folks should have the freedom to live wherever they want in this town. We must fight this ordinance, tooth and nail! We must!"

A furious chorus ignited, assailing the lecture hall with unseemly talk. The chairwoman shot a pigsty filthy look at James as she frantically banged her gavel. She got no initial response so she banged harder and harder, her face reddened with strain and just suppressed anger. The uproar subsided like a dying storm, descending into murmurs once more.

"Mr. Walker is correct," the chairwoman stated, recovering a façade of composure. "We will fight this ordinance tooth and nail. But we will do it with dignity, not histrionics. Civility will win the day."

Though he refrained from another outburst, James didn't much agree with what she'd said. He had grown tired of being civil. Civility only got Colored folks pushed one step backward for every step forward, meaning that they ended up in the same spot. He would wait to see what the local NAACP leadership would do to address the matter of the ordinance, but he intended to carry out his own design if he was not satisfied by theirs.

V.

"You are truly a gifted one," Miss Ruth spoke wistfully, shaking her head as she and Nathan sat facing each other in the earthen floor of her cabin. "I think that its time I teach you what I've been holding back. I don't know that there's much more I can do with you once that's done."

It had been six months since Nathan's initial stay with her. The usual long, hot summer had come to Alabama. Having been exposed to the old woman's tutelage every other weekend had resulted in Nathan developing great control over his powers. He had also learned great judgment in exercising that control.

Thanks to his elderly teacher, Nathan was now separated him from other young children by more than just incredible powers and preternatural intelligence. His sense of consequences also placed him on another plateau.

More than anything, he did not want to hurt anyone or ruin anything by using his powers. He had waited with great patience for Ruth to show him what she was now about to. He was full of nerves and anxiety now that the time had come.

That desire to perform well was balanced by worry. He sensed that his teacher was not well.

"Miss Ruth," he asked. "Are you alright?"

She cackled and offered him a bemused smile. "You know that I'm not, child. You sensed it from the moment I hugged you hello."

She rubbed his head. "Don't trouble yourself over me, boy. Old Ruth has had a long and eventful life. The Lord will take me home when he sees fit. You best ready yourself for what I aim to teach you."

Nathan closed his eyes and crossed one leg over the other. His hands rested on his knees as he erased all thoughts from his mind. His conscious and sub-conscious merged, becoming a great black void.

Now, you are ready, Ruth's voice reached his elevated consciousness as a loud echo. *Follow me.*

His mind's eye latched on to the immensity of hers as it left the old cabin and ascended into the cold night.

Ruth's eye blurred past the forest floor, zipping through the brush and climbing the tallest trees. It grazed consciousness after consciousness, simple and clever, finding them all full of vivaciousness.

The eye settled upon an old and tired essence, a creature that lived in constant pain. Nathan stilled himself, allowing his mind's eye to observe the old woman's communion with the weary soul.

Hello, ancient one, she thought. *I can feel your pain. It is great pain. Is it not-ancient one?* Nathan felt the creature's aura flash cold as it accepted Ruth's presence.

I know much about pain, ancient one, Ruth continued. *I know much about you. I know that you have had a long life and are now tired. You can no longer keep up with your family. You have all but lost your appetite for grazing. It would be best if a wolf pack leaped upon you, put you out of your misery. But those creatures are long gone from this land. And no hunter would consider you a prize. So you'll continue to suffer, until the day you finally expire. Perhaps that day will be long in coming.*

Ruth paused for a few beats, allowing the creature to process her sentiments.

There is no need for you to perish so indignantly, my friend, she continued. *If you will yield yourself to me, I can end your pain. I can end it quickly.*

An image of a quick and peaceful death passed into the creature's mind. *If you will come to me, I can end it. If you but yield, I can give you peace.*

The old woman fell wordless then, sending the creature images to guide it to the cabin. Nathan absorbed it all, knowing that he must learn how to do this himself. After an interminable amount of time, the old woman spoke to the creature again.

I see you have come, she thought. *Sleep well, my friend. Sleep well.*

Nathan felt Miss Ruth focus her entire consciousness into a shattering psychic blow, causing a powerful jolt as the animal's consciousness dissipated. Searing pain racked Nathan's mind's eye as the triple link was broken.

Nathan labored to breathe as he wiped sweat from his brow. He looked to his right and saw the old woman, sweating and trembling. She always grew flushed and sweaty when using her powers to slay an animal, but this time she looked downright feverish. She pitched forward, spewing green bile into the earthen floor.

She staggered to her feet and wiped a trickle of blood from her nose. She balled her fists, steadying herself. Wiping spittle from her withered lips, she smiled the ghoulish smile Nathan had seen many times before.

"I'm alright, boy," she said. "Not ready to check out just yet. Go see what I slew."

Nathan stepped out into the hot, sticky night. An emaciated old deer lay just outside of the cabin. It was motionless, having passed on from its painful existence.

VI.

A throng of well dressed Negroes held close ranks as they marched down Pennsylvania Avenue. The local branch of the NAACP had stirred their assembly, to protest the new housing ordinance that would place Baltimore on par with the Jim Crow South. City Hall was their destination.

James Walker strutted like a king rooster at the head of the crowd, having been instrumental in persuading this course of action. His lovely wife matched him step for determined step.

The distance from the stretch of Pennsylvania Avenue where the march began to City Hall was about three miles. The marchers covered it with joy, pride, defiance, and determination. Young and old held hands and sang Negro spirituals as they advanced. The throng multiplied as onlookers felt galvanized and fell in with their ranks.

All was well until the crowd crossed onto Saratoga Street. Here they were no longer protected by the invisible boundary line that would soon have legal designation as their area. Downtown Baltimore and most of the areas that lay to the east of it were not Negro friendly, unless said Negroes ventured into them to drive cars, clean house, nanny, butler, or perform any other number of servile tasks for white folks. It was even fine for Colored folk to do a little shopping or dining, as long as they used the rear entrance or sat way in the back, where decent white folks could ignore them.

Such areas were not places for Negroes to try to make their presence felt as real citizens. Downtown Baltimore was far from an ideal place for Negroes to raise a ruckus.

Thus, the marchers found their route interrupted at Saratoga and Paca, when a quartet of clunky police cars stopped at the edge of the block. The officers were so anxious in arriving on the scene that they came within a hair's breadth of having a four car pile up.

"Just what the hell do you folks think you're doin'?" A burly officer emerged from the lead car. A fearsome scowl covered his face as he smacked his Billy club against his thick palm. A lilting, just shy of sing-song tone undercut the menace in his voice, betraying him as an Irishman.

"We're just on our way to City Hall, officer," Madame Chairwoman answered in the calmest of tones. "Where we intend to exercise our right to peaceful assembly."

"Is that right?" the officer growled, advancing a step. As he did so, his three comrades rested their hands on the butt ends of their pistols.

James could feel some of the crowd shift just a hair backward. He knew that fear was starting to take hold already. "That's correct, Officer Hutchens," he spoke up, having read the officer's badge. "Every citizen of this country has the constitutional right to peaceful assembly. And as none of these good folks have any weapons of any sort," he continued, pausing to open his suit jacket and reveal the lining, then holding out his arms as if inviting a search, "our little march inarguably qualifies as peaceful. You can search each and every last one of us if you don't believe so."

"Maybe I don't want to bother with searchin' you black filth," Officer Hutchens spoke with a smile. A mischievous light danced in his eyes as he advanced toward James. "Maybe we figure if we say you've weapons, everyone will believe us."

James smiled and shrugged his shoulders. "If it were but a few of us here, it would surely play out just that way. But there's more than a hundred of us assembled, Officer Hutchens. You really think the word of four white cops is better than the word of more than a hundred Negroes?"

Officer Hutchens's face contorted into a red mask of hatred. "You're a talky nigger. Know that boy? Maybe I'll just run you in. Let you cool your heels for a couple of days in the city jail."

John shook his head as if he pitied the officer. "You could do that. But that would only bring you more trouble in the long run. See, this march was organized by the NAACP. Surely you've heard of that organization?"

Officer Hutchens gritted his teeth and shook his large head. "I've heard of the bastards, aright. Niggers and Jews in bed wit' one another. It's all Communism, you ask me."

"Communism or no, the NAACP has many Jewish lawyers working within our ranks. You run any of us in or do anything that you can't explain perfectly to the letter of the law, and they'll expose you. It would all make the papers; that's for sure. Such publicity would be quite embarrassing for the Police department. They'd need a fall guy for it." James sighed. "Might be a risk to your badge."

The menacing officer shrunk away at that, right hand instinctively caressing the silver shield on his chest. The devilish glint returned to his eyes a moment later.

"Could be this nig- negro's right boys," he said, turning to his fellow officers. "It's a beautiful country we live in. Even darkies got a right to peaceful assembly."

He faced James again, his lips parted into a predatory grin. "Course we can still do just as he said. Search each and every one of these folks. Be sure they're unarmed, as he claims."

Every Negro present was made to stand against the nearest wall. The officers took their sweet time searching each of their number. They also took numerous liberties, fondling many a woman's breast or squeezing their buttocks, and tossing the men roughly about. After what seemed like a humiliating eternity, the ordeal ended and the crowd continued on its' way.

A good number of those assembled disappointed James by slinking away. The officer's degrading tactics essentially sent them home with their tails tucked between their legs, despite the exhortations of James and the chairwoman.

Though he did not verbalize his sentiment, James thought of all who abandoned the march as weaklings and cowards. He felt glad that a significant majority remained as they continued down Saratoga Street. Reporters fell in among the marchers at Charles Street, snapping pictures of what they sensed to be a seminal event.

Soon they reached Baltimore's seat of government, a huge gothic style building located in the center of Downtown. Stone steps half the width of a football field ascended to the imposing entrance. A long black railing bisected the steps at their center, with identical ones at the far left and right. The remaining protesters' voices exploded in cacophonous chants as they made their stand in front of those grand stairs.

"Stop the Colored Housing Ordinance. Stop the Colored Housing Ordinance!"

"If Negroes can pay taxes and work, Negroes can live where they can afford!"

"This is Baltimore, not Mississippi!"

"Who knew Jim Crow's reach was so long?"

"Stop the Colored Housing Ordinance! Stop the Colored Housing Ordinance!"

They continued for more than an hour, chanting and walking back and forth in front of the building with such exertion that they all dripped with sweat.

Dozens of policeman gathered at their perimeter, placing threatening hands on Billy clubs or the butts of pistols. The protestors did not lose resolve, having been well drilled on such intimidation tactics during the planning of this action.

They knew that as long as there were reporters present, the police wouldn't dare use undue force. Soon, a tall, brown haired white man exited the massive doors of City Hall. He ran nervous hands over the front of his expensive, double-breasted suit.

"Please, quiet for just a moment!" He yelled down at the crowd. "Please be quiet!"

Madame Chairwoman moved her arms up and down, palms facing the ground.

The crowd quieted as soon as she did so.

"Alright, we're quiet, sir," she said, folding her arms across her chest. "What is it that you wish to say?"

"I am one of the Mayor's aides," the man uttered, wiping his brow. "You may know that he and the City Council are presently in session?"

"We know that very well."

The man cleared his throat. "Well, your actions have proven very disruptive to that session."

James found himself smiling along with Madame Chairwoman.

"By 'actions'," she said, "do you mean exercising our constitutional right to peaceful assembly? We've broken no laws."

The mayor's aide placed a hand to his chin and nodded. "That is correct. You've broken no laws. But you have made the conducting of our session extremely difficult. That is why I've been sent out here – to discover your requests for ceasing said disruption."

"That is very simple, sir. We request that city ordinance number 2179, otherwise known as the Housing Segregation Ordinance not be passed into law at the upcoming General Assembly. We request that the Mayor and City Council recognize that the NAACP, acting on behalf of the good Colored folks of Baltimore City- assert that we Negroes, we Colored, will not accept being forced into one small portion of a burgeoning city. We Negroes request that we maintain the right to live wherever we choose, so long as our wages afford us to."

"Is that right?" the mayor's aide asked. There was a rueful smile on his face.

"That is exactly right," Madame Chairwoman said, placing her hands on her hips. "And that is all that we request."

The mayor's aide took a deep breath. "Very well, then. I shall relay your wishes." He turned and hurried inside.

The crowd waited for more than twenty minutes before the aide returned. Every Negro assembled stared at him in silence, anxious to hear what he had to say.

The aide cleared his throat, emitting a nervous cough. "Our esteemed Mayor Preston and the City Council have sent me to inform you that the Negro view on City Ordinance 2179 will be greatly considered during the upcoming General Assembly. We will do all that we can to please all parties involved."

A great uproar broke out amongst the crowd. Negroes cheered, hugged, and slapped each other's palms. Although he didn't believe a word of what the aide had just said, James swept Naomi into a bear hug. Experience had taught him not to trust a white man in a suit or a uniform. He believed there to be a dearth of white folks worth trusting at all. Though he knew that the battle was far from won, just getting politicians to promise to consider the wishes of Negroes was a huge victory. What had just happened was a great accomplishment. Proud moments like this made him feel justified in the promise he'd made to fight to advance the Negro cause for as long as he drew breath.

VII.

Ruth pointed a bony, gnarled finger at Nathan. "Listen to me good, boy," she said.

"Yes, ma'am?" Nathan perked up, setting aside the charred venison on his plate.

"What I did earlier is the only way things are to be done. You get my meaning?"

Nathan shrugged.

A dry laugh escaped the old woman as she smacked her own forehead with her palm. "Of course you don't. I swear you're so sharp, sometimes I forget that you're not yet six years old. I guess even an old woman like me can't help talking silly at times."

Her mirth dissipated in the next instant, replaced by a hacking cough that subsided after a few moments.

Nathan thought at her. *Are you alright?*

Don't trouble yourself, little one, she answered inside his head. *The Lord's not calling me, yet.* She cleared her throat before speaking aloud. "What kind of deer did I kill tonight, son?"

"An old, sick one."

"That's right!" Ruth said. She smiled and clapped her hands. "And that's the only killing a seer should do – a mercy killing. Otherwise, it's like sinning against the good Lord who blesses us with such powers. You understand me?"

Nathan thought for a moment before speaking her inside her mind. *But you always have rabbit or squirrel. Are they all old or sick?*

The old woman wheezed dry laughter, followed by another hacking cough. She lifted her water glass from the earthen floor and pressed it to her lips.

You're a sharp one, alright, she thought at him. *I've told you that a million times and you always prove me truthful. Thing is, child- rabbits, squirrels, and the like are lowly creatures. Not good for much more than eating, multiplying, or becoming food. It's alright to kill a certain number of them, rabbits in particular. It's a miracle when one of those critters lives more than a year or two, anyway. Even if they don't get eaten by another critter, their high strung little hearts give out quickly. Animals like deer and bear on the other hand, are of a higher nature. Animals like deer and bear are majestic.* "God blesses such beasts with long life," she said aloud. "So it's wrong for a seer to slay one, unless it's on already on its last legs."

Is it wrong for hunters to kill them then? Nathan sent another thought.

Ruth shook her head before verbalizing her answer. "Not if the hunter is killing them to feed his family. But nowadays, more and more hunters kill for sport, not necessity. Those who do so don't know any better."

They can't sense the inner workings of God's greatest creatures, she slipped into inner speech once more. *They have no notion that killing such beautiful creatures is any different than squashing a bug. But folks like us are closer to the Lord, Nathan. We're closer to all the animals great and small, simple and majestic. Folks like us know better.* "Don't we boy?"

Nathan answered the question aloud, as it had been asked. "Yes we do, Miss Ruth."

"Very well, then. That will end this lesson. Enjoy your venison, for it is a truly special meal around these parts. After that, we'll say our prayers and it's off to sleep with you. I want you ready for your folks bright and early come morning."

"Yes, ma'am."

Nathan returned his attention to his food. His first taste of deer meat was quite enjoyable. As he chewed, he wondered when he would get his own opportunity to kill an animal.

Next time, son, Miss Ruth spoke inside his head. *Next time you come.*

7

Sacrifice and Consequence

I.

James knew that something was amiss from the moment Mr. Breslin came whistling into the store. The Irishman strutted toward his tenant, holding out a pile of papers in triumphant fashion.

The two policemen whom accompanied Breslin only reinforced James's dread. Worse still, one of them was Officer Hutchens, the man James had gotten one up on during the protest march less than two weeks earlier.

Menace oozed from the big cop's smile as his Billy club waited, drawn and ready. There was no doubt that he craved revenge for how James had bested him. Hutchens's younger cohort wore an anxious expression, but his drawn Billy club could do just as much damage as his leering partner's.

James and Naomi ceased the chore of wiping off counters and tables as the unwelcome trio approached. Man and wife froze in place, James behind the counter and Naomi at a table. The desire to have the store in immaculate condition before the day's first customer arrived was replaced by stark fear of what might happen next. "We have business, James," Breslin began.

A few seconds was all that it took for James's pride to override his fear. He sat the rag he held down before standing tall and ramrod straight. "What business is that- Breslin?"

"I've told you before that I prefer Mr. Breslin from the likes of you." The redhead stopped a few feet from the counter, with the officers standing close behind him.

"And I've told you before that I'll start calling you Mr. Breslin when you start calling me Mr. Walker," James retorted.

Breslin laughed himself into a fit, the sound and force of it expanding until he bent over at the waist. As his landlord carried on, James caught the victorious glint in Officer Hutchinson's hateful eyes.

Breslin challenged his tenant with cobalt blue eyes after managing to compose himself. "You have gotten quite uppity, haven't you? No matter. You'll be brought down a peg, very shortly."

Alarm flashed in James's eyes before being usurped by disgust. "What are you getting at, man?"

II.

Though nearly a year had passed since the incident with John Turner, Nathan continued to block off his own powers. Not using his powers at all was a far more attractive alternative than losing control of them and harming someone.

Ardent practice refined his ability to shut himself off like one might douse a lamp or shut off a faucet. He used his full concentration to drown out the light of his other consciousness each time it threatened to break through.

What had been sweat inducing and draining of mind and body grew easier each time he did it. For the past few months, the only manifestations of Nathan's extraordinary abilities were insignificant, such as the sense that he was about to step on a crack in the sidewalk or that someone around him was in a bad mood.

After the incident with John Turner, Nathan could have become something of a bully himself, but nothing could be further from what he wanted. He only wished for a simple life- to do well in school, play with his cousins and neighborhood friends, and work in the family store. He realized all of those desires without obstacle, until the morning when his psychic senses faced violent assault as he sat in Grammar class.

Head sweating, his inner self suffering jackhammer like pounding, he asked for a pass to the restroom. He was leaning over a faucet in sore need of cleaning when the damn of his awesome abilities burst. Every psychic barrier that he had worked so hard to construct crashed and shattered in an instant, leaving nothing to block the power of his mind's eye.

Nathan slumped to his knees in front of the faucet, his arms reaching up to grab its' edge. A terrible vision besieged him- a vision in which his father died.

III.

Concentrate now, Nathan, Miss Ruth thought. *Concentrate.*

Nathan stood outside of his mentor's cabin as a red sun set over the forest horizon, seeming to caress the treetops. Nathan obeyed the familiar guiding voice in his head, emptying himself out as he had done many times before. His mind's eye became a powerful searchlight, seeking a forest creature to link with.

It made brief contact with dozens of vibrant creatures- owls, rabbits, snakes, squirrels, a possum that had just gorged itself on grubs, a raccoon he had linked with once before, and a red fox. The eye even reached down to brush against the hive consciousness of a swarm of red ants.

The eye did not settle on any of those consciousnesses. Its' possessor sought a target of a specific nature.

Exploring the forest with his psychic vision as his body stood still, Nathan took no notice that the sunset had been supplanted by darkness.

Nor did he notice the confident expression his wizened tutor wore as she regarded him. He sent his mind's eye out further still, until he felt the sensation of cool waters run lazily through his mind. Wetness permeated his consciousness, making him feel as if he were swimming naked though the stream himself.

Nathan's mind's eye settled upon the consciousness of a creature that was in great pain. Whatever the creature was, it made its' home near the water. Nathan could sense that it had been wounded in an encounter with another animal.

Nathan probed with care, unearthing the creature's memories of being bitten by a cottonmouth. It had escaped before the viper could deliver enough venom to ensure quick death, but a lethal dosage had still been delivered. The creature had spent most of the day surrendering to the deadly toxin that ravaged its' bloodstream.

Nathan sensed that the creature would die a slow, suffering death unless he intervened. *Can you hear me, friend?* He took care in communicating, caressing it with his thoughts. *Can you hear me, dear friend of the forest?*

A lukewarm sensation passed through Nathan's mind. The creature accepted his presence, but did not yet know what to make of it.

Hear me, friend, Nathan transmitted. *I know that you are in great pain. I have come to relieve that pain. I offer you peace.*

He filled the animal's consciousness with thoughts of rest and relaxation. In return, a warm sensation passed through Nathan's mind.

Yes, my friend, Nathan sent a reply. *I know that you would like that. All that you have to do to have that peace, my friend, is to crawl to me.*

A hot, hissing sensation passed through Nathan's mind, almost severing the link. He counteracted it with images of a clear lake with beautiful foliage growing at its' edge. The creature he communed with grew calm.

I know that it pains you to move, friend of the forest, Nathan thought. *But I can ease that pain long enough for you to make your journey. When you come to me your suffering will end. Do you believe me?*

Another warm sensation passed through Nathan's consciousness.

If you are ready, my friend- I'll show you the way.

Very good, Miss Ruth interjected in Nathan's mind. *Do what you promised as you guide it. Take its' pain away.*

Nathan did as he was told, using his mind's eye to guide the creature from its burrow, through the now moonlit forest. At the same time, he concentrated on removing the pain that racked its' body. Doing so resulted in him absorbing the creature's pain into himself. The torment was as shocking as it was excruciating.

Miss Ruth pushed at him, keeping him from breaking the link in his suffering.

It will be over soon, boy, she soothed, flooding his mind with serene images. *The pain is only temporary.*

Temporary though the pain might have been, it took every ounce of determination that Nathan possessed to press past it. With Nathan's guidance, the creature made it to the edge of the brush at the forest road without any other denizen of the night bothering it.

Seconds later, Nathan sensed its' movements cease.

It's at your feet. Strike it down now, boy. Poor critter.

Nathan did as his mentor told him, focusing the power of his mind into a single mental blow.

The creature's consciousness went blank in an instant. In that same instant, Nathan's pain dissipated.

"Good job, son," Miss Ruth said, her voice tinged with joy. "Now open your eyes and see what you felled."

Nathan's eyes beheld a huge, plump rodent with a paddle for a tail. He had killed the first beaver he'd ever encountered.

IV.

Breslin smiled as he flung the papers towards James. "Read them and weep," he said.

Hot anger coursed through James as he swept the papers up from the counter. It was a notice to appear before the local magistrate for an eviction hearing, on the grounds of causing repeated public disturbances and leading dangerous activities, using the store as a base of operation.

"These charges are false!" he said, dropping the document in disgust. "I have done nothing of the sort!"

"What is it, honey?" Naomi asked, walking around the interlopers to stand at her husband's side. None of them budged to give her any room.

"It says… it says I am to report for an eviction hearing!"

Naomi became as outraged as her husband. "On what grounds?"

"On the grounds of your husband here's a rabble rouser," Officer Hutchens growled. "We don't take kind to rabble rousers in Baltimore. 'Specially not black ones. Now, the Mayor and City Council are kind enough to offer to give you Negroes your own part of town. Lots of your kind are happy wit' that. Then you got the likes of your husband, leading marches… rallies and all."

"Quite troublesome," Breslin said, wagging his finger. "I just couldn't accept someone operating that way while living on my property."

"You ought to have sold it to me," James said. "I have money to buy this place several times over!"

Breslin laughed. "Sure you do. But, you see, money isn't everything."

James balled his first, staring at Breslin and the officers.

"Baltimore isn't the town for what you're tryin' to bring about, boy," Officer Hutchens spoke with a grin. "Your kind is treated more than fair here, but there's some things that just can't be accepted."

"Like a Negro being held as an equal?" James's voice trembled.

"Now, no one said all that." Breslin had the audacity to adapt a patient, almost paternal tone. "The Negro is separate but equal, if I recall correctly. Oh, by the way- you don't have a prayer of winning the hearing. The judge is a long time friend of my family. He also can't abide by rebellious Negroes. I warned you about stirring up trouble last year- didn't I?" Breslin's smile illustrated his gloating mood. "I guess you'll soon have to find another means of funding your rabble rousing."

James found the white men's gloating manner to be far worse than the likelihood of being evicted. His next words to Breslin spewed forth on a crest of hate. "You're a filthy, fucking bastard, you know that?"

Shocked that any Negro (even one as headstrong as James) had the audacity to curse him, Breslin's jaw collapsed toward the floor.

Naomi clasped a mortified hand over her mouth, as terrified as she was certain that the point of return had just been passed. Officer Hutchens licked his lips as he moved within inches of the counter, Billy club held aloft.

"You're going to apologize to Mr. Breslin for that, boy."

V.

Horrible images continued to assail Nathan as he used the sink to pull himself to his feet. His forehead trickled sweat as he breathed labored breaths.

He held his hands to his temples as he looked around, trying to figure out what he must do. He decided that he could not go back to the classroom. Even if his teacher believed he was sick, she would only send him to the school nurse. Even if the nurse determined that he was ill enough to go home, she would try to contact an adult to come get him rather than dismiss him.

There was too little time for that. While the school nurse was trying to make a call, his parents could be dying.

Nathan swooned, sensory overload threatening to knock him back into the floor. His eyes settled on the bathroom window as he used every iota of fortitude that he possessed to steady his body and mind.

The window stood rudimentary, little more than a looking glass through which the rear of the schoolhouse could be seen. There were no latches or cables to open it with. Nathan lifted one leg high and kicked the glass as hard as he could (causing a small crack to bloom in it). He alternated legs, kicking it four more times before it shattered. He climbed out without hesitation, shimmying to avoid being cut by loose shards.

He ran, striding hard and fast as soon as he hit the ground. He thought he heard Principle Trotter calling after him, having come to investigate the noise from the breaking glass. The voice was faint and weak, as if it were trying to reach Nathan through an underwater tunnel.

Nathan resolved himself to facing the consequences for breaking the window and leaving school later. Right now, he had to get to *Walker's* as soon as possible. If he arrived in time, he might manage to stop the terrible vision he'd had from becoming reality.

VI.

"You're real good at this stuff, Nathan," Miss Ruth said. "You know that?" *I mean you're just as graceful at this kind of thing as a big old sea turtle, swimming the Pacific Ocean,* she thought at him.

The old woman and the boy sat in a familiar position on her earthen floor, empty dinner plates in front of them. Nathan licked his lips, having very much enjoyed the taste of more venison.

"I'm glad I've been able to teach you so much in such a short time," Miss Ruth said aloud. "Don't know if I could show you much more if I had ten more years to do it in."

Nathan stared at his teacher. *You're not just sick- are you, Miss Ruth? You're dying. Aren't you?*

A warm flash passed through his mind, following by a shred of darkness.

Everybody's dying, boy, Miss Ruth thought at him. *I'm just a little closer to reuniting with the good Lord than most. He's been waiting for me a long time already, that's for sure.*

How old are you, Miss Ruth?

Huge laughter escaped the old woman, causing her few remaining teeth to rattle. *Older than you can imagine, child*, she thought. *Say, haven't your folks ever told you its' not polite to ask a lady's age? Even an old bag of bones like me?*

I'm sorry, ma'am.

Don't be. There's not a soul alive that needs to apologize to the Woman of the Gulf Woods. I've seen and done just about everything the Lord's aimed for me to do. Yes, I've been around long enough to outlive all of my children and my grandchildren. Working on the great grandchildren, too. I've been to, fro, and beyond doing what the Lord set out for me. Dozens of special individuals like yourself have come to me during the long decades I've lived in these here woods.

She reached across the earthen floor and pulled Nathan into a fierce hug. He felt the considerable strength remaining in her brittle, shriveled frame.

With everything I've seen and done, I've wondered if the Lord would ever take me or if I'd be cursed to live on and on, until everyone I might ever have had history with died. Then I saw you.

Intense warmth flooded Nathan's mind. The feeling he experienced was the mental equivalent of sitting before a fire on a cold winter night.

Even before your folks brought you here, I saw you, Miss Ruth continued. *The good Lord was kind enough to alert me to your coming. I saw you and knew that once I'd taught you, my work here would be done. Well, I've taught you now, boy. And you've learned fast. There's only one more thing I have to do for you. After that, the Good Lord just might see fit to call me home.*

VII.

"I'm not apologizing for anything," James growled. "And I'm no boy."

Naomi trembled, noticing that the younger officer had moved in close to Hutchens, his club also poised to strike. She grabbed her husband by the meat of his arm.

"Maybe you should apologize, honey," she said. "We don't need this kind of trouble. We'll just go peacefully, try to straighten this out later."

"Yeah, nigger," Officer Hutchens hissed. "If you're smart, you'll listen to this black bitch."

VIII.

Nathan was three blocks from home when the psychic force within him exploded, knocking him to the ground like a right cross landed by Jack Johnson.

Passersby gathered to gawk as his eyes rolled back in his head. Spasms racked his body as his feet kicked like a three year old in the midst of a particularly bad tantrum. He was not aware of the kind woman who bent over him and held his head up to keep it from banging into the curb. He was also unaware of the young man who went running off in search of medical help.

His arms flailed about until a mailman and another young man each seized one. Streams of saliva poured from his open mouth, the copious spill an unwanted reward for the woman holding his head aloft.

A warm puddle spread across the front of Nathan's pants and down his leg. He was ignorant of the urine and all else occurring in his physical environment. His only awareness was of the fact that his father was dying.

IX.

Miss Ruth released Nathan from the hug she held him in and seized him by the wrists. Nathan felt her hot breath on his face. Feeling complete trust in her, he did not cower or pull away.

A great force passed between them as she held him. Nathan's mind filled with images beyond count, words beyond measure. Though his eyes were wide open, he saw nothing of the tiny cabin they inhabited or the lush forest landscape that waited outside the structure's unadorned windows.

While his outside eyes fell blind, Nathan's powerful mind's eye saw with more clarity than it ever had, adjusting to the breakneck pace of the old woman's transmissions with ease.

Nathan processed image after image of those like himself and the lives they lived. The first person he saw was a Creole woman, perhaps 30 years old. She settled along the Louisiana Bayou, making a living as a fortune teller. Nathan watched as the woman held back, never revealing larger truths to those who came to have their palms read. The extent of her true powers was never known because of her restraint.

Madame Bluefield was her professional name, Miss Ruth thought at him. *She made a humble but stable living as a minor curiosity. A peaceful and honorable living for our kind.*

The image of Madame Bluefield gave way to that of a charcoal-skinned man running from a group of bloodhound-led lawmen. As the man sprinted and gasped his way through the woods, that image also dissipated, giving way to a scene of the same man traipsing through a manor house at night, intent on stealing the owner's goods.

He was one who misused the sight, Miss Ruth addressed Nathan once more. *Used it to steal and rob. Only on this occasion, it failed him. He did not see everything as it unfolded.*

The man descended a flight of stairs, preparing to exit the house with a sack full of jewels and finery. His plan for escape crumbled when he came face to face with a drowsy young maid.

The brave young woman picked up a candlestick and tried to bash the thief in his head. He dodged just enough to take the blow on his left shoulder, shoving her with both hands before she could manage another swing. The candlestick clanged to the floor as she stumbled.

She recovered her footing and scrambled to wrap her arms around him. "You filthy thief!" she shrieked. He tried to shake her off, but she was much stronger than she looked. His sight seized him as they struggled, sounding like an alarm in his head. The owners of the house were just up the road, heading back from their evening outing by carriage.

The panicked thief rushed forward, launching himself and the maid toward one of the stone walls of the house. Her head met it with a sickening thud, causing all resistance to leave her as her feisty body became a limp mass and crumpled into the floor.

The thief fell down the rear stairs in his haste to exit. Greed drove him to stop to recover each piece of booty that scattered about. He resumed flight as the unsuspecting owners pulled their carriage up front.

That scene gave way to another of the same man being led to a hangman's platform in the town square. A crowd of townspeople jeered, throwing eggs and stones in his direction. The man made no attempt to dodge or avoid the projectiles.

He sneered at the audience as they hurled racial epithets and other hateful words at him. He declined the opportunity to ask God for forgiveness or speak any other last words.

Not a single muscle moved as the noose slipped over his neck. The hangman released the lever, collapsing the wooden platform beneath him. The crowd cheered and screamed as the criminal's feet bucked and he gasped for air that would not come. Those assembled fell silent at the sound of his neck snapping. A young blond woman swooned, her beau keeping her from falling to the naked ground. A fresh tumult of cheers erupted moments later. Many of the onlookers sang and danced with macabre joy.

That's what can happen when our kind misuse our God given powers, Miss Ruth cautioned Nathan. *Better to keep them close to you, and not go around trying to abuse them for personal gain, especially not personal gain that involves taking from others.*

I know you probably think that you would never do anything like that, but its' easy to think that when you're so young and pure. But you're going to get older, boy, just like everybody else. And life's going to be as hard on you as it is on us all. Your emotions are going to make you want to act on your powers. You won't be all serene as you are now, especially when you get to be a young man. That's why I wanted to show you what can happen if you don't do right by what God's blessed you with.

She squeezed his wrists even harder, until they started to bruise, but he felt no pain. He wasn't aware of anything that transpired outside of his mind's eye.

A cavalcade of terrible images flooded him. He watched as seers used their powers to punish lovers who had spurned or been unfaithful to them. Other seers used their powers to perpetrate business scams. Some used their powers to pummel their rivals in physical confrontations.

Each incident that Ruth replayed for Nathan ended with the seer being chased into hiding, jailed, or killed.

I'm worried about you, boy, she thought at him. *Worried about what will happen when the world is unkind enough to you to make you feel the anger our kind is bound to feel. If you go down a bad path, it'll be worse than with any of those folks I just showed you.*

She released both her mental and physical grip on him. Nathan's mind thudded back into awareness of the physical realm. It was then that he became aware of the soreness in his wrists. He alternated rubbing each one with the opposite hand.

Nathan saw that his mentor's eyes had become wild and feverish. Both of the colors in them burned with great intensity and her body was soaked with sweat.

"That's why I'm going to help you block most of your power off," she said, wheezing out the words. "So it won't get the best of you later. I can only do it if you allow me too, though. You're already more powerful than I am and you can stop it if you like. But I'm telling you what would be best. You trust your old teacher, don't you?"

Nathan nodded. He did trust her, even more than he trusted his own parents. They had never disappointed him or been unjust, but they were not like he and Miss Ruth. They were not his kind.

"Alright, then," she said, reaching her bony hands out to him. "All you have to do is clear yourself out for me. Just as if you were seeking an animal to link with."

Nathan flinched at the unnatural heat in her hands, taking her measure as he held them. Her breathing had more or less returned to normal, but such heat was a sure signifier of fever. She seemed even weaker than usual.

"Will it hurt you to do what we're about to do?" his voice grew shrill with concern.

She cackled without humor, throwing her head back. "Dear child, it will kill me. Surely, you know that."

X.

James leapt over the counter with the grace of a cat. He twisted to his left when he landed, dodging a blow from the big officer's Billy club.

As Hutchens raised the club again, James seized his wrist in a two-handed grip, squeezing it so hard that the club squirted loose and clattered across the floor.

"Stop it, James," Naomi pleaded. "Please, stop!"

Her voice registered as a far-away whisper, muffled by the rage that had consumed him. It was a rage born of a lifetime of hard work and shrewd actions to try to better things for himself and others, only to have the racist white society he inhabited take it away at the drop of a hat. It was a rage born of having to leave his family land like a thief in the night, avoiding a torture and lynching for which his would be murderers would not have been punished. It was a rage born of later learning that the land he'd inherited had been desecrated by fire in manifestation of those same white men's hatred.

All that James had ever owned in Alabama was no more. Now Breslin had the audacity to gloat about the foul legal machinations he'd performed to try and take away all that James had established in Baltimore as well? To add further insult to injury, the man's police bodyguard had spoken to Naomi as if she were some worthless dog.

If these bastards could get away with treating him like some criminal, then it was time he lived up to it. They could take his store, but he aimed to take pieces of their wretched hides.

Such were the thoughts consuming James Walker's enraged mind as he punched and slapped Officer Hutchens about his store. He was so angry that he did not hear the other policeman shout a final warning for him to stop, but he did feel the bullet explode into his back.

XI.

Miss Ruth pressed down on her pupil's hands, digging her nails into his knuckles. He felt no pain because his consciousness had deserted the physical plane.

Nathan had done as instructed, making his mind into a blank void. Soon the essence of his teacher filled him, the way that torrential rain might fill a gulley. Great waves of psychic energy jolted him as they poured in. The initial shock almost caused him to close himself off, but he rode it out.

You're already more powerful than me and you can stop it if you like. He remembered the words she had spoken aloud mere moments ago. *But I'm telling you what would be best. You trust your old teacher- don't you?*

Yes, he did. He trusted her enough to allow her to do something that would cause her death. He felt her strength depart at a rapid pace as her psychic energy continued to flood him.

He fed off instinct as one psychic jolt after another rocked him, rolling with the mental blows as a prizefighter would roll with punches. He withstood the tempestuous barrage long enough for it to morph into something smooth and controlled.

Miss Ruth's voice came to him in a mental whisper. *Hear me well, child. I am not long for this world. I am ready to pass on to the Lord. But, I have left a sort of echo of myself, of the control that I've learned during my long life. That remnant will always be with you, unless you should choose to cast me out. It will be your lock, your harness. It will help to keep the great power that you have under control, until you gain the maturity to choose wisely and control yourself. I don't expect you to understand everything I've said. You're just a small boy, no matter how powerful you may be. Just know that I've done the best I could by you. With the proper control and judgment you might do a world of good, with the great power you have. Without restraint and good judgment, you might cause a great deal of suffering and destruction. I believe that you will do far more good than bad, for your soul is pure. Had I not believed that, I would have killed you.*

Killed me?

Yes, I would have had to kill you if I had detected the slightest bit of evil in you.

I'm not evil, Miss Ruth.

A warm flash passed through Nathan's mind. *I know you're not, boy. I must be going now. But I will always be with you. Before the greater part of me departs*

this plane for good, I want you to enjoy the feeling that you have right now. It feels
wonderful, doesn't it?

Yes. Yes it does, Miss Ruth.

Nathan felt clear headed and complete, engulfed by a sense of tranquility.

Stay just as you are for a while. Stay as you are because you might never feel
so full of peace again. After a time, you may return to your physical body. Then
you'll find what is left of mine. Do not be alarmed.

I won't be alarmed, Nathan promised. *Miss Ruth?*

Yes, child.

Are you going with God, now?

Indeed, I am dear boy. Indeed, I am.

An airy, loving feeling flashed through Nathan's mind- the psychic
equivalent of a kiss on the cheek. Then the old woman was gone.

Nathan remained in his psychic sanctuary as she instructed. It was a
wonderful state of being.

He felt in touch with the moon and the stars, the past and the future, the
woods and the streams and everything beyond. He felt like the universe was
limitless. He felt limitless.

After a time, he decided to ease his psychic essence out of the nirvana he had
attained and back into his earthbound body. He settled into his flesh like a
beachgoer in cold water, beginning by dipping his toes in. Soon, both feet were
wet. Then he waded up to his waist. He paused as his body adjusted to the
temperature, until he felt comfortable enough to plunge all the way in.

He opened his physical eyes to behold the dried out, limp husk that lay before
him. Nathan couldn't help thinking that Miss Ruth's remains resembled a rubber
chicken.

Her once spectral eyes had become white pits, devoid of pupils. Her once wrinkled skin was now as smooth as a baby's and lacked so much as a single pore. Her once claw-like, discolored nails were flat and white, as if they had just been manicured. Her sackcloth dress dangled from her shriveled remains.

Nathan felt no alarm, but he did feel very sad. Moonlight crept into the cabin as he hugged his departed teacher and cried out in grief. All through the forest, the animals cried with him.

XII.

James crumpled into the floor like a great tree felled by a lumberjack, coming to rest with no further sound or movement. Mr. Breslin stood stunned, eyes wide in horror.

Officer Hutchens turned and slapped his young comrade on the shoulder. "That a boy, Turnblatt," he said, admiring what was left of what he thought of as the nigger who had been assaulting him just moments earlier. A feral scream disrupted his enjoyment.

Naomi charged at Officer Turnblatt with a large knife in hand and eyes full of malice. Already regretting what he had done to her husband, the young officer decided to flee from her. He didn't want to harm anyone else, let alone a woman. His partner shared no such sentiment.

XIII.

Upon returning to Miss Ruth's cabin, James and Naomi were shocked to find their Nathan all alone. He stood in the morning sun, looking not the least bit bothered.

"Where is the old woman?" James asked, not wanting to let on how alarmed he was.

"She died last night," Nathan answered. He spoke with the casual air of someone commenting about the weather.

James and Naomi turned to each other, mutual shock rendering them unable to speak.

"Don't be alarmed," Nathan said, sauntering up the dirt path in front of the cabin and hugging both parents at waist level. "It was her time."

"Okay, son," James found his tongue after a brief struggle. "Okay." He looked into Nathan's strange eyes while patting him on the head. "How did she die?"

"She.." Nathan started to tell the truth before realizing that his parents wouldn't understand. "She passed in her sleep."

"That poor old woman," Naomi said.

"Its okay, Mama," the boy spoke with a smile. "She's with God, now. Good people get to go with God when they die. You taught me that."

"Yes, I did," Naomi said, forcing a smile of her own. She fought back tears as she swept the child into her arms and planted kisses on his cheek and forehead. "I swear I don't know what to do with you sometimes, son."

James's eyes scanned the periphery of the cabin before he walked up the steps and peeked inside. A puzzled expression spread across his face. "Where is her body, son?"

Naomi set the boy down.

"I buried her," Nathan spoke in a flat tone, as if what he said wasn't the least bit remarkable.

"You buried her. As small as you are?"

"Yes. I buried her, Papa. I buried Miss Ruth."

"But how? I don't see any dirt on you. Nor do I see any shovels around here. Not that a shovel that a little one like you can hoist has been invented yet."

"Perhaps he didn't need a shovel, dear," Naomi said, speaking with a tone of eerie resignation. She held her palms out in surrender, as if to say we have no choice but to accept that he did as he said.

James gave a slight nod, spreading a set of long fingers across his forehead. "No. I guess he might have other ways," He said, recovering the composure that had threatened to escape him. "You want to show us where you buried her, son?"

Nathan nodded and walked around the side of the cabin. James and Naomi followed the boy until he stopped in front of a patch of earth that was about twenty feet past the rear of the cabin. The area was marked by a makeshift cross of branches that jutted from the ground.

James and Naomi stared at the makeshift burial plot, their faces a mixture of sadness and awe.

"It's okay," Nathan said. He moved between them and took each of their hands. "This is what she wanted."

"Did she tell you that?" Naomi asked.

Nathan shook his head. "She didn't have to tell me. She knew that I would know."

"Well, I don't know," James said. "Doesn't she have any family left? It doesn't seem right to leave her out in the woods like this."

"She is a part of this forest," Nathan said. "She belongs here. And she has outlived everyone in her family who knew her well."

There was no immediate reply to Nathan's assertion. Instead, they all stood in silence, the boy who was like no other boy and in many ways not a boy at all, and the parents who adored and cherished, but were in awe of him.

XIV.

A massive blow from Officer Hutchens's Billy club pelted Naomi's skull, sending her into the floor alongside her fallen husband. The dull, sickening thud of the blow portended serious injury. So did Naomi's prone, twitching body.

"Crazy black bitch," Officer Hutchens gasped as he wiped blood from his weapon. "A shame it had to come to this. I don't know what got into those two niggers."

"I can't have this s-sort of in...incident on my property," Breslin stammered, trickling sweat. "I can't have this."

"Hutchens- you- you son of a bitch!" Officer Turnblatt screamed. His face was as red as Breslin's hair. "You didn't have to do that to that poor woman!"

"Oh? I didn't have to do that to that poor woman?" Officer Hutchens said. "We can argue the merits of my actions later. Just as you can thank me for saving your pimply white ass later. Right now, we'd better get out of here before the place is crawling with jigs. We don't have enough bullets to shoot them all if a riot breaks out."

The senior of the two officers snatched the stunned property owner by the arm and hauled him from the store. "Let's get the hell out of here, Breslin," he said. "Legalities will be the least of your worries if you stay any longer."

"What about the woman?" Officer Turnblatt asked as they hustled along the sidewalk. There were already several gawkers attracted by the gunshot. "I think she was still alive."

"We'll send for the ambulance as soon as we're safe," Officer Hutchens said, diving into the police car and shifting into drive as his cohorts joined him. "You ain't gonna put the safety of some nigger bitch who meant to stab you ahead of your own. Are you?"

8

Hospital

I.

Nathan opened his eyes in slow motion, finding himself lying on a humble, uncomfortable bed in a room with dim light. He felt groggy and weak.

He blinked as he looked upon Virgil, Alma, David, and Eli.

"We thought you might not wake up 'til winter," Virgil said. The smile on his face was at odds with the somber mood that permeated the room. "You had a serious attack the other day. The doctor gave you something to put you under, but he didn't figure you'd be out for two days."

Virgil leaned over the bed and patted Nathan's arm with a strong hand.

"Yeah, cousin," David said. "We're awfully glad to see you awake."

"The doctor says you had a massive seizure," Virgil continued, nodding as he spoke. "Drew your blood. Been runnin' tests to see if you got epilepsy. But…"

Nathan sat up in the bed, his spectral eyes shining like starlight. "I don't have epilepsy, Cousin Virgil. I got into such a state because I saw what happened."

Alma recoiled at Nathan's tone, grabbing her husband's arm for comfort.

"What did you see, little cousin?" she asked, her blood running cold.

"You know what I saw!" Nathan shrieked, banging his fists on the meager pallet. "You know what I saw!"

"Wait a minute, now," David reprimanded his cousin, glaring at him. "Don't go yelling at my mama. I don't care if you are in the hospital."

"Hush now, boy!" Alma silenced her eldest. "Take your brother into the hall."

"But, Ma…"

"You mind your mama, boy," Virgil growled. "And be quiet out there."

Nathan wore a wild glare as Virgil and Alma stood arm in arm, a mixture of sadness and confusion painted on their faces.

Nathan's visage softened. There was no sense in being angry with the only family he had left. They hadn't told him what happened because they didn't want him to have another attack. They had no idea why he had jumped out of a window at school prior to having what they thought of as a seizure in the middle of the street. No doubt they figured him for a loon- that he couldn't handle knowing what happened to his parents.

Virgil and Alma had no way of knowing what really happened to land Nathan in this hospital bed, no reason to imagine that Nathan had seen the very tragedy that they attempted to conceal from him unfold.

A single tear escaped the brilliant prism of Nathan's left eye to flee down his face. He wiped it away, trying to be brave.

"I'm sorry, Cousin Alma." His voice quavered. "I had no right to disrespect you. I suppose I deserve a spanking."

Alma's eyes widened as she released her husband's arm. She leaned over to kiss the patient on his forehead. "Don't be silly, child. We know you're not yourself. You've had a terrible shock."

Nathan stared into her eyes. "Was it as bad for y'all as it was for me?"

She blinked in confusion. "I don't understand…"

"I saw it, Cousin Alma. I saw what happened to my parents. So y'all don't have to try to keep it from me. Because I already know."

Alma shrank from the bed, gasping and placing her hands over her mouth. Virgil placed a strong arm around his wife's shoulders, turning her and drawing her against his broad chest.

"How?" Virgil asked. "How could you know what happened to them when you were found throwing a fit in the street, five blocks away at the time it happened?"

Nathan took a deep breath before answering. "I saw it in my mind, Cousin Virgil. Saw my father lose his temper and light into that big cop. The one who hates Negroes. That's when the other cop shot him in the back."

Virgil said nothing, only staring at his young cousin in disbelief. Feeling his wife swoon, he helped her into the rickety chair near Nathan's bed.

Nathan continued, his strange eyes burning brighter than Virgil had ever seen them. "After that, Mama, she went after that other cop with a knife. That's when the big one hit her with his nightstick. He swung it just as hard as he could."

Nathan balled his fists, digging his nails into his palms. "He didn't have to hit her so hard. He enjoyed that part."

Virgil glanced at Alma and saw her near catatonic with shock. He made no move to intervene.

"I saw it all in my mind, just minutes before it happened," Nathan continued. "That's why I acted so strange ....why I dodged out of school and was running home. I was trying to warn my folks- keep what I saw from coming true." Tears streamed beneath his fingers as he hid his face in his hands. "But, I was too late."

"My God," Alma whimpered. "Oh, Dear God."

Nathan's tremulous voice conveyed his grief stricken spirit. "I was too late."

His sobbing began as a single flame, then spread to consume him like wildfire. His body shook in time to the song of his misery as it soared through the halls of the hospital.

A nurse appeared in short order, bearing the stern countenance of a drill sergeant and the rugged body of a farmer's wife.

"What's the matter with him?" she asked no one in particular. She went straight to Nathan, not waiting for an answer.

"Poor child," she said, shaking her head. She turned to Virgil and said, "The boy's overcome again. I suppose he's not yet ready for visitors. He'll need another sedative."

She headed for the hall. "I'll have to get the doctor, now. And you folks will have to leave him be."

II.

Nathan felt groggy and weak when he next awakened. He recalled two nurses holding his arms as the attending doctor injected him with a needle that looked fit for an elephant.

He oriented himself to his surroundings, realizing that he was no longer in a hospital recovery ward. His new location was a long corridor arranged in a fashion very much like an army barrack. He lay atop a flimsy cot that was even less comfortable than his hospital bed. There were lines of identical cots to his left, right, and across from him.

He heard inane muttering three cots to his right, causing him to turn and see a frail boy with crazed eyes. Across the room and to his left, a bald boy kneeled, playing solitaire over his cot. Playing solitaire wasn't strange, but the way the card player's mouth hung open, spilling drool all over the cards and cot was. His face was a blank page as he competed against himself.

Observing these boys and a few others led Nathan to deduce that he was in a psych ward. He had heard of such places- places whose sole purpose was to house crazies. He hadn't imagined the existence of one just for kids.

Nathan also noticed that his co-inhabitants were mixed company. Perhaps the bounds of segregation did not apply to patients suffering from mental illness.

Is that what the doctors and nurses who had treated him thought? What Virgil and Alma thought? That he had lost his mind?

If so, he had helped them reach that conclusion. He realized that he had gone wild with grief and guilt every time he'd gotten his bearings.

The guilt tore at him worse than the horrible grief did. Since he was a young child, everyone who'd known about his sight had cautioned him to avoid using it in a self-serving fashion. His only major violation of that guidance had been his handling of John Turner. The thing with John had scared him so much that he'd tried not to use his abilities at all. He'd pushed them deep inside, submerging them with such severity that they sometimes seemed to disappear. Choking off his powers left him unable to sense his parents' tragic fate until it was too late to save them.

The knowledge that he could have saved his parents (had he not run from himself) would haunt Nathan for the rest of his life. Well, he wasn't going to run anymore.

He had a big task ahead, a task that he wouldn't be able to undertake unless he could contain his emotions long enough to shed the appearance of losing his mind. If he didn't do that he'd end up in a real sanitarium, not just a hospital psych ward.

Nathan had no intention of that being his fate. His ward mates were rife with negative and uncontrollable psychic energies, the echoes of which threatened to flood his mind's eye. A sanitarium would be much more of the same. If he were trapped within a sanitarium, the constant exposure to the psychic echoes of madness might drive his senses haywire. More importantly than that, he might never marshal the focus necessary to strike down those who struck down his parents.

Book II- Wrath

1

Homecoming\ Learning to Hunt

I.

The sight of Naomi shattered Nathan's heart into a thousand pieces. Before she even spoke, the doddering grin and childlike innocence of her eyes told him that she was but a shadow of the maternal figure he had always known.

So, this is what that policeman's stick did to her? Nathan thought. He decided that his dead father had fared much better than his mother.

"Hello, Mama," he managed, eyes fixed on Naomi as Virgil and Alma flanked her in their living room.

"Hello!" Naomi replied, her grin widening as she waved like an excited child. "Hello..."

"Nathan," Cousin Virgil reminded her, his cadence slow and patient. "Remember we've talked about this, Naomi. Nathan is your son."

"Yes, Nathan!" Naomi said, clapping her hands. "Nathan! My son!"

Virgil took Alma's hand and led her from the kitchen, leaving the boy alone with what remained of his mother.

They regarded each other, Naomi still grinning while Nathan sighed.

"Are you sad?" she walked over to him. To his mortification, she put her hands to her cheeks and stuck her tongue out at him. "Don't be sad, mean boy."

Nathan found himself smiling just to placate her. This is going to be like having a little sister, he thought. Mama Naomi is going to be like my little sister now. It's not fair for her to have to be this way. But then, life had never been fair to him and his loved ones.

First, his biological mother died while giving birth to him. Now, his father was dead and poor Naomi (whom he loved just as if they were flesh and blood) was reduced to idiocy.

Virgil and Alma had explained the effects of Naomi's brain damage as best they could before Nathan saw her, but he still wasn't prepared for the encounter.

It's not right, he thought. Those white cops walked free, while his father rested in a grave and his mother was ruined for life. There were no witnesses to the incident other than that bastard landlord. That left the words of three white men against what the general public perceived as wild accusations. Of course, the general public that counted in Baltimore was white. They were quick to label Nathan's father as a crazed Negro who dared to assault a policeman, leaving the other officer no choice but to shoot him. The NAACP and its' lawyers could prolong the struggle to paint things with a different brush for as long as they desired to, but the world was more comfortable with that notion.

"Do you know me- Mama?" Nathan grimaced as he asked, testing the memory of the simple creature before him.

"Yes," she chirped. "I know you... you are." Her face frowned in concentration. "Nathan. That's right." She clapped and giggled. "You're my son. Nathan!"

She squealed like the young girl she had become, pulling Nathan into a hug. Having grown some as of late, he didn't have to reach as far to return it as he had in the past. Still, she had about five inches on him. That didn't prevent her from seeming a thousand times smaller.

II.

Virgil came into Nathan's room after dinner. When the Walkers lived in this house upon first coming to Baltimore, Nathan and Eli shared a bunk (while David slept on his own bed across from them). But Nathan now had his own quarters, as did Naomi.

"How are you holdin' up?" Virgil sat next to his young cousin, on the edge of the mattress.

"Alright. I guess."

"Alright. You guess?'" Virgil said, turning his large head to the right to face the boy. "You don't have to act tough, little cousin. Ain't a grown man alive that tough."

Nathan bit his lip and cleared his throat as he cast his eyes along the floorboards. "Just trying to keep myself together," he said. "Don't want to end up back in the psych ward."

"You ain't gon' end up back in no place like that." Virgil rested a strong hand on Nathan's shoulder. "Anybody can bear what's happened- its' you."

Virgil turned away from Nathan, eyeing the wall in front of him. "Now, I ain't gon' lie to you. There was no rhyme or reason in what happened to your folks. Your father- all he ever did was try to help folks. Try to make it better for other Negroes. He could've just worked at that store, made all the money he could, sat back an' counted it."

Virgil cleared his throat. "Instead, he got involved with the NAACP, holdin' rallies an' meetin's an' such. I figure that's why what happened happened. White folks are afraid of Negroes who don't want to stay in there place. We're alright so long's we don't step on their toes."

Nathan couldn't help himself. "You mean like you don't?"

Virgil cleared his throat again before smacking his right fist into his left palm. His bulky shoulders climbed level with his neck before he took a deep breath.

His posture relaxed as he spoke. "That's right, little cousin. Like I don't. Now I know you think your father was a braver an' better man than me an' I'll be the first to admit you're right. But he's gone, an' I'm here. An' since I'm the only male kin you got to help you out, I got to see after you. So that's mainly what I come to talk to you about. About when you intend to start school back up."

Nathan thought long and hard. It wasn't a question he'd considered at all in the weeks following his father's death and Naomi's injury.

"I don't know, Cousin Virgil. I guess I'm just not ready, yet."

Virgil turned his head in Nathan's direction again. "Cain't say I blame you for that. It'd be a lot to deal with, I suppose. Think I'll go talk to the headmaster at the school, see if you can't do some of your work at home for a while. How's that sound to you?"

Nathan met his Cousin's eyes for a fleeting moment before turning away. "That'll be alright, I guess."

A deep belly laugh rumbled out of Virgil. "Damn right it will. I know you won't have no problem with assignments either, bright as you are. Hell, you could problee teach classes yourself, already."

Virgil's next words lacked mirth. "If you ain't gonna be in school, we'll have to figure somethin' else for you to do during the day. Cain't have you roamin' the neighborhood or twiddlin' your thumbs all mornin' an' afternoon."

He stood and stretched his stout frame. "I guess you could give me some help around the studio. Help me set up my supplies and clean up. Maybe you could even pose for me some. That's all I can think of, right off. But iss a start."

He turned toward the door. "Well, I guess I'll be leaving you now, little cousin. We'll be talkin' lots more. Me an' Alma got to look after you. Your folks would've wanted that."

That last statement burdened Nathan's mind long after his cousin's departure. "Your folks would've wanted that." As if both James and Naomi were dead. Nathan guessed they both were- at least all the parts that counted. There was someone occupying Naomi's body, but that someone was far removed from the woman who raised him.

Nathan reflected on what his cousin said about him needing to do something during the day if he wasn't in school. He figured that he might die of boredom if he had to spend all day helping out in the man's studio.

He didn't want to see Virgil at work, anyway. Not when Virgil was sure to allow some white man to take credit for a good deal of his best work. Nathan didn't want to witness his older cousin sell himself short every day any more than his father had wanted to see such before that policeman shot him.

None of that would have been an issue if *Walker's* were still open. The storefront stood unadorned now, the namesake sign that used to hang over its' entrance having been removed. Nathan was sure that his father's scummy former landlord was devising plans to make money on the place despite the tragedy that had occurred within.

But Nathan had other plans for the property formerly known as *Walker's*. He intended to fix things so that Connor Breslin never profited another dime from it.

III.

Nathan focused on strengthening his abilities every night, while his relatives slept. The knowledge that neither his parents nor Miss Ruth would have desired such did nothing to deter him.

After all, it wasn't as if his father knew everything there was to know about everything. If he was so smart, Nathan thought, he wouldn't have attacked that policeman. If Mama Naomi had been so smart, she wouldn't have attacked the other policemen either. If they both knew so much, they'd be alive and in one piece.

As far as Miss Ruth was concerned, Nathan knew that she had meant well. But her teachings made a lot less sense to him at eleven than they had at five. She always spoke of taking caution in wielding his power, but she had used her powers all the time- even to slay animals.

Why should things be different for me? He thought. Because I live in the city instead of the woods? Because I'm so young? Because I'm more powerful than she ever was?

He'd tried her way- tried to keep his ability caged in. His reward for that approach was the loss of his parents.

Never again, he promised himself. Never again will I sit by while this cruel world does whatever it pleases to me and the people I care about. I have the power to make a difference and I will do just that.

Training himself wasn't easy, what with the old woman's warning sentiments buzzing within him like a swarm of angry bees. *Do not misuse your powers*, they nagged. *Do not be self-serving.*

Time and again he overcame the resistance of Miss Ruth's spectral imprints, just as she told him he'd be able to. She'd told him that his powers could only be limited if he allowed them to be. Well, he would no longer do so.

Still, the blocking energy she'd implanted in him caused him great difficulty. The physical fatigue he felt after focusing his powers was another problem. Using his mental powers drew upon his physical energy just as much as hard manual labor might. The more impressive the task Nathan attempted, the more drained he felt after its completion.

He started small, sending his mind's eye out into the night to link with animals. Although he had not attempted to do so since he arrived in Baltimore as a seven year old, he found that he took to it like a bear to catching salmon.

Nathan first linked with a rat as it scurried along the foul smelling sewers and trash strewn alleys of Baltimore. The next night, he toured an opossum as it explored the treetops of a wooded area. His greatest joy came from linking with a wolf far in the northernmost hills of Baltimore County. He ran with the pack and howled with the moon without leaving the comfort of his bedroom.

When communing with animals became second nature, he moved on to entering the minds of humans (overcoming the echoes of Miss Ruth that admonished him not to do so).

Nathan found humans as easy to inhabit as animals (though their spirits were far richer and their emotions much more varied and complex). He delighted as he entered the mind of Reverend Anderson, the exalted leader of Bethel AME church. The good Reverend was engaged in a romp with Meredith Charles (lead soprano on the church choir) as Nathan did so.

Nathan saw and felt everything as the Reverend enjoyed the fringe benefits of his office. Reverend Anderson's mind pulsed with psychic sensation of an intensity that easily matched the pleasure of his body. Fleeting thoughts of wife visited him in the throes of his animal lust. The Reverend felt both terrified and excited that she might find out about what he was doing.

Nathan didn't know what to make of such strange thoughts. He wondered what the good Reverend's wife might do if she found him out, imagining that it wouldn't be pretty.

A fiery eruption blasted Nathan's senses at the moment of the Reverend's release, followed by an intense feeling of relief. Nathan felt his own body shiver as he returned to it. Fevered and weak, he stuck his right hand inside his pajama bottoms.

A thin sticky substance coated his thighs. His warm penis trembled. His first sexual experience had been through another man, an adulterous preacher at that. He enjoyed the sensations that had been transmitted to him through the Reverend, but he enjoyed the fly on the wall feeling far more.

After a second night of the Reverend and his exuberant soprano, Nathan moved on to more important matters. He practiced forcing a person to destroy something.

IV.

Calvin Dockery was a robber and rapist, doing the former because he had no better way to earn a living. He committed the latter because he hated women. Each member of the weaker sex was trash to him, every one of them as lowly as his whore of a mother.

Calvin's mother never earned a dollar doing anything that didn't involve parting her legs or using her mouth on a man. Night after night of his hellish childhood, he'd lie on his tiny bed, trying his best to sleep amidst bestial groans and grunts. She further exacerbated his discomfort by neglecting to feed, cloth, or bathe him in a proper manner.

Calvin's mother seemed to resent his very existence, perhaps never considering that he'd had no say in whose birth canal he was pushed forth from. She dropped him off at a boy's home when he was eight years old, promising to return after she found legitimate work. They both knew that she would neither find such work nor come back for him.

For eight years, Calvin ate the same plain food (save for holidays), did the same mundane tasks and learned the same ridiculous Catholicism. For eight years, he was paddled by nuns or confined to his tiny quarters during the many occasions when his behavior was deemed unacceptable.

Calvin pretended to absorb the religious teachings force fed him but the reality was that he figured Mother Mary for a whore like any other woman. He figured that the nuns had all been whores as well. He noticed that no pretty young ones worked among him and the other orphans. He believed that the nuns who tended to his sorry kind had spent all of their pretty young days whoring (just as his mother had).

Their kind couldn't fool Calvin. They'd only turned to Jesus when they felt themselves growing old. Not because they loved the Lord, but because they were trying to atone for all the whoring they'd done as young women. They were all afraid of going to Hell.

Calvin figured that hell couldn't be much worse than what he'd already lived through. When he was sixteen, he high tailed it out of the orphanage with just the clothes on his back and a sack on his shoulder.

He learned to survive on his wits, scrambling to pay for cheap, crowded, vermin and roach infested rooms. It wasn't unusual for him to sleep as one of four to a room, in the most God forsaken parts of town. He learned to keep one eye open as he dozed. It was the only way to be sure none of the hard cases rooming with him tried anything.

It bordered on impossible for an unskilled young Negro like Calvin to obtain consistent work. If those nuns had known anything, they would have spent a lot less time trying to force feed the Gospel and a lot more time teaching something that might have helped a fellow to earn some money. Calvin thought that Negro nuns had to be ten times more stupid and superstitious than their white counterparts. He wondered if all those old Colored women ever considered how ridiculous it was for them to even choose to be nuns.

It didn't take long for Calvin turn to a life of crime. He started out running with a few toughs, robbing folks who walked too close to alleys or were foolish enough to walk through dark areas alone.

The cops caught him after a year or so of that. He served five years of hard labor, on a chain gang on the outskirts of Western Maryland. He broke up rocks in a quarry, loaded and unloaded railroad cars. The prison system never seemed to run out of backbreaking things for he and his fellow convicts to do.

Calvin found work even harder to come by once his time was served. Abandoning a life of crime was not an option.

He decided to do all of his criminal deeds by his lonesome from that point forth, thinking of things as less complicated that way.

One hot summer night, he crouched near a dumpster in a dark alley in Old West Baltimore. He waited hours for some unfortunate fly to buzz too close to his web.

Frustrated and close to choking with thirst, he decided to begin the trek back to his pitiful lodging when he heard laughter approaching from the left.

As the laughter drew closer, Calvin saw a beautiful young woman hanging on the arm of her guy. She looked well fed and content, with caramel brown skin and stylish, respectable garments. A great wall burst within him, releasing all the anger and hatred he had felt since his helpless, miserable childhood. He would never get to touch a woman like her. The only women he'd touched had been lowdown whores that he'd spent a few ill gotten dollars on. That kind of women who would think nothing of spreading their legs in the very alley he crouched in. He found that kind of woman repulsive within seconds of gaining a sexual release.

Calvin slapped or spit at such women when he was done with them, sending them fleeing from his presence.

Why was he consigned only to such lowly trash? Because he was trash himself, that's why. He was trash because his mother had been trash. According to Calvin's worldview, trash could only beget trash.

Calvin could never have a woman like the beautiful one he watched, but he could make her feel as stained and helpless before fate as he did. For all he knew, she was just a well appointed whore, anyway.

He pulled a sheer stocking over his face and sprung from his hiding space as the couple passed him, raining a flurry of punches upon the young man's head. The woman screamed as her gentleman company fell unconscious to the ground. Calvin slapped her hard enough to draw blood from her mouth. He dragged her into the alley and behind the dumpster. Pinning her against the brick building, he smiled in pleasure at her shallow, terrified breaths and panicked eyes.

"Pl-please," she gasped, "please, don't hurt me."

Calvin realized that his own breathing had grown ragged. Not in terror, but excitement. He unveiled his knife and pressed it against her pretty brown throat.

"I ain't gon' hurt you, pretty," he said, kissing luscious lips that had grown cold in terror. "So long as you're quiet and still, I ain't gon' hurt you at all."

Quiet and still she was. It seemed pathetic to him, her sobbing and gasping much too quiet to be heard by any passersby.

The young woman shuddered in revulsion as Calvin entered her. Her shuddering intensified when he spasmed, filling her with his criminal seed. Calvin fixed his pants - then kissed his victim's forehead. A geyser of tears erupted from her anguished eyes. She slid down the brick wall, curling into the fetal position alongside the dumpster.

"There now," Calvin said, putting his knife away. "I told you I wouldn't hurt you. You better go check on your fellow. I think he hit his head pretty good on the pavement."

Thus, Calvin discovered the pleasure of rape. It was far more satisfying than anything he might have imagined. He was even more pleased when weeks passed without the authorities looking for him. He soon reasoned that the police were in no hurry to solve crimes against Negroes, not even rapes. Also, it was a humiliating crime for women to come forward with. A woman whom admitted she had been raped would be seen as damaged goods by any potential suitor. There was no better feeling than the terror and utter helplessness that Calvin saw in some bitch's eyes as he had his way with her. Confident that he'd never be caught, he grew determined to commit the act again and again. All he needed to do was pick his spots, not go overboard with it. He'd have to show discipline like he'd learned from those old nuns. He often had a good laugh wondering what the old hags would think of his application of that principle.

Calvin allowed himself four rapes per year, one for each season. He committed the deed in areas a good distance apart- always against Negro women. He loved them young, curvaceous, and pretty (as his whore of a mother had been).

Calvin figured that he'd never have to stop raping, so long as he stayed smart about it. He had no reason to suspect that someone had become aware of his crimes. He had no reason to suspect that he would be punished for every unfortunate woman he victimized.

V.

It took Nathan nine days to unearth the treasure trove of atrocities in Calvin Dockery's mind. The rapist's evil nature afforded Nathan an opportunity to kill two birds with one stone. The young seer could make the streets safer for young Negro women and destroy Walker's in one fell stroke.

No, child, a faint voice sounded within him. *That is not the way. You must allow God to punish the wicked.*

God is taking too long, Nathan argued with the remnant of Miss Ruth that sought to be his conscience.

The good Lord is never late. Your soul will be lost if you choose this path. Your power is not to be used in this fashion.

Leave me be, you old spook! Nathan's psychic voice shrieked. *Leave me be, now!*

He felt the sensation of a great weight being lifted from his mind as the old woman was banished for the time being. He had no doubt that her attempts at interference would continue. He also knew that try as she might, she couldn't stop him. No one could stop him from doing what he intended to do.

VI.

Calvin bolted upright in his tiny, well-worn bed. The room he stayed in was tiny enough to suit the bed, but at least he had it all to himself. He still had to share a bathroom with the rest of the borders at this house on the south end of Pennsylvania Avenue, but that was a sight better than sleeping with no-account Negroes all around him. He had no question that he was a no-account Negro himself, but that didn't mean he wanted to be surrounded by his own kind.

Alone as he was, there was no one to see the vacant expression in his eyes as he dressed and headed out into the cold autumn night. Calvin had no intention of raping or robbing during this excursion into the dead hours. Indeed, his intentions were not his own at all.

A mindless compulsion forced him toward *Walker's*, the popular store that had closed down after the fellow who ran it went bonkers and tried to kill a police officer. Calvin felt silly about marching through deserted streets to a place that would have been vacant at this time of night even if it was still in business, but he marched nonetheless.

Calvin broke a ground floor window and crawled in once he reached his destination. The desolate interior looked as if it had never hosted bustling activity. The only evidence that the store might ever have been in business was the deserted counter top and stove nestled in the rear corner.

Having no memory of approaching it, Calvin found himself standing in front of the stove. He thought he heard a faint hissing sound. He did hear a faint hissing sound. Looking down at his right hand, he saw that it held a book of matches. He emerged from his trance just long enough to wonder just what the hell he was doing.

You're about to blow yourself up along with this store, a voice spoke inside his head.

No, I'm not, Calvin argued, trying to put the matches away. "Why would I want to do something like that?"

He realized that the hissing sound was stove gas. Someone had turned it on.

Not someone, the voice in Calvin's head corrected. *You. You did it because I forced you to, just like you forced yourself on all those girls. It's not a lot of fun doing something against your will. Is it?*

"Who are you?" Calvin whimpered. Sweat poured down his face as he struggled to put the matchbook away.

I'm death to you.

No, please, Calvin begged the presence in his mind. His eyes widened in horror as he watched himself tear off a match and poise to strike it against the book. *Please, don't do this to me!*

A high, cackling sound filled his mind. He recognized it as laughter. Someone laughed inside his head.

You're begging amuses me just as much as those women's begging amused you. And it will gain you just as much mercy as you showed them.

Calvin became aware of the powerful smell of gas that permeated his surroundings. He had been here long enough for the place to grow thick with it. He wondered why he hadn't passed out.

You are conscious because I allow you to be! The voice shrieked. *I wouldn't want you to miss your own barbecue.*

Barbecue? Calvin thought. "No! No, please!" he shrieked. "I swear I'll never rape any more. I swear I'll never do it…"

The match struck the casing, giving birth to a brilliant blue flame. The flame ignited the gas and extinguished Calvin's time of raping or even drawing breath.

VII.

A great wall of flame burned itself into Nathan's psyche as he experienced the psychic residue of Calvin's physical trauma (the loss of oxygen, the charred flesh, the force of being thrown by the explosion).

Although the mental link had been severed at the moment of Calvin's death, Nathan still paid a heavy toll. He lay whimpering and fevered in his bed, his body slick with sweat. His eyes fluttered, revealing red orbs in place of his normal green and gold luminescence. A trickle of blood spilled from each nostril. His body trembled as if someone had stuck him in a meat locker and he could do nothing to help himself. *I didn't expect this*, he thought, before his mind went blank.

VIII.

Nathan took great care in sitting up, treating the task like a labor of Hercules. David was seated in a chair by his bedroom window.

"So, you're finally coming out of it?" David asked in his deepening, thirteen-year old man-child voice. He walked over and handed Nathan a glass. "Here. Drink some water." He returned to his seat, smiling as Nathan gulped down the contents.

"Yeah. You're feeling better now." He nodded as he spoke. "Before we had to force you to eat and drink. Had to spoon feed you, like you were a little baby."

"How long have I been in this bed?" Nathan asked, raising an eyebrow.

"So you don't remember none of it, huh? Cousin, you been in this bed for four days now."

"Four days?" Nathan shrieked, craning his neck to look to and fro.

"Easy now," David said, lowering Nathan onto his back again. "Don't get too excited. You might be all alert now, but we still don't know if you're better. We gotta let Doc Tilden have another look at you before you start moving about. I'll tell everybody you're awake. Feel like some food?"

David's question caused Nathan to realize that he felt as if he could eat an entire horse, hooves and tail included. "Yes. I'm very hungry."

David chuckled. "Well, that's a good sign. I'll come bring you a plate right away."

David returned with a large bowl of tomato soup, explaining that the doctor had warned Alma not to try to give Nathan anything solid just yet (out of concern that he might not keep it down).

After Nathan demolished that bowl of soup and two others, Cousin Virgil came to see him. He kept an even tone as he explained that David had discovered

Nathan moaning, feverish, and with a bloody nose, after Nathan didn't come down for breakfast.

After sticking a thermometer under his tongue, Alma discovered that he had a fever of 101 degrees. They sent for Doctor Tilden right away.

The chestnut skinned doctor prescribed medication and strict bed rest for Nathan's skyrocketing temperature. He also drew Nathan's blood, sending it to City Hospital for analysis. He urged Virgil and Alma to be patient, saying that the results would take a few days.

"He called this very mornin' to tell us what the tests turned up," Virgil spoke with a pained smile on his face. "Damnedest thing-you takin' ill like that, but the results showed nothin' wrong witchu. Doc Tilden said the only thing he's ever known of the like was folks makin' themselves sick on account of a broken heart or some great loss."

He placed a hand on Nathan's knee. "I know you done had a terrible loss. We all have, but it was worse for you. Still, you were actin' about as well as could be expected before David found you that mornin'. The type of people Doc Tilden was talkin' about stop eatin,' stop drinkin,' shut themselves off to other folks. Pretty much stop livin'. That's not how you acted."

Virgil pounded the bed in a moment of frustration. "I plain don't git it, little cousin. I plain don't git it." He chuckled in embarrassment as he realized himself. "Forgive me, boy. I sure kin be silly sometimes. Sittin' here tryna figure out somethin' a doctor couldn't even figure, when I should just be glad you're feelin' better. That's the important thing." He stood up and headed for the door. "Want some more soup?"

Nathan smiled. "I'd really love some chicken."

Cousin Virgil tossed his head back, clutching his gut in hearty laughter. "I'll jus' bet. Any more soup an' it'll be comin' out your ears- right? I'll see about Alma bakin' you some yardbird. That way it won't be too greasy."

"Thank you, Cousin Virgil."

"No problem," Virgil said, in a somber tone. "One more thing- your mother's itchin' to see you. We been keeping her away on account a we know it's hard for you to see her like she is. Figured it wouldn't help too much witchu being sick an' all. But your fever's broken an' she's still your mother. So when will you see her?"

Nate placed a hand against his forehead, waiting a few moments before answering. "I'll see her tomorrow morning, I suppose."

It saddened him to see Naomi when she came to his room. She babbled on like a little girl as she squirmed in her seat at his bedside. She was always giggling, clapping her hands, stomping her feet, and singing childish nursery rhymes.

Like a kind big brother, Nathan pretended to enjoy her antics. All the while, he thought of punishing those who had done this to her.

IX.

Nathan seated himself at the small desk in the corner of his room after supper. He was busy with a school assignment when Virgil walked in.

"You must be a sight better," Virgil said, wearing a warm smile. "You can do school work an' all, now."

Nathan shrugged. "I could do half of this stuff in my sleep. It's just arithmetic."

Virgil chuckled, plopping down on the edge of Nathan's bed. "Just arithmetic- you say? Well, Nathan, your old cousin here never could git the knack of figurin' numbers. You though…you just as bright as your daddy, maybe brighter even."

His face flushed as he realized that Nathan might not be ready to have his dead father spoken of in such a casual fashion. "Sorry, little cousin. I…"

Nathan smiled, looking up from his schoolbook to make eye contact. "It's okay, Cousin Virgil. I don't mind you talking about my daddy. Memories are all that we have left of him."

"Ain't it the truth?" Virgil nodded, leaning to his left to pat Nathan on the shoulder. "Anyhow, seeing how you're better an' all, I figured I should come tell you all about it."

"All about what?" Nathan pretended ignorance, when in fact he already knew what Virgil meant to tell him.

Virgil swallowed hard, his prominent Adam's apple bobbing like a beach ball on a rising tide. "The store- your folks' old place- it burned down."

"It burned down?" Nathan allowed his voice to crack as his eyes widened in a perfect approximation of shock.

Virgil nodded.

"But how?"

"Damnedest thing. They found what was left of some vagrant in there. Seems the fool broke in and blew the place up. Nearest the cops can figure, he turned the stove on, let the place fill up with gas, and dropped a match. Barbecued his self right along with it."

Nathan fought the impulse to smile, replaying "I wouldn't want you to miss your own barbecue," his taunt to the departed Mr. Dockery. Punishing that scum while also destroying what was taken from his father was worth every bit of physical suffering he endured in the aftermath.

"Why would anyone do something like that?" He asked.

Virgil shrugged. "Beats me, little cousin. Last I heard, the fella couldn't even be identified, he was cooked so crisp."

He stood up. "Only thing I got to say about it- it wasn't good that some fella burnt himself up like that, even if he was just a loon. But I don't mind your folks old place burnin' down. I'd rather have it gone than go to somebody else. That store should have rightfully been your father's. If the landlord hadn't been so hateful of Colored folks, he would've sold it to James outright. The shame of it is, even though the place burnt down, his lilly white behind'll problee still make a mint on it."

"A mint?" Nathan's surprise became genuine. "How can he make money off a building that's been destroyed?"

Virgil smiled. "It feels kinda nice when you say things like that, little cousin. Lets me know that even though you're so smart, I still know a few things you don't. Only cause you're so young, though. Breslin's gonna clean up 'cause like any businessman worth his salt, his property was insured, unless he's a damn fool- which I know he ain't. Once the insurance company is satisfied he didn't have anything to do with the place going up in flames, he stands to collect more than what the property was worth in one piece. That, little cousin, is how the rich get richer."

Nathan frowned. He hadn't known about the insurance. Helping that bastard Breslin make more money had been far from his intention. No matter, he wasn't finished with the man yet. If Nathan had his way, the bastard wouldn't get a chance to enjoy the insurance payout.

2

First Hunt

Connor Breslin owned sixteen acres of choice land in the village of Lauraville, on the outskirts of Northeast Baltimore. There were several horse stables and a guest house on the verdant property. Rolling greens gave way to a stately mansion, the show piece among the handsome acreage. The architectural style was Italianate, bearing a low pitched roof and tall rectangular windows. Its' three stories of height spread out among 20,000 square feet. It contained a total of eight immense bedrooms and four baths, along with a grand kitchen and dining hall.

Though it was nearly 2 AM, Breslin did not lie in the grandiose bed he shared with his wife. He kept his own counsel in a study that was larger than an ordinary homeowner's bedroom instead. A well stocked liquor cabinet stood at his disposal in the corner of the room. His family and the servants in the quarters below might have been well asleep, but Breslin could not have been more wide awake. His constant sleeplessness had become par for the course, accompanying increased drinking and a much diminished appetite.

His wife, young daughters, maid, and butler worried about his bloodshot eyes and weight loss. Friends and business associates wondered if he had taken ill.

Night after night, Breslin attempted to inoculate his troubles with large amounts of brandy. Night after night, he only managed to drink himself senseless. The troubles returned without fail the next morning, often accompanied by a pounding hangover. Having a breakfast drink to level off the effects of the previous night became habit.

His dear Abigail did not take his excessive alcohol consumption sitting down. "All of this drinking- along with the fact that you hardly eat," she complained. "Are you trying to kill yourself?"

He always assured her that he had no such intent, that he wasn't doing anything he couldn't handle. She didn't believe him, and he wasn't sure he believed himself.

Abigail threw all of his bottles out on several occasions. Breslin stifled the urge to slap her each time that she did, losing no time in sending his butler to replenish his supply.

He didn't like his drinking or gaunt appearance any more than his wife did. He liked hangovers even less, but all of those effects were a fair price for the hours he spent passed out, oblivious to the world and incapable of thinking of the departed James Walker and his unfortunate young wife.

He'd never been more than a social drinker before the Walkers' demise, a near teetotaler. The generous amount of alcohol he'd kept in the house was for guests at the regular parties that he hosted- fellow businessman and country club members.

He no longer had any desire to host affairs or even individual guests. How could he act carefree and sociable when lives had been both lost and destroyed because of his actions?

Breslin knocked back another glass of brandy as he ruminated, allowing the alcohol to burn his chest and warm his stomach. He glimpsed his reflection in the burnished end table when he set the glass down. Bloodshot eyes, pasty skin, a hangdog expression and unkempt red hair gave him the appearance of the undead.

"Yer fallin' apart, auld Connor," the Irish brogue he kept suppressed poured out in his drunkenness. "Yer fallin' apart."

He laughed at himself, thinking that he sounded just like his father, whom had lived in the old country until the age of 37. Connor on the other hand, had left Belfast at the tender age of 10, which was plenty long enough to develop a sharp brogue.

He became the butt of mean jokes and other prejudice while attending school in America. He devoted countless time and effort to ridding himself of the accent. He succeeded, too, even if his old man disapproved.

He now knew that if he got drunk enough, all his work at sounding American went out the window.

Breslin shook his head, thinking that his elocution efforts weren't the only work to go out the window. Hell, James Walker's hard work could be described as having gone into the grave. It wasn't right what I did, Breslin thought. Yeah, I was worried about him making trouble, but I never even warned the man before taking action. Just had the judge draw up papers to toss him and his family on their rear ends. We might have been able to come to some sort of agreement before things went that far. I didn't have to do what I did, then lord it over him like that. If I'd acted a bit more kindly, he might still be alive.

But you didn't act more kindly, an angry voice sounded in Breslin's head. Breslin jumped in surprise, a flailing arm knocking over the glass on the table.

The voice he'd heard was not the incessant droning of his conscience. It sounded like something else- like someone else. "I'm hearing things," he chuckled, managing to stifle his brogue. He sat the glass upright and straightened his ruffled shirt.

It's just the guilt, along with the damn booze, making me loopy. I must do something to ease my conscience. It's time I start sending money to Walker's family.

What makes you think his family would want your blood money? The angry voice spoke again. *What good would it be to them?*

Although he'd managed to convince himself that it was just a manifestation of his tormented conscience, Breslin decided to engage the voice. *Why, it could do a lot for them. Medical care for the woman. It would guarantee that the boy will be comfortable.*

Ha-ha-ha! The alien voice laughed. *How could an eleven year old boy ever be comfortable without his parents? And the woman doesn't need medical care- She needs an intact brain! Can your money buy that? Can it?*

No, Breslin thought, rising from his seat with liquor glass in hand. *I suppose it can't. But that's the only way I can help.* He headed to the liquor cabinet and uncapped a tall decanter of brandy, poising himself to refresh his glass.

An urge to smash the bottle against the oaken face of the cabinet overcame Breslin before he could pour. Several small lacerations trickled blood from his hand after the impact. Brandy ran across the top and down the sides of the cabinet. Shards of glass marked its surface, and the carpeted floor beneath.

Hurts doesn't it? The alien voice taunted. *You know, I made you do that. And I'm about to make you do much worse.*

Connor started to scream "Who are you?", only to discover that his mind couldn't force his mouth into action. He clasped his unharmed left hand over his damaged right. He shocked himself by digging his fingers into his own cut flesh. The pain, though excruciating, paled in comparison to the stark terror that overtook him. There was a voice inside his head- a voice forcing him to harm himself. That voice would not even allow him a scream to express his terror.

Are you ready to die? The voice asked.

Realization struck Breslin like a strong wind. *No!* He begged. *No! I don't want to die. I am not ready to die!*

Breslin's bladder emptied, sending hot urine down the legs of his silk pajamas.

It figures you'd say that, the voice sounded almost kind when it came again. *You know who else wasn't ready to die?*

Despite his terror, Breslin couldn't resist asking. *Who?*

My father, you bastard! The voice screeched, becoming a banshee wail within Breslin's mind. Breslin's blood ran cold as it assailed him. *My father, James Walker!*

Your father? Breslin swooned, trying to return to his previous seat on the room's luxurious couch, but finding himself unable to budge.

Resigned to his imminent death, he decided to spend his last few moments engaging the hateful voice in conversation. Perhaps he could learn a little from his murderer while he still breathed. Perhaps he was already asleep and would wake up on that couch, not twenty feet from where he now stood, wondering how his imagination had managed to manufacture such a vivid and ridiculous dream.

That's right. I am James Walker's son- Nathan. I've always been a special boy, though my folks mostly made me keep it to myself. I bet you figured me for just another little black boy just like my father was just another black man. I bet you figured us all to be just some lowly niggers.

No, Breslin protested. *I don't use that word.*

You don't use that word? Well, pin a medal on you! I guess that makes everything alright. You refuse to sell your property to my father because of his skin color, but it's alright- because you don't use that word! I've got news for you,

Breslin. Whether or not you use that word, you destroyed our family. You know that? You destroyed us!

I didn't mean for anyone to get hurt, Breslin whined. *I only meant for…*

Us to lose our business and our home-right? You're a monster, Breslin.

Breslin swung his left fist up in a vicious arc, smashing it into his own forehead. The stinging pain was secondary to the shock that he felt.

You and your police friends will all pay for what you've done. I'll start with you.

Breslin's mind felt as if it had been seized in the world's strongest vise. He walked out of the study and headed into his voluminous kitchen, bladder squirting with each step. His bowels joined the fray, as he reached into an oaken drawer and removed a large butcher knife.

He knew what was about to happen, yet he was powerless to stop it, powerless to even beg for mercy. He gripped the instrument of his own demise with both hands, turning the handle away from his body. He wondered how it could be that his damaged right hand had no trouble doing its part.

The cold steel blade hovered over Breslin's left breast for a split second before he plunged it into his own heart.

Death was instantaneous. His body collapsed, back first, onto the immaculate tiles of the kitchen floor. There he lay until morning, blood pooling around the knife's buried blade.

Lying in his Pennsylvania Avenue bed, Nathan fought to keep from unleashing a hellish scream. He slipped into oblivion, feeling as if his own heart had been punctured.

3

Aftermath

I.

Virgil Tilden Walker sat down at his kitchen table on the morning of November 21, 1913. He began unfolding that day's edition of *The Sun* while waiting for his wife to finish preparing breakfast.

The promising aroma of bacon and grits lost his attention to a sensational headline printed on the front page. The headline read: "Local Business Man Dies of Self-Afflicted Knife Wound."

Virgil lost no time in devouring the account of how Connor David Breslin, age 39, had been found in the kitchen of his mansion just south of Hamilton Township. The article explored Breslin's success as an heir to a father who amassed a fortune in real estate and transportation.

According to the article, Breslin seemed to have the perfect life. The wealthy businessman owned numerous properties in the area, had a lovely wife and beautiful daughters, and was well respected by the community at large and his illustrious peers.

He'd had some difficulty in recent months. A trouble making Negro tenant was killed by police inside the Pennsylvania Avenue property that Connor had sent the officers to evict him from. There had been great outcry from the NAACP and Baltimore's Negro community over the incident, fueled by the fact that the policemen involved were not charged with any wrongdoing.

Less than a month after the incident first hit the press, Breslin's Pennsylvania Avenue property fell prey to a powerful explosion and subsequent four alarm blaze. An unidentified man was found inside of the wreckage, burned beyond recognition.

The results of the ensuing police investigation suggested that the burned man had set the blaze with purpose, destroying the building and killing himself in the process. It had taken several weeks for dental records to reveal the man as Calvin Dockery, a once incarcerated young Negro who had grown up in an orphanage run by an order of Negro nuns and who had no close friends.

Passing acquaintances revealed no reason for Dockery to commit suicide in any fashion, let alone the spectacular one he chose. Breslin's family and friends also revealed little reason for him to plunge a knife into his own heart (though some did concede that he seemed haggard and stricken since the death of his former tenant). Still, no one could have anticipated that he would commit suicide.

The author of the article speculated that the death of Breslin's former tenant at the now destroyed Pennsylvania Avenue property might destine a terrible aftermath for all involved.

Virgil grinned as he finished the article. "Serves him right," he chirped.

Alma placed the finished bacon atop a napkin lined plate, allowing for some of the grease to soak through. She walked over to her husband and rested her hands on his meaty shoulders.

"What are you so excited about?"

"Just readin' this article in the paper, is all," Virgil said, tilting his head to smile up at her.

"Must be a good one."

"Sure is. 'Member Breslin? James' bastard landlord? The one brought them cops around, ended up gittin' 'im killed."

Alma cleared her throat, feeling uneasy about the direction her husband was headed in. She eased into the seat next to him, smoothing her apron so that it laid flat. "Of course I do, honey."

Virgil snorted and clapped his hands, followed by tapping the headline several times with his index finger. "Says right here the bastard killed his self."

Alma's eyes expanded. "What?"

"That's right. He was found in the kitchen of his big mansion with a big ole knife shoved in his chest. All evidence says he done it his self." Virgil laughed.

Alma frowned. "And you think that's something to celebrate? I'm surprised at you, Virgil Tilden Walker."

"And I'm surprised that bastard really got what he deserved. But that's a good surprise."

"Ain't nothing good about a man losing his life like that. Him dying like that won't bring your cousin back. It won't fix his wife either."

"I know that," Virgil spoke in a kind tone, as if Alma were a confused child. "But it sure does even things up a bit."

Alma bolted from the table and stood in front of the stove, her back to her husband. Her next words crawled from a pursed mouth. "I'm truly disappointed in you, Virgil. You just lost your dear cousin a short time ago. We got to care for his poor wife because of the state she's in. And the man's poor son keeps getting stricken with strange fever and attacks. All the suffering in this house and you want to gloat over someone else's misfortune?"

She turned to face him, eyes hot with intensity. "It ain't right, Virgil. Even if that man did wicked things to this family, it ain't right for you to act that way. It ain't right and it ain't Christian."

Virgil's delight over Breslin's fate departed as he realized how right his wife was. Being a Christian meant loving and forgiving your enemy, no matter how difficult it was. Lord knows forgivin' Connor Breslin will be a sight easier now that he's dead, Virgil thought, suppressing a snicker for Alma's benefit.

He rose from the table and kissed Alma on the forehead, drawing her into his stout arms. "You're right, Darlin'," he admitted. "That was mighty ugly talk on my part. Kin you ever forgive me?"

Alma tried to keep her face stern, but she couldn't fight back a smile. "What choice do I have?" she pecked him on the lips, returning his embrace.

"None at all," Virgil chuckled, giving her one last squeeze before releasing her. "I'll go an' git ever'body up for your delicious breakfast. See if Nathan feels well enough for some country fare."

Yes, Alma's right, Virgil thought as he went about his stated tasks. It wasn't right for me to act that way. But the papers are right about something, too. James' death seemed to bring ruin to them that had something to do with it.

As he entered his young cousin's room, Virgil wondered if anything might be in store for the two police officers whom had killed James and busted Naomi's brain. Virgil's thoughts were interrupted by the sight of Nathan caked with sweat, bed sheets strewn about the bed. The boy moaned and clutched at his chest in his sleep.

"Oh, no," Virgil gasped as he approached his ward's bedside. "What's happenin' to you now, child?"

4

Fear

I.

After the unfortunate incident at *Walker's*, Officer Galen Hutchens grew even more resigned in his myopic disgust toward Negroes. The NAACP in particular provoked his ire by seeking to force legal consequences against him and his partner. Hutchens's hatred led him to nickname the organization: "The Nigger Brigade and Their Kike Lawyers."

The big Irishman fought tooth and nail when he was transferred to the Northwest Baltimore police district as part of the collateral damage from the incident. Well to do Jewish and Pollock businessman comprised a large percentage of the population, making for a boring beat.

Hutchens believed that his superiors had reassigned him because they feared for his safety, thinking that if he stayed in Old West Baltimore some angry niggers would try to make reprisals for what he'd done. Though he had no choice but to tow the departmental line, Galen would have relished the challenge. Busting heads was nothing new to him and any nigger who messed with him would end up as least as bad off as that uppity spook Walker's woman. Few darkies were as brave as the fool Walkers had been anyway.

Hutchens had patrolled Pennsylvania Avenue and its neighboring streets for years, leading him to the discovery that most niggers were quite submissive. Only a few generations removed from slavery; they knew the natural order of things. They might be bold and brazen amongst themselves, but for the most part they knew better than to get out of line with a white man. Law officers like Hutchens were much more feared than ordinary members of the superior race.

Spooks like James Walker were exceptions to the rule. Arrogant and ungrateful, niggers like he and his NAACP buddies wanted more and more. They acted like being given their own section of Baltimore wasn't enough. What did they expect? To live among whites as equals? As far as Hutchens was concerned, they were not equal and never would be. To treat them as equals would only cause the downfall of society.

He shuddered whenever he imagined a Baltimore overrun by spooks free to come and go as they pleased. That would never do, he thought. Never.

II.

Once the police department found him innocent of misconduct, Terrence Turnblatt resigned his position. Wracked with guilt over what he'd done, he desired to do so right away. At the behest of his superiors, he stayed on for an investigation that was really just a cover up. "If you don't come to bat for it, us policeman will have to worry about being policed by jigs and lawyers", they said. "Then this city will really go to hell in a hand basket."

They beseeched him to put on a good show for the department, even though they knew that he believed himself wrong in shooting James Walker. "Stick to your guns for you fellow officers," they urged. He hated that phrasing. After what he'd done, he hated hearing the word gun at all.

Officer Hutchens claimed that James Walker had held him in a death grip, choking the life from him prior to the shooting. In actuality, the Negro had only landed a few punches and slaps. Hutchens seemed embarrassed at the time, but far from injured.

Though he liked Hutchens even less after he lied, Turnblatt didn't dare look down on his erstwhile partner. After all, it was not Hutchens who elected to use

deadly force against James Walker when he didn't need to. That had been
Turnblatt's doing.

A fusillade of better responses sprinted through Turnblatt's mind after he shot
the unarmed man. He could have just hauled the Negro off of his partner or hit him
over the head with his service weapon. He could have even shot James Walker in a
part of the body that would not have caused a mortal wound (such as a shoulder or
knee).

He had done none of that, because fear had overcome him when he pulled the
trigger. That mindless fear resulted in him taking a man's life.

Unlike Hutchens, Turnblatt didn't believe that Negroes should be treated like
dogs just because they were Negroes. No matter the color of their skin, they were
humans just as he was. He would have thought that a fellow Irishman like Hutchens
could appreciate that to hold any other view was wrong. With all the prejudice the
Irish had experienced, how could they look down on another race?

No matter what the department's farce of a finding stated, Turnblatt refused
to delude himself into believing that his actions could ever be excused.

On the morning of his resignation he went to Mother Mary Hall, a small
Catholic church in the southeast Baltimore neighborhood where he grew up. He
met with Father Tommy O'Hallaran and announced his intentions to enter the
priesthood. Growing up, he had always wanted to be either a cop or a priest. He
now hoped that becoming a man of the cloth could bring some atonement for his
last disastrous action as a lawman.

So he and Hutchens walked their diverging paths. One kept a new beat,
minutes apart but worlds away from where he was hated and reviled. The other
immersed himself in his already beloved Catholicism, Seminary serving as the
genesis of an arduous march toward a life of cloth.

The estranged partners did not encounter each other again until they learned of Connor Breslin's fate.

III.

Galen Hutchens wore a rueful smile. "I never figured you for a collar, Terry," he said. "I knew you'd quit the force over bein' all torn up about what happened, but I never figured you for a collar."

He grabbed his bottled beer by the neck, swilling it like a desert traveler at an oasis. The two former partners were dressed in ordinary shirts and trousers. They faced each other across a circular wooden table inside *Kellerman's* (a popular Irish-American tavern).

"It's something I always considered as a boy, as a way of helping people."

Hutchens snickered. "That or the police force, huh? I guess maybe you should've tried the cloth first. Might of saved us some trouble."

"Maybe," Turnblatt said, shrugging his sinewy shoulders. He picked up his glass cola bottle and took a sip. "Anyhow, I'm only studying for the priesthood presently. I have quite some way to go before my ordination."

"Yeah, I know. You're in Seminary or whatever." Hutchens looked past his former partner, scanning the tavern for eavesdroppers. The expansive interior was occupied at only a quarter of its capacity, due to it being a weekday afternoon. The barkeep took his time filling mugs for customers who drank without hurry. A pair of friendly billiards games unfolded a comfortable distance away from the rear corner where Hutchens and Turnblatt sat.

Turnblatt mocked Hutchens with a smile. "Someone after you?"

"I don't know," Hutchens replied, a serious expression on his face. "Whaddoyou think?"

Turnblatt sighed, tapping impatient fingers on the table top. "What's this all about?"

Hutchens sighed and cleared his throat. "You hear about what happened to that nigger's old store?"

Turnblatt's face reddened. "I beg you not to use such hateful terms in conversation with me."

Hutchins's eyes widened. "Hateful terms. You mean nigger?"

"That's right."

The big man burst into laughter, slapping the tabletop. "You're a funny one, Terry. Don't want me to call the fellow a nigger, but you got no problem puttin' a bullet in his back."

Turnblatt's eyes hardened as he leaned across the table. "I'd do anything to have that moment back."

Hutchens returned a stare every bit as intense and unblinking as his former partner's. "Sure you would, Terry. Sure you would." He took another swallow from his beer, set the bottle down with a clink, and laughed. "That was a tense moment. Wasn't it? Anyhow, you hear about what happened to that Negro's store?"

"Sure I have. It was a very strange occurrence."

"That's for certain. Hear about what happened to Breslin?"

Confusion conquered the hostility on Turnblatt's face. "No. I don't believe I have."

Hutchens frowned. "Just 'cause you're studying for the priesthood doesn't mean you ought not stick your head out of the cathedral from time to time. I figure a clergyman can help folks a lot better if he keeps his pulse on the outside world."

He pulled a newspaper section from his back pocket and unfolded it on the tabletop. Placing his finger on the headline of the article about Breslin's death, he said, "Read it and weep, Terry. Read it and weep."

The text of the article caused Turnblatt to slip into momentary catatonia. He felt his breathing grow ragged, but was powerless to stop it.

A strong hand shook his right arm, drawing him out of his anxiety attack. "Get a hold of yourself, Terry. Come on, now. Breathe deep."

Breathe deep. It was perhaps the truest words of wisdom the big lummox had ever spoken to Turnblatt. Breathe deep he did, until he recovered his ability to focus on his surroundings.

He looked at Hutchens, a compassionate expression on the man's face the likes of which he had never seen.

"You alright?" the big man asked. "It was quite a shock to me, too. Had to knock down a few beers to calm myself." He stood up and walked over to Turnblatt, placing a large hand on his right shoulder. "Listen, I know Seminary students ain't sposed to drink. But, I think the good mother would make an exception for you under the circumstances."

Turnblatt declined the offer with a shake of his head.

Hutchens fixed his gaze on the smaller, younger man. "Suit yourself." He started toward the bar. "But I'll have another."

Returning with his desired prize, Hutchens settled back into his seat and took a few swallows. "I think I see a pattern here, Terry. A bad pattern at that."

"I don't understand," Turnblatt said.

Hutchens laughed without humor. "You'll understand if you want to. You're plenty smarter'an me and I figured it out right away."

"Figured what out?"

Hutchens sighed. "I don't believe either Christ or the Virgin Mary'd take kindly to a future priest bein' dishonest with himself, Terry."

Turnblatt's eyebrows climbed skyward as realization struck him. "Surely you don't think?"

Hutchens nodded.

"You think that those two events are more than mere coincidence?" Turnblatt asked.

"I'm damn sure they are. The thing with the crazed ni-negro blowin' up the store is one matter. But you met Breslin 'fore we went to do 'is biddin'. That rich bastard was on top of the world. You sense any reason he might want to kill 'imself?"

"I suppose not," Turnblatt admitted. "The paper seems to want to paint it like he might've done it over guilt, but we were the ones responsible for what happened that day. All he did was request an eviction notice, something that landlords do all the time. I could see him maybe feeling guilty enough to drink heavily and stop eating right, but not suicide. Not over something he only had a small part in."

"Course not. Course he didn't kill 'imself." Hutchens leaned in close and dropped his voice to a whisper. "Tell you what I think."

"What's that?" Turnblatt followed suit, leaning close and whispering as well.

"I think somebody murdered 'im," the big Irishman said. "Did a real good job, too, makin' it look like suicide."

Turnblatt's eyes widened. He found himself looking around, making sure that none of the other tavern patrons noticed them. They didn't.

Hutchens continued whispering his theory. "I mean, think about it, Terry. Most suicides leave a note, you know. And most suicides are folks who've led a miserable life or are just plain crazy. Not this fellow. You met this fellow. Not'im."

Turnblatt nodded. His throat felt parched. He polished off his cola, wishing the priesthood allowed him to drink beer. "But who?" he asked. "And how? Who could pull something off like that?"

"The fellow you shot had family, you know," Hutchens said, grimacing. "A coosin. A stout, strapping nig- negro. Definitely strong enough to overpower Breslin."

Turnblatt shrugged. "That might be so," he said. "But even if this cousin is physically capable, how could he even find out where Breslin lived? Once that was accomplished, how could he get into that mansion, in and out of a wealthy white community, undetected?"

Hutchens picked up his beer bottle and drained its contents in one long draught before answering. "I just can't figure that part. Maybe he ain't the one. But I can't figure nobody else. What I do figure is that we need to look into it, 'cause if all this stuff really is connected…"

Turnblatt finished his former partner's thought. "Then trouble is headed our way."

A four alarm blaze roared in Hutchens's eyes. "You're damn right it is, Terry. You're damn right it is."

IV.

Thanksgiving was a bittersweet occasion at Virgil Walker's house. The bitterness was caused by the absence of Virgil's departed cousin, James. The sweetness was due to James's son recovering from a prolonged fever and violent vomiting. Before he fought through it, the family worried that they might lose him.

Dr. Tilden cared for Nathan as best he could during the illness, making daily house calls. He was forthright about not having seen anything like what had befallen the youth. It was the second occasion since his father's death that a mysterious and violent illness had stricken Nathan.

Nathan suffered for the better part of four days, becoming a fragile and miserable wretch. He recovered on Thanksgiving Eve, his color and vitality returning in full. Save for a few pounds off his already thin frame, it was as if the illness had never happened.

Making yet another house call, Dr. Tilden gave the boy a clean bill of health.

"He's just fine." The doctor spoke to Virgil and Alma near the front door, away from the boys and Naomi. "I've never seen anything like his recovery."

"God is good," Virgil said.

"God is good," Alma agreed. "There's no arguing that." She frowned. "But, this is the second time the poor boy has taken ill. Recovered or not, that ain't good."

She turned to Dr. Tilden. "You sure he doesn't have some kind of condition?"

Dr. Tilden shook his head. "There's no sign of any physical malady. I would have guessed it might be influenza. But influenza is highly contagious and the boy's symptoms haven't spread to anyone else in this house. I suppose it could be psychosomatic."

"Psycho what?" Virgil raised his eyebrows.

"Psychosomatic. There's a school of medical thought that believes that a person who has suffered some kind of trauma can become ill through force of will. Nathan has suffered some very tragic circumstances at a particularly tender age."

Virgil nodded. "No arguin' that. So you're sayin' the boy might've made his self sick on purpose?"

"The mind is a powerful thing, Mr. Walker."

"Yes, indeed," Alma agreed. "But still, giving his self a fever and all? Vomiting like he did? It ain't like the child's a magician."

Dr. Tilden chuckled. "Magic would hardly be necessary. There's no hard scientific proof that a traumatized person can't force such extreme symptoms on himself." He cleared his throat. "Nathan's blood tests should come back some time tomorrow. We'll know for sure then if there's any actual physical problem. But I don't expect the results to be any different from the last time he fell ill."

Virgil smiled. "Do us a favor, Doc?"

Dr. Tilden raised his eyebrows.

"Unless the tests say he's about to keel over and die any second, don't bring us those results until after the holiday. We'd like to enjoy it without worries."

A broad smile engulfed Dr. Tilden's face. "Virgil, I would not dream of intruding upon your family's Thanksgiving. Nor mine."

Virgil chuckled, extending his hand. Dr. Tilden shook it with strength.

"You're all right with me, Doc."

"Thank you. I think well of you folks, as well. It's a great thing you all are doing, taking in your cousin's boy and widow like that."

Alma shrugged. "It's just the family thing to do."

"Family or not, it's still a deed of the highest kindness."

Husband and wife remained by the front door after the doctor departed. Virgil wrapped a big arm around Alma's shoulder, pulling her close to plant comforting kisses on her cheek.

"I heard what he said, Virg," she sighed. "But psychosomatic don't quite explain it for me. How can that boy go from being so terribly ill to the picture of health?"

"Now, you know what Pastor says," Virgil offered. "The Lord works in mysterious ways."

Alma smiled as she turned to face her husband. "You think God healed him?"

"Of course I do, honey. This time and last."

Nathan's recovery did resemble an act of divine intervention to the family. He ate like a horse during Thanksgiving, devouring heaping helpings of turkey, stuffing, collard greens, macaroni and cheese, potato salad, candied yams, sauerkraut, and cranberry sauce.

"What's everyone looking at?" he asked between mouthfuls, noticing the curiosity they all regarded him with.

"We're looking at you, little cousin," David said, laughing. He gave Nathan a good natured slap on the arm.

"You're eating like a horse, Nathan," Naomi giggled, her little girl's voice full of wonderment. She dropped her fork and launched into a dead on pantomime of a person shoving food into their gullet with bare hands.

Eli laughed to bust a gut, until Alma silenced him with a glare. She then turned to Nathan's mother.

"Now, Naomi. We mustn't carry on at the dinner table."

Naomi pouted, poking her lips out like the young girl she'd become. "Sorry, Cousin Alma."

"It's okay," Nathan said. "She was just trying to make her son laugh."

"Son?" Naomi looked confused for just a second, before her eyes brightened. "Oh, yes. You are my son."

"That's right, Mama. And I love you."

Naomi squealed in delight, jumping from her seat to hug him. "I love you, too. I'm so glad you feel better." She pecked him hard on the cheek.

"We all are," Virgil said. "We're all very glad you feel better."

"I'm glad I feel better, too," Nathan said, smiling. "And not a day too late. It would have been terrible to miss all this good food."

Later that night, Nathan lay in bed considering whether he should kill Officer Hutchens or Officer Turnblatt next. He hadn't even known the policemen's names at first, but he didn't need any *Sun* coverage to obtain that information.

He tracked them instead, finding the task to be very easy. He emptied his mind as Miss Ruth taught him, sending his mind's eye to the rubble that remained of *Walker's*. There he locked in on the psychic traces his parents' victimizers left behind.

Once he had their trail, it was easy to enter the policemen's minds and use them as binoculars to look out into their individual, private worlds. Just as with Breslin and Dockery, Nathan knew where the officers lived. He also knew their comings and goings, family, and acquaintances.

Nathan knew that he could take either of the officers at any given time. Still, he didn't want to move too soon.

The memory of two illnesses cautioned him that using his powers for violence took a hideous toll. He absorbed a great deal of the pain of those he attacked, the shock of his consciousness spreading to his body. The result was enough to put him out of commission as it just had, necessitating serious recovery time.

I'll suffer the pain so that I can make them pay, Nathan thought. I don't care how sorry Turnblatt might be- that he left the police force and is now studying for priesthood because of his guilt. If Turnblatt's guilt was as great as he thinks it is, he would confess that what he did to my father was outright murder. He doesn't feel guilty enough to accept legal justice for what he's done. Well, I'll see to it that the cowardly back shooter pays a true price for killing my father. No matter how much I have to harm myself, I will see to that.

Although Hutchens had not killed his father, the boy's supernova of anger for him far exceeded his volcanic anger towards Turnblatt. Hutchens's only regret about what happened was that it got him reassigned to a part of town where he wouldn't have a satisfactory number of dark skinned folks to harass.

Hutchens had escalated the entire incident by insulting Nathan's parents with his racist remarks. Aside from that, he had made Naomi simple for the rest of her days.

What Hutchens did to Naomi was worse than murder. Nathan's anger boiled as he thought of his mother at the dinner table hours earlier, behaving just like a little girl. The same woman had once been a paragon of intelligence and quiet dignity, one who had no problem holding her own with a man of James Walker's ambition and drive. A single blow from that hateful bastard's nightstick changed all that.

Nathan couldn't wait to take his revenge. He couldn't wait to taste the two policemen's suffering. But wait he would, because he wanted to be well recovered before he punished them.

He decided to allow a few more weeks to pass (maybe even a month or so), just to be safe. He planned to make Hutchens and Turnblatt suffer at his leisure. He didn't suppose that even the best laid plans of a psychic are subject to change. Nor did he imagine that the most prescient of psychics are vulnerable to unpleasant surprises.

5

Confrontation

I.

Doctor Tilden's sunny disposition confessed the good news before his mouth confirmed it.

"The boy is alright, then," Virgil said, smiling and motioning for the physician to enter his home.

"A picture of health. His blood showed no traces of abnormal maladies. No influenza, nothing wrong at all."

"Nothing wrong?" Alma chirped, peering over Virgil's shoulder. "Then how?"

"Psychosomatism, as I said before. It's a powerful condition."

Virgil turned to see Eli perched on the stairs. "What'd I tell you about signifyin'?" He growled. "Git on up to your room while grown folks are talkin'."

"I was just coming to ask if I could go outside," The small boy whined.

"I ain't ask for no back talk, Eli. Git on up those steps."

Dr. Tilden smiled as he watched the boy traipse away. "They have to try, don't they?"

"Mmmm-hmmm," Alma said, nodding. "We didn't imagine you'd come by so early, Doc Tilden. If we had, we would've saved some breakfast for you."

"That's not necessary. I was up at the cock's crow this morning, so to speak. Turns out the blood results were ready late last night. I hurried over to share the good news as soon as I got them."

He shook Virgil's hand and patted Alma on the shoulder. "I should be going now. You folks have a good day."

"It sure will be a good day," Virgil said, wearing a huge smile. "Nice as our Thanksgiving was, you jus' made this day after even better."

"I'm glad," Dr. Tilden said, turning to make his leave.

"Hold on there a second, Dr. Tilden," Alma said. "How about you spare a minute for a muffin and some coffee? While you're enjoying it, you can explain a little more about psychosomatism."

Dr. Tilden smiled as he looked at Virgil. "Your wife is very persuasive."

Virgil smiled. "Persuaded me right to the altar."

Alma responded to Virgil's wisecrack with an arm punch. "Don't go lying to that good man. You know you begged me to the jump the broom with you. You knew there weren't no more trains like me coming along."

Virgil winked at the good doctor. "Let the church say amen to that."

Eli marched into his cousin's room as the adults sat down to the dining room table. Nathan sat at his desk, his back to the hallway. "What you doing, Nate?" Eli called over his shoulder.

Nathan stood and turned to face the younger boy. "I was reading." He pointed the book he held in his right hand toward Eli for confirmation. "But, I guess I'll be talking to you now, since you've come to bug me." He closed the book and placed it on his desk.

"What book is that?"

Nathan frowned. "What do you want, boy? I know you didn't come here to ask about a book."

Eli giggled. "Sure didn't," He said. "I came to tell you what I heard Doc Tilden say to my folks about you."

"Signifying again? You know your father's going to get you for that."

Eli smiled. "I didn't mean to. I was just going downstairs to ask if I could go outside in a little bit."

"Sure you were."

"Honest. Anyway, the doctor said the blood he took from you came back just fine. Said you didn't have inflenzia or anything like that."

"Influenza," Nathan corrected.

"Right. Inflenzia."

Nathan shook his head, deciding not to waste his breath again.

Eli continued. "Says you got cycleslo-cycleslomizm, though. Whatever that is."

Nathan chuckled. "Psychosomatism, you mean."

"Yeah. Cycle, Cycle…."

"Don't hurt yourself, little cousin." Nathan placed his hands on Eli's shoulders.

"Well I can't say it quite right. You ever heard of it?"

"Yes, I've heard of it. It means that the doctor thinks I made myself sick with my own mind."

Eli stared at his older cousin for a beat. "Because of you being sad about your folks and all?"

Nathan nodded.

Eli stared for another beat. "Is it true?"

"No, boy," Nathan said, punching Eli's arm. "I wouldn't make myself sick, even though I do feel sad a lot. I want to be healthy. Maybe Dr. Tilden's wrong this time. You know? Adults don't know everything."

"I know that, silly," Eli said, smiling for an instant before growing serious. "But they know a lot more stuff than kids do."

"What are you two talking about?" David said, his steadily growing frame darkening Nathan's doorway. At thirteen, he stood within an inch or two of his father's unremarkable height.

"We're just talking," Eli said.

"We're just talking," David mocked Eli's shrill voice.

Nathan laughed while the runt of the house ignored his older brother's teasing.

"Y'all want to go outside and play?" Eli asked.

"What do you say, Cousin?" David asked. "Want to play with the little bugger for once? Its' been a while since we beat the pants off him in some games."

Nathan smiled and nodded. That smile twisted into a rictus of dread in the next moment as he sensed the worst kind of trouble rushing toward him and his remaining family.

II.

Officer Galen Hutchens swaggered down Pennsylvania Avenue in full uniform. None of the niggers he passed on the chilly post Thanksgiving morning seemed to recognize him as one of the officers who'd been responsible for the death of one of their most prominent neighborhood figures. None of them looked at him straight on as they rushed toward whatever their destination might be.

Hutchens was almost disappointed that none of the passers by cursed or confronted him for what he'd done. He hadn't had a confrontation with a nigger since the Walkers reaped their rabble rousing crop. In fact, he hadn't seen any meaningful action at all.

The Jews and Pollocks on his new beat were much more orderly sorts. Even if they hadn't been, busting another white man (no matter what the creed) could never be as pleasurable as rousting one of these darkies.

The niggers that he passed may not have given him cause, but Hutchens was about to have a confrontation nevertheless. He'd done a little snooping and found Virgil Walker's address. He had a strong notion that the nigger had something to do with Connor Breslin's death, though he couldn't figure out just how. He intended to look Virgil in the eyes and find out whether his hunch was right.

Years on the police force had honed Hutchens's ability to discern the truth from a man's eyes. His instincts were so keen that it didn't even matter if the man trying to fool him was a nigger. Once he looked into that jig Virgil's eyes, he would know the truth and take appropriate action.

III.

Nathan came running down the steps an instant after Dr. Tilden left. "You have to get ready, Cousin Virgil," he said.

"What are you talkin' about, boy?" Virgil said, frowning.

"There's trouble coming. Trouble coming in a few minutes. Things'll turn out bad if you're not ready."

Virgil and Alma exchanged quizzical looks, as if to say: "What on Earth is this child babbling about?"

"Maybe you should lay back down, Nathan," Virgil said. "Maybe your fever's comin' back."

"I don't have a fever," Nathan said, his eyes wild. He darted forward, grabbed Virgil's hands and placed them against his forehead. "See?"

Virgil pulled his hands back in surprise. "No, I guess you don't have fever. Still, somethin's vexin' you to act like that. I think you best head back to your room for a spell."

Knowing that he didn't have time to argue, Nathan closed his eyes and projected an image of his parents' downfall to his older cousins. The nightmarish details flooded their minds, leaving them shaken.

Releasing them from his power, Nathan used his trembling right hand to wipe sweat from his forehead. Virgil and Alma stared at their young charge with disbelieving eyes.

"That's what I saw before what happened to my folks," Nathan said, his voice tremulous. "I have always seen things. But I didn't see that in time."

A voice in the first stages of manhood called from the stairs. "How come y'all are just standin' there like that?"

"Git on back to your room," Virgil ordered. His voice bore none of the authority it usually did when he bossed his older son.

"No," Nathan said. "Let him come. Eli and Mama, too. They all need to know what's about to happen."

Every member of the household gathered and linked hands in the living room. Nathan wielded his powers of the mind with great care, transmitting an image of the hateful officer heading their way. They all "saw" the thoughts that spurred Hutchens's impending visit (the suspicion that Virgil was involved with the destruction of Walker's and Breslin's death).

Nathan did not show his relatives that he was the perpetrator of those events. He did show them that Officer Hutchens's seeking of Virgil was unauthorized and unknown by his superiors.

The police department wanted the big Irishman as far away from Pennsylvania Avenue as possible. They certainly didn't want him anywhere near the remaining Walkers.

Nathan eased his hand out of Virgil's, severing the link. One by one, everyone released each other's hands.

Save for Naomi, the entire family stood with their mouths wide open. The girl-woman was frantic, a small child in the throes of terror. "That's the bad man," she cried, snatching at her hair. "The bad man who hurt me! That's the bad man!"

"Calm yourself, Mama," Nathan commanded, causing her to fall silent. "We'll send him away without any problems. He won't hurt you again."

"But how?" Virgil asked. "How will we do that?"

"Here's how," Nathan began. He wore a sly smile as he gave instructions for how they all should behave during the impending exchange.

Everyone readied themselves according to Nathan's instructions. Virgil added the extra precaution of having David sit ready with Virgil's pistol. They waited for the hateful policeman to arrive, praying that the forthcoming encounter did not end in disaster.

IV.

The Walker's second caller of the day pounded on the door as if he meant to break it down.

Alma's hands rested on Virgil's shoulders as he looked through the peephole to confirm the cause of the disturbance. It was Officer Hutchens, of course, red-faced and in full uniform.

"Who is it?" Virgil feigned ignorance.

"It's the police," Hutchens bellowed. "Open the door, right this instant!"

Virgil affected a calm bearing as he eased the door open. The reality was that he was afraid of what this man might do, though nowhere near as afraid as he would have been without the benefit of Nathan's assistance.

Virgil smiled as if the officer were a long lost friend. "What kin I do for you, officer?"

"You can start by cuttin' the crap, shade. I know I'm no regular officer to you. You ought to recognize me."

"Yes, sir," Virgil admitted. "You're one of those officers got mixed up in that business at my cousin's old store. What kin I do for you, sir?"

Hutchens looked confused for a moment before recovering the scowl on his face. Virgil knew that the officer had expected him to react with anger or fear.

"There's been strange goin's on in the wake of that business," Hutchens growled, moving nose to nose with the stout Negro. "I've reason to believe you might know somethin' about these occurrences."

Virgil didn't blink. "I kin assure you we know nothin' of any occurrences past a few blocks of our doorstep," he said, taking a graceful step backward. "But do come in. I'll be glad to help you in any way I kin."

"Really?" Hutchens sneered, stepping inside. "You'd help the man accused of bearin' a hand in your coosin's death. Of dealin' 'is wife a brain blow?"

Alma excused herself, walking past them to close the front door. She stood as still as death, her face that of a card sharp as she regarded the exchange between her husband and the ornery lawman.

Virgil shrugged, speaking in a sober voice. "Sir, I'm nothin' like my cousin. I'm a humble man. I understand the Negro's place in the world. All I want is my home and to make a humble livin' to support my family. But James, he was ambitious and impatient. He wanted ever'thang in life that a white man might have, includin' power. He was determined to git it- sometimes so much that he acted crazy. I know that y'all went there to throw him out on the street that day. But, I believe the rest was because of him and his wife losin' control of their selves. Attackin' officers of the law. They should have known better."

Hutchens's smile was akin to the open mouth of a crocodile. Here's a nigger who knows his place in the world, he thought. Still, he supposed the darkie could be acting. There were niggers cunning enough to do that sort of thing. He couldn't deny that the man's cousin had been very clever. He decided to put a scare into the spook, just to be sure.

"Could be I pegged ye wrong, boy. Best sit down and smoke it over, anyway."

Unbidden, he plopped down on the living room couch.

"Can I bring you anything?" Alma asked, smiling. "Cookies? A sandwich?"

"'Ow 'bout a beer?"

"We don't keep any beers in this house."

"I'll bet you don't. Not any that you'd spare on me, anyhow. That's alright. I'll just sit and talk with your 'usband."

Alma departed with urgency, continuing to perform her role to a tee. She strained her ears as she clinked dishes about in the kitchen. David, Eli, and Naomi crouched in silence at the top of the stairs, wanting to hear as well. David clutched the loaded pistol in his right hand. He had a job to do should things not go as planned, a job he intended to do well, consequences be damned.

Virgil continued to exude calmness as he eased into a chair opposite the big officer. "What is it you think I might know about, Officer?" he asked, shining his most pleasant smile.

Hutchens frowned before sighing in disgust. "I appreciate the friendly nigger routine and all, but ye don't ask me any damn questions. I ask you. Got it?"

"Yes, sir." Virgil nodded, the smile disappearing from his face. He suppressed the urge to laugh at his own performance. It was true that he'd never been as bold with white folks as his departed cousin, but he'd never been quite this submissive either. Not that Officer Hutchens needed to know that. He'd find out that Virgil had his own form of steel soon enough.

"Now by chance, do you read the newspaper? I know not all you niggers can read."

It took all of Virgil's self-control to avoid firing back, "I'll bet a chimp could read better than you, you big lout!"

At the top of the stairs, Eli covered Naomi's mouth before she could exclaim in protest against the mean man. David ran his free hand over his father's gun, almost hoping he'd have reason to use it. Meanwhile, Alma just avoided dropping one of the dishes she washed to the floor.

Nathan remained in his room, using a small bit of his mind's eye to observe the interaction. He didn't want to use his powers again so soon, but he was not going to allow any of his remaining family to be harmed. Nor would he allow David to ruin his life by wielding a gun against a police officer. If Officer Hutchens pushed too far, he'd just have to deal with him a sight earlier than he'd anticipated.

"I read plenty good, sir," Virgil said, continuing his calm façade. "An' I git the paper ever'day. Read it front to back."

"So then you know about what happened to Conner Breslin? Your dead coosin's former landlord?"

"Yes, I do, Officer." Virgil shifted in his seat. "I also know about what happened to the store. Didn't have to read no paper to know about that. S'been the talk of Old West Baltimore. Got so we politely had to ask folks not to talk about it wit' us. James bein' our passed family an' all."

"Passed is right," Hutchens snickered. "That fellow passed on instantly. One shot- bang! Greener pastures!"

Though he wanted nothing more than to pummel the gloating bigot, Virgil did nothing more than raise his eyebrows. The rest of the non-paranormal members of the family matched his restraint.

Feeling his own anger approach eruption, Nathan forced it back. He promised himself that he would punish this man far worse than he had Dockery and Breslin. Now was not the time, though. He meant to do so when the bastard was far away from this neighborhood.

"That was a very cruel thing for you to say, officer," Virgil spoke with indignant calm.

"Yes, I spose it was," Hutchens admitted, his visage softening just a bit. "I mean you've been very cooperative. I ought not to of said that."

Virgil shrugged, as if to say, "Forget it. Let's move on."

Hutchens continued. "Point is- I think there's a pattern to those two events. First, some nut blows up the building. A crazed nigger with no known connection to it. Next, Breslin kills himself. I figure those two things 'appenin' ain't coincidental. I figure maybe someone's got it in for anyone and anything involving your coosin's death."

He leaned forward, fixing a blue eyed stare upon Virgil while dropping his voice into a menacing whisper. "Figurin' like that's what brought me to your door. I figured-Who else would want to avenge that nigger other than the people who loved 'im?"

Virgil cleared his throat and relaxed his body. He returned the officer's stare, though his eyes betrayed not a hint of aggressiveness. His visage retained the same calm expression it had worn since he answered the door.

"I cain't answer that question, officer," he said. "But I kin tell you this. If a police officer's superiors ever found out that he had dressed up in his uniform on his off day- marched to some poor citizen's house- a citizen who had already suffered deaths in his family in a scandalous incident that was just startin' to fade from the press- if that citizen's house wasn't even on the policeman's beat, that policeman might have to endure more than havin' to work foot patrol on account of havin' his vehicle taken from him. That policeman might git more than the slap on a wrist of two weeks paid leave, followed by bein' switched to another precinct in the city. I kin tell you that."

Sweat beaded on Officer Hutchens's forehead as every drop of color drained from his face. He sat in stunned silence for a pregnant span of time.

After he recovered from the shock of Virgil's well spoken words, he stood up to leave. "You don't know anything about those occurrences, then?" he asked, his voice lacking conviction.

"No, Officer Hutchens," Virgil said, managing to restrain a grin. "I don't know anything about them."

"Very well, then." The defeated officer went so far as to tip his hat. "Good day to you."

Virgil, Alma, their two sons, and Naomi all burst into laughter as soon as the officer's shadow fled the front doorstep.

"I'll bet that wasn't what he 'figured' would happen," Virgil said, clutching his wife, children, and Naomi to him. He felt glad that he'd done as Nathan said, though thinking of the boy's ability gave him a chill.

Just then, Nathan came down the steps and headed toward the rest of the family. Though he looked a little peaked, he wore a big smile. "I'm so glad you're all okay," he said.

"Thanks to you," Virgil said. "How are you able to do such things, Nathan?"

"I was born this way." Nathan lowered his strange eyes to the floor. "I was born with the sight."

Naomi was the first to break the awkward, prolonged silence that followed that statement. "Its' okay, Nathan," she said, hugging her son and dancing about. "Cousin Virgil scared the bad policeman away, thanks to you! You're really somethin', Nate!"

That I am, Nathan thought. I am really something, but just what, I don't know.

V.

Officer Hutchens felt proud that he possessed the fortitude to refrain from wetting his pants in light of the exchange he just had with Virgil Walker. That nigger had known every unglamorous detail of what he'd been up to. He didn't see how such a thing was possible.

The police department had kept its' discipline of Hutchens close to the vest, erecting a façade of outward support. It was possible that the nigger could have gained the information that Hutchens was reassigned to a different sector on his own. He might have even guessed it. But there was no way some ordinary nigger like him ought to know anything about the ins, outs, and consequences of authorized and unauthorized police investigations.

The things that nigger had surmised were impossible- and that one wasn't half as sharp as his dead cousin. A confounded feeling hounded Hutchens as he hot footed it out of Old West Baltimore.

On the way to Virgil's house, he would have welcomed a confrontation with any nigger in the street. Now he wished he were invisible. He wanted nothing more than to abort this ridiculous mission unnoticed.

The next streetcar arrived within a few merciful minutes. Hutchens sighed in relief as he boarded, heedless to the curious black passengers whom had never seen a fully uniformed policeman riding public transportation. He folded himself in his seat as small as he could (again wishing that he one could see him).

He exited the first street car downtown and transferred to another line that would pass the Southwest Baltimore block where he resided. He was glad that most of the passengers on this car were respectable looking whites. They greeted him with all the manners of their finer race, smiling or tipping their hats in respect for his uniform and the order it represented. Hutchens breathed easy, returning the ragged tooth smile of the old woman he sat next to.

It had been crazy of him to approach that jungle bunny Virgil like he did. Hazardous as it had been, the trip wasn't fruitless. He had learned that the nigger knew too much. He now knew that it was in his best interest to have Virgil Walker suffer the same fate as his cousin. The only question for Hutchens was how to do it so that no one could point a finger at him.

VI.

Virgil came into Nathan's room just as his younger cousin started to doze off. He pulled the seat from Nathan's writing desk over to the bed before settling into it.

"I cain't make heads or tails of it, little cousin."

"Heads or tails of what?" Nathan sat up in bed, resting his back on his pillow, which rested against the wall behind him.

"I don't git how you could a jus' been born havin' powers of the mind like that."

"Some things are not to be understood," Nathan said. "Some things are only to be accepted."

Virgil chuckled and patted Nathan on the knee. "Those are words beyond your years, but right on the barrel, for sure. Still- it's hard to accept havin' all this laid on me. You gotta admit- what you kin do- iss kinda like somethin' out of a storybook. Hell, I always just thought you were real smart and mature for your age."

Nathan widened his eyes in mock surprise. "I am really smart and mature for my age."

They both laughed. "No doubt about that," Virgil said. "But…."

"But today you found out there's a whole lot more to me than that."

Virgil nodded. "Damn right there is. Say…did your folks know about this?"

"My daddy told me I've shown signs since I was a baby. I had a vision that some men were coming to kill him. That's the real reason we came to Baltimore."

Virgil swallowed hard, his Adam's apple bobbing up and down. "I always felt like y'all had come here awful sudden. I'd been urgin' your father to head North for years before he up and left Alabama, in what I thought was out a the blue."

Tears welled in Nathan's eyes. "I saved him that time. But this time, I couldn't." His lips trembled to accompany his voice. "I couldn't save him because I'd been suppressing what I am. Keeping my self blocked off, because I didn't want to cause problems. If I hadn't been doing that, I might've seen what happened sooner."

Virgil grabbed his young cousin by the undersides of his arms, snatching him from the bed and hoisting him to his feet. He locked eyes with the tremendous responsibility James had left for him.

"Or you might not've," He said. "Maybe you weren't meant to see what would happen. You got your talent, but you still ain't all knowin'. You ain't God, boy. Jesus Christ, neither. You think your father would want you beatin' yourself up about what happened?"

"No," Nathan said, his voice soft.

Virgil smiled as he released his hold. "Damn right, he wouldn't. Your father chose to live his life a certain way. He knew the risks- but he still had to do what his spirit drove him to do. Knowin' James, I think he'd rather be dead than to act any different from how he did. You just keep in mind it was a white policeman who killed him. Not somethin' you failed to do."

I know that, Nathan thought. Just like I know that white policemen and his bastard partner who just left here are going to pay. I'll see to that.

"What are you smirking for, boy?"

Nathan spat a quick lie. "Just thinking about how that cop switched up real nice, once you started telling him how things were."

Virgil chuckled, giving Nathan a genial shove. "That was real nice. Thanks to you, little cousin." A quizzical expression emerged on his broad face. "Say do you know anythang about the stuff he was talkin' about?"

"No," Nathan shook his head, again lying with ease. "No, I don't."

"I spose not," Virgil said, shrugging. "Anyway, I wouldn't mind too much if that big ox was right. You know? About bad things happenin' to them that hurt your folks. If that's the case, maybe he'll be next. Git what he deserves."

Nathan nodded. There's no maybe about it, he thought. He WILL get what he deserves. But first, he will suffer.

6

Second Hunt

I.

On the evening of Monday, November 29, 1913, a weary and worried Terry Turnblatt headed home. The many duties of studying for the priesthood were not responsible for his condition. His perhaps unjust killing of a man did not cause his condition, either. Enrolling in Seminary had been the beginning of a life long penance for that, a penance that he hoped would absolve him in the eyes of the Heavenly Father.

What weighed on the aspiring cleric was his second encounter with his former partner within a week. During the first of those meetings, Hutchens postulated that someone was out to get everyone whom had been involved in the tragic incident at *Walker's*.

Hutchens proved to be far more paranoid during their just concluded second meeting. They'd met at *Kellerman's* once again, occupying the same booth they had before. This time, the watering hole was far more crowded with hard-working Irishmen, thirsty for drink after long days of toiling in the concrete jungle.

Turnblatt thought that he had disabused Hutchens of the ridiculous notion that James Walker's cousin was responsible for the attack on Connor Breslin. Hutchens's ranting during the second meeting deep sixed that belief. Between savage gulps of beer, the big man leaned across the bar table, growl-whispering an account of the visit he'd paid to the Walkers that past Friday.

"You shouldn't have done that," Turnblatt said. "The department wouldn't take kindly to it."

"I know they wouldn't take kindly to it!" Spittle sprayed from Hutchens's lips. "I also know there's no way they'll believe that darkie's out to get us. They'd think such a tale too tall to swallow. 'Til we turn up dead, that is. Now I'm tellin' you, we got to take care a that jig before he takes care a us."

Turnblatt's eyes ignited like fireworks, threatening to explode skyward. "You can't be suggesting that we kill him."

Hutchens laughed, the sound as dry as it was mirthless. "Course not. I'm talkin' about payin' someone else to do it. Pref'rably another darkie. After its' done, I'll take out the scamp we hire. Shut 'im up so there's no connection. See?"

Dear Jesus, Turnblatt thought. This poor soul has gone mad.

"I don't expect you to have a hand in that part of it, of course. Your studyin' for the priesthood and all. Hell, I wouldn't have mentioned this to you at all if I had a choice. Thing is, I ain't exactly got enough money to pay for it all."

Turnblatt's shocked response came just a hair above a whisper. "You really expect me to help you finance a murder?"

Hutchens drained his latest bottle in one long draught before unleashing a volcanic eruption of a belch. He added the bottle to the row of empties in front of him. "Figure its' that or end up dead soon enough, yourself. Think of all the good service to the Lord that'd be wasted then. This could be the last worldly thing you'll ever do. Figure you'll more than make it up to Christ and the Virgin Mother later."

That's it, Turnblatt thought. My former partner's insanity has gone too far. He knew right then and there what he had to do. "How much would you need from me- for a thing like that?" He whispered, leaning forward.

Hutchens smiled like the Devil as he stood and whispered a figure in Turnblatt's ear.

"I'll need some time to think it over," Turnblatt lied as Hutchens returned to his seat. "Give me until tomorrow evening."

Hutchens nodded. "Fair enough," he said. "Fair enough."

Turnblatt hesitated before extending his hand. Hutchens's eyes danced with excitement as he gave it a firm shake. Turnblatt concluded that the man had descended into utter lunacy.

"I'll be going now, then," the Seminary student said, making his leave.

"Course," Hutchens said, smiling and tipping an empty bottle at his former partner. "Bein' in Seminary and all. Me- I think I'll have a few more beers."

That was how Turnblatt left his former partner- knocking back beers with mental wheels turning toward the arrangement of murder. Turnblatt's wheels turned in a far different direction.

He could not and would not be part of the murder of another innocent man. Speed walking toward home, he further reconciled himself to what had to be done. As crazy as Hutchens was becoming, he didn't put it past the man to try and harm him if he didn't agree to his wicked plot. After all- why leave a man who could tell on you alive?

Well, telling on that lunatic is exactly what I intend to do, Turnblatt thought.

Early in the morning, he would pay a visit to his former unit captain. He would lay it all out for old Rollins- everything from Hutchens's paranoid musings to his unauthorized investigation and harassment of Virgil Walker and his nefarious murder plot. He had complete faith that the department would believe him and deal with Hutchens in swift fashion.

Virgil Walker would not be harmed. Neither would Turnblatt. The aspiring priest brimmed with the belief that Christ would not allow any different result.

What would you know about Christ? An angry voice trespassed in Turnblatt's thoughts. *What would you know about God?*

A jarring sensation accompanied the voice, causing Turnblatt to wobble as if he had just taken a punch from Jack Johnson.

"Hey, fella," An old man called from his seat on a set of pristine marble steps. "You alright?"

You're fine, the voice said. "I'm fine," Turnblatt said.

I don't want you walking down these streets. There are still a few people out. You will walk the rest of the way through the alleys.

*But I don't want…*Turnblatt's complaining thoughts were interrupted by another jarring sensation.

I don't care what you want! The invading voice shrieked. *I'm steering this ship now.*

An unseen force seized the Seminary student, moving him toward the alley just as a puppeteer might manipulate a marionette. Helpless to resist the course navigated by the alien presence in his mind, Terry Turnblatt only hoped not to be bitten by any of the dogs or rats that frequented this backdoor route.

A warm flash passed through Turnblatt's mind. He thought of mocking laughter. *The rats and dogs are the least of your problems,* the voice spoke. *Soon you'll have no problems at all. Other than the fate of your eternal soul.*

Who are you? What do you mean?

Who am I? I am your punishment.

Punishment for what?

Don't pretend like you don't know! A mad rush of images passed through Turnblatt's mind. He saw himself back at *Walker's* on that terrible morning, standing idle as his partner goaded the store's namesake proprietor with foul insults. He saw himself first freeze up, then panic, shooting the enraged Negro in the back. He saw himself leave the scene with Hutchens and Breslin, thinking only of himself and not what would become of the fallen Walkers as he fled.

Who are you? He asked again. The fact that his body moved without him commanding it was no longer his most pressing concern.

I am the one your victims left behind.

What?

I am their son, Nathan. I'm not a normal child. I've always had these powers. You, your partner, and that bastard landlord have given me reason to use them. Your partner is right about someone being out to get those who hurt my folks. It wasn't Cousin Virgil, though. It was me. I got Breslin first, fixed him good. It's your turn, now.

Please, Turnblatt's internal voice whined, as he felt his bladder release. *Please don't do this. I didn't mean to kill your father. I wish I hadn't killed him.*

I know you do. That's why I'll show you some mercy by killing you quickly. Your partner won't be so lucky.

But I don't want to die at all. Not now.

My father didn't want to die when he died either, but we all have to go sometime.

Turnblatt realized that his body had stopped moving. He looked through eyes that no longer belonged to him and saw that he stood near the rear exit of a deli, less than two blocks from the room he rented.

But I was making my penance to God, Turnblatt protested. *I would have done so much good.*

Maybe God will have you, the voice said. *But I'm not him. And my father would have done much more good than you could ever imagine! You killed him*

before he really got started, so I'm just returning the favor. Do unto others…
you're studying for the priesthood, right? I mean, you were studying for the
priesthood. Now…

The invading voice fell silent. Turnblatt flexed his fingers, realizing that he
was in charge of his own body again. He started to dash from the alley before
feeling himself yanked backward, like a dog on a leash.

Thought you would get away? The voice asked. *Thought I would let you get*
away with murdering my father? It's time you join him now.

Turnblatt had been facing away from the brick-walled sides of buildings that
formed opposite flanks of the alley when he started to run. He now found himself
shifting to face the brick wall to his left that stood around the side door of the
delicatessen.

Turnblatt surprised himself by thinking, Maybe dying here won't be so bad.
At least I'm in the neighborhood, near one of my favorite places. Sure wish I
could've had one more of those corned beef sandwiches before I checked out.

As soon as he thought this, he found himself sitting at a table to the left of the
deli's counter. He lifted a thick, delicious smelling sandwich to his lips. As always,
it was a work of simple culinary art, the generous slices of meat slathered with just
the right amount of mustard. The soft bread was piping hot. Turnblatt took his time
eating, savoring each delicious bite.

The vision dissipated as soon as he swallowed the last morsel, leaving him to
realize that he had backed all the way to the wall opposite the deli's side door. He
took a running start and launched himself into the brick structure, head bowed and
jutting forward like that of a mountain ram.

II.

Nathan caused Turnblatt to bash his head into the brick wall three times before he died. A broken neck accompanied the dead man's smashed and bloody skull. Cerebral fluid leaked from the ruination.

Nathan's immediate consequences for committing the murder were a throbbing headache, utter exhaustion, and a strange sensation in his eyes.

Nathan had no idea what caused the latter symptom, but he knew the headache resulted from absorbing the psychic impact of the head trauma that Turnblatt endured. He felt just as certain that his exhaustion was not due to inhabiting Turnblatt. Turnblatt had been the weakest willed of the three men he'd killed so far. He accepted his imminent death without much resistance- probably because he felt so guilty about what he'd done.

No, the exhaustion Nathan felt was a result of once more fighting off the remnants of Ruth's essence. She had interfered from the grave again- demanding that Nathan not punish such a sorrowful man while trying to block him off with her diminished presence.

Ruth's determined effort bought Turnblatt a few more seconds before Nathan fought her off and seized control of his victim once more, this time finishing the desired deed.

Nathan had chosen well in disposing of Turnblatt in a dark and deserted alley. He felt certain that no one saw his victim appear to be yanked backward by an invisible force. Nor had anyone seen Turnblatt bludgeon himself to death against a brick wall. Someone was bound to discover his body in the morning, just as Nathan wished. After that, it wouldn't take long for word to get back to Officer Hutchens.

Nathan felt no worry about Hutchens panicking and trying to hurt his family because he understood that the man was really a coward. He expected Hutchens to flee like a frightened rabbit instead, insuring that no one would see Nathan punish the big man.

Nathan didn't anticipate any further need to use his powers for violence after he was done torturing and killing Hutchens. Once he completed his vengeful vendetta, he'd settle into living as normal and unassuming a life as possible.

Nathan now felt certain that the ailments he suffered after attacking his victims were affected by the method in which he killed them. He was prepared to suffer great injury in light of that knowledge. The agony he'd have to tolerate would be an even exchange for the privilege of making Hutchens suffer worse than anyone he'd struck down so far.

7

Conscience and Panic

I.

Nathan knew that Virgil sat at his bedside even before opening his eyes. The brawny painter had done his best to act more like a father than a cousin since James died. Nathan appreciated Virgil's kindness and caring, but it didn't come close to filling the aching void his deceased father had left.

Although Virgil smiled in concert with the rising sun that peaked through Nathan's uncovered bedside window, his eyes screamed concern.

"You feelin' okay, little cousin? You don't look so well."

Nathan started to lie before he caught a glimpse of Virgil's thoughts. Those thoughts reflected a disturbing image of a boy who looked pallid with illness, whose spectral eyes had grown dull in their bizarre coloring.

"I have a terrible headache," Nathan confessed.

"How long've you had this headache?"

Nathan looked around, pretending to get his bearings. "Since late last night- I guess."

Virgil frowned. "Since late last night? Why didn't you wake me or Alma?"

Nathan shrugged. "I thought I could sleep it off."

Virgil snickered. "I guess you cain't always see the future." He leaned close. "Listen to me, boy. From here on out, I want you to always tell me when you're not feelin' well. You got a lot of strange talents, but you ain't a doctor. An' I hardly think iss a good idea to go to sleep wit' a headache. Maybe I should send for Doc Tilden again."

"No!" Nathan shrieked, waving his hands in front of each other. "Please don't do that, Cousin Virgil. Please! I've had all the poking and prodding I can stand for a while. It's just a headache. That's all. Everyone gets headaches."

Virgil nodded, satisfied to acquiesce to Nathan's wishes. He had no way of knowing that Nathan had just used a tiny amount of psychic power to influence him. He thought having visions of the future was his young cousin's sole talent. He'd heard tell of such things before, being from the Deep South. Therefore, the boy's clairvoyance hadn't been a difficult thing for him to accept. Still, he might have been terrified if he knew what else Nathan could do.

"Know what I think, Nathan?"

Nathan shrugged, although he knew full well what was about to be said.

"I think when you git one a the visions you have, it takes a lot out a you. I figure if that's right, a doctor's care cain't help you too much, no way. That's how come Doc Tilden never found anything wrong with your blood test an' all. And I kin understand you not wantin' to be examined for a while. Lord knows the man been makin' so many house calls here lately, I'm ponderin' gittin' Alma to fix up a room for 'im. Not that we got any more rooms to spare. Ole Doc might just have to bunk in the basement."

He stood. "I spose if 's'just a headache, some rest'll do you fine. I'll git Alma to check your temperature an' bring you some water."

Nathan felt mixed emotions as Virgil exited. On one hand, he was glad that Dr. Tilden wouldn't be around unless Alma found that he was running a temperature. He knew that wouldn't happen. If anything, he felt as cold as a snake's blood.

On the other hand, Virgil's conclusion that he became fatigued after having one of his visions wasn't a good development. How long until Virgil realized that

Nathan's illnesses struck him in conjunction with the deaths of those he was settling things with?

Virgil might be gullible enough to let a white man profit from the exquisite art he created, but he was not stupid. Nathan decided not to dwell on the possibility for now. He'd cross that bridge when he reached it.

Alma entered his bedroom in short order, wearing a kind but concerned visage. Pink curlers filled her hair. She wished him good morning and handed him a tall glass of water. After he gulped down half of it, she stuck a thermometer under his tongue.

"Temperature's normal," she said, smiling and rubbing his head. "I guess tiredness is all that's ailin' you. Tiredness an' stress."

She leaned over him and planted a tender kiss on his cheek. "You'll stay in bed for the day, unless you start to feel better. We'll bring you your meals. Don't worry, Nathan. You'll be fine." She took a long look at him. "You're made of stern stuff, just like your father. All Walker men are made of stern stuff."

She left then, carrying out the water glass he had finished. As she departed, Nathan considered how great she and Virgil were. In the wake of his parents' demise, they'd taken him in, no questions asked. They doted on him and his stricken mother just as much as they doted on their own sons. And that bastard Hutchens wants Virgil dead, he thought. The swollen pig wants to take all that I have left.

Nathan had no intention of allowing that to happen. He would rest, all right. He would rest for the remainder of the day, gathering his strength for a special punishment for the big cop. Officer Hutchens would learn the true meaning of suffering before he died.

II.

Galen Hutchens had good reason to dislike being summoned to the Captain's office. Things hadn't turned out well for him the last time it had happened.

"You'll have to be moving on, Hutchens," Captain Rollins had said, speaking without even a scintilla of emotion, as befit the company man that he was. If he were sorry to see Hutchens go, he would never show it. "The higher ups want you walking a beat in Northwest. They figure you won't get into any dust-ups with the Jew and Pollock businessmen."

Seated across from Rollins's huge, cluttered mahogany desk, Hutchens's jaw plunged toward the floor. He asked when he was due to push on after he managed to collect himself.

"Today," Captain Rollins said, maintaining firm eye contact. "Right now." He pushed a sheet of paper across the desk. "Here's the transfer order."

Hutchens felt his face warm as he picked up the order and ripped it to shreds. He did not doubt that he'd turned a bright crimson.

Captain Rollins didn't blink. "That doesn't do a bit of good, Galen. You still have to go."

"Northwest," Hutchens hissed, lips curled into a sneer. "That's not police work, Captain. That ain't real police work!"

"Yeah?" Captain Rollins's eyes flashed hot. "Well neither is busting some Negro woman's head, especially with the lot of them already full of piss and vinegar over the Segregation Ordinance. You caused a lot of problems for the department with that goddamn NAACP. Just what we need. A bunch of angry Negroes and their Jew lawyers breathing down our collective necks! We've been wearing the black eye you and your partner give us ever since. This is your penance for that. Be glad you still have a job."

Hutchens exploded from his seat and slammed a heavy paw onto Rollins's desk. Rollins responded by setting his jaw and fisting his hands as he rose to his own impressive height. The two large men regarded each other like a pair of rival bulls about to lock horns.

"You think that's right?" Hutchens demanded. "Or are you just pissin' out the company line?"

Rollins relaxed his body and opened his hands. "Doesn't matter what I think, Galen. Things are what they are."

"That's for certain," Hutchens grunted. "Things are what they are. Even if the whole thing stinks worsen a hog's shit pile."

He turned and stormed out of the office, pushing past his fellow officers congregated in the open air area of his now former precinct. Not a word passed his lips or theirs as he crashed through the front door. A harsh wind awaited him outside. It blew him all the way to his new beat.

Now Hutchens had been summoned by the captain of that new beat. He wondered what the hell the matter could be. Stopping just outside Captain Green's door, he had time to wonder if he had played the wrong hand with Turnblatt. Maybe the high and mighty, want to be priest was only pretending to need time to think about my offer, he worried. Maybe he blew the whistle on me. He decided that couldn't be, telling himself that if Turnblatt had let the cat out the bag, he most likely would've been arrested. Conspiracy to commit murder was a serious crime, even if Hutchens was a cop and his conspiring was only done against niggers. Maybe it was even more serious to plot so against niggers, what with the current tensions in the city.

Face flushed and coated with perspiration, Hutchens paused with his hand on Green's doorknob. The robust Jew saw his subordinate through the glass square at the top of the door and motioned for entry.

Hutchens had figured Green for Jewish since his first day at the Northwest Precinct. The man's huge and angular nose left no doubt. Hutchens assumed his born surname to be Greenberg, Greenbauer, or something of that sort. Hutchens didn't like taking orders from a kike, and he hated being summoned to a kike's office even more. He turned the knob at the pace of a fatigued snail, resigning himself to whatever his fate might be.

III.

"Sit down, Hutchens." Captain Green pointed to the chair opposite his desk.

Just as Rollins's had been, the massive oak structure was cluttered with papers. Green stroked the caterpillar above his top lip with his left hand as he ran his right hand once through his balding blond hair.

"It's about your former partner," he said, his slow cadence indicating great care in choosing his words.

Hutchens's heart fluttered. So this is how it's going to be? Maybe he was wrong in thinking he'd be arrested for planning a murder for hire. Maybe plotting a murder against a nigger only got a cop kicked off the force. That would be a horrible enough punishment in itself.

"What about 'im, sir?" Hutchens croaked.

"He's dead."

Hutchens gasped as he placed a large hand over his left breast. Green watched him without any outward expression of emotion, giving his subordinate time to recover from the shocking news. Eternity wouldn't have been long enough.

"When?" Hutchens managed, collecting himself. "How?"

"Last night. He was found in the alley of a deli, not two blocks from his home. His skull was smashed all to hell and he had a broken neck. He even leaked brain fluid. Hutchens?"

"Yes, Captain?"

"This detail won't be released to the press. But initial findings point to suicide."

"Suicide?" Hutchens shook his head. "He wouldn't do that. Not Turnblatt, sir."

Green frowned and raised his eyebrows. "Why not him? I know all about what you two were involved in before you came to this precinct. Him joining Seminary and all - it had to be guilt that drove him to that. Maybe pursuing the priesthood didn't do enough for that guilt. Could be it got to be too much for him."

Hutchens shook his head like a dog drying itself after a bath. "No. I don't buy it."

Green sighed and shifted in his seat, folding his hands in his lap. "Physical evidence doesn't lie, Hutchens. The coroner is a good friend of mine. He says it looks like your former partner must have charged that brick wall like a billy goat, ramming his own head into it several times."

"Someone else could've done that to 'im."

"I don't think so," Green said, shaking his head. "There was no sign of struggle, not one other mark, anywhere on his body. There's nothing to indicate that anyone else was with him at the time."

Hutchens nodded, digesting all of the details. "It was the nigger's coosin," he spat.

Green blinked. "What?"

"It was the nigger's coosin. The one Turnblatt shot that day. He's been after us. Everyone who was there. He's after us."

Captain Green smiled as one might smile at an idiot child. It occurred to Hutchens that Turnblatt had smiled much the same way during their last palaver at *Kellerman's*. The poor, disbelieving soul never even made it home after they parted.

"You're in shock, officer," Green said.

"I am not in shock!" Hutchens felt himself dissolving in a solution of terror and anger. "I know exactly what I say! That dead nigger has a coosin who's out for revenge. He's kilt Connor Breslin and now Terry. He'll surely look to me next!"

"Connor Breslin?" Green's eyes turned in unison with the wheels of his mind. He stroked the caterpillar that obscured his top lip again. "Oh, the landlord who was mixed up in that business. That man committed suicide as well. I'm not going to pretend that I think it's a coincidence, two who were there both ending themselves. No, I think that neither one of them was able to live with what happened that day. It seems everyone involved in that ugly incident was irreparably damaged. Including you."

Green sighed. "Listen…I know you've been through a lot and this is quite a shock to you, but…but what you're suggesting is ludicrous!"

Hutchens sprang from his seat, ears flushed and nostrils flaring. "You don't think it very unlikely that two men involved in the same incident would commit suicide? And what would Breslin's reason've been? Was he a drinkin' buddy of yours? That how you've so much insight into what he was doin' before he died? No, I don't think you knew the man at all. So your theories don't mean shit!"

Captain Green rose to his feet and rolled up his sleeves, revealing bulging, hairy forearms. "You're in a very bad place, Officer Hutchens. You are not speaking rationally at all. It is a well known fact that Breslin stabbed himself in his own heart, in his kitchen. There was no evidence of anyone else being present at the time save for his wife, his maid, and his daughters. They were all sleeping at the time of his demise."

"I didn't say any of them killed 'im, did I?" Hutchens growled. "I said that nigger's coosin did it. I know he did."

Green shook his head. "I think it was a mistake for the department to transfer you to Northwest. What you really need is some time off."

Hutchens started to blurt, "I don't need any time off, you stupid kike. I need to get that nigger before he gets me", but thought better of it. He couldn't convince a man like Green through mere argument. Men like Green gave no credence to things they couldn't prove or understand. Proof or not, Hutchens realized he'd be dead soon enough if he sat around and waited. He didn't know how that nigger Virgil had done it, but he knew that it had been done. He also knew that the nigger would come for him very soon.

With Turnblatt dead, Hutchens didn't have enough money to finance a murder for hire on his own. Still, he wasn't going to allow Virgil to pick him off at his leisure. There was only one thing left to do, so he made up his mind to do it and face the consequences afterward. Any consequence that involved him still breathing was far preferable to the alternative.

III.

You cannot do this, the disembodied voice shrieked. *You cannot do this! You again*, Nathan thought. *Why won't you just leave me be? I can't accept you giving yourself over to evil. Giving myself over to evil? What evil thing have I done? Murder. Murders! This is not why God blessed you with such power.*

Oh? Then, why did he? Tell me why he did, you old woman. No, not old woman- old ghost. You're an old ghost, now, an old ghost who haunts my mind. I think its' time for you to move on.

I'm greatly saddened that you've grown hardened enough to speak so cruelly, the presence that remained of Miss Ruth replied. *The world's been vile to you, I understand. It's been vile to us all. But that doesn't justify what you've done.*

All I've done is punish those men for what they did to my folks? What's so wrong about that? Doesn't the bible say an eye for an eye?

Yes, it does say that. But such reckoning is for the Good Lord to bring about.

And the Good Lord uses human vessels to do his work. Didn't you tell me I was the Lord's vessel?

Yes. You were meant to be the Lord's vessel. But, I fear that Satan's gotten the better of you.

No. Satan has destroyed my family, Nathan asserted. *He used those evil men to destroy my family. So now, I will destroy them. I will destroy all of them. And you will not stop me!*

Even with power as great as yours, you can't control every outcome, Miss Ruth cautioned him. *There are always consequences that even those with the sight can not foresee.*

Nathan unleashed a psychic scream. *I have done nothing wrong! And I'm tired of you, buzzing in my mind like a swarm of flies. Go away from me, old woman. Go away and stay away! I think I'll send you away.*

No. You can't mean that. You don't know what you're doing.

I know exactly what I'm doing! Nathan stopped debating and fell into the deepest concentration possible, summoning all of his vast psychic powers. He sensed what remained of Ruth's essence, as it braced for the force he was about to unleash. He felt nonplussed, remembering her revelation that he could drive all of what remained of her away. He was determined not to let anything interfere with his vengeance, not even the essence of the old woman who had taught him so well.

He unleashed his psychic force like a powerful explosion, intent on driving what remained of Ruth into the spirit world for good. She resisted him with all of her considerable power, intent on derailing him from a path of destruction.

They impacted like two runaway trains colliding at top speed. In the aftermath of that collision, Nathan sensed that Ruth had gone. Darkness remained in her place, an unrelenting, paralyzing darkness.

IV.

Virgil both worried about and felt confounded by his young cousin. The boy had slipped in and out of consciousness all morning, his eyes fluttering open at irregular intervals.

Virgil had sent for Dr. Tilden, only to discover that the man had left his office for another house call. He and Alma decided that it was best not to move the boy, suspecting that his malady may have something to do with his powers of clairvoyance.

Other than prying Nathan's lips open to give him water at regular intervals, they remained still, keeping a worried vigil over his bedside. Their other charges (the two boys and Naomi) were trusted to look after themselves.

Once, when Virgil went to David and Eli's room, he saw them kneeling with Naomi, their hands joined in quiet prayer. Virgil stepped inside, taking hands and joining them.

None of Nathan's family wanted anything to happen to him. David and Eli had bonded with him as if they were all brothers, while Virgil had assumed the mantle of father figure. Alma had not forged as powerful a bond with the boy as her husband had, but her heart still hurt for him. Even in her traumatized simple mindedness, Naomi continued to think of him as her son. Her brain-damaged notion of a son was not much more sophisticated than how a child might think of a dog or a fancy doll. Still, her heart ached for him. She felt terrified of what might become of him. What none of the intact Walkers could know was that another member of their family was in far greater danger than Nathan was.

V.

Stark terror ravaged Nathan's consciousness. His body had shut down, as had his powers of the mind. Damn that old woman, he thought. She had tried so hard to stop him from doing what was only right that he'd spent himself overcoming her.

He had expected pain and fatigue as a result of dueling with her. He had not imagined physical and psychic paralysis. He wondered if this was what being in a coma was like.

He felt cocooned, able to "see" his immediate surroundings with what little psychic power remained, but unable to interact or truly be "seen" by others. Sure, Virgil and Alma could see the occasional twitch of a limb or pathetic fluttering of eyelids that lacked the strength to remain open. But, they could not detect the warning harbored in his mind.

Nathan would have told them that a dangerous man was headed their way, if only he were able. That was not so, thanks to Ruth's meddlesome spirit. His only hope was to emerge from his condition before Hutchens arrived. Every time that he tried to send a warning to his family, his thoughts dissipated upon contact with a black barrier that separated his mind from theirs.

He wished that he could bring Ruth's essence back from the void where he had sent it, just so that he could torture her for what her actions might soon cause. If anything happened to his loved ones, he just might try.

VI.

Galen Hutchens was not the least bit concerned with departmental rules when he snuck his old squad car off the lot. He had no access to one in his new assignment as a beat cop in Northwest, nor did he have an automobile of his own.

I'll surely lose my badge and probably serve prison time for this, he thought. People will surely label me a murderer or a crazy, or both, after all's said and done. Maybe they'll say the stress and the liquor drove me to it. I am drunk off my Irish ass, that's for sure. But what I'm about to do won't be the act of a crazed, drunk, nigger hating Irishman.

No, Hutchens didn't like niggers very much; that point was beyond argument. Still, under normal circumstances, there was not a nigger alive important enough for him to hunt down and murder.

But these were not normal circumstances and Virgil Walker was no normal nigger. A wraith in the night was what he was, a wraith hell bent on revenge. It had been at night that Virgil destroyed his cousin's old store, at night that Virgil disposed of Connor Breslin, and at night that Virgil murdered poor Turnblatt.

It was an undisputable fact that Terry Turnblatt had been a good man. He didn't deserve the fate he met. Nor did he deserve the departmental line that his death was a suicide, just as Breslin's death was thought to be. Though Hutchens knew that Breslin's death hadn't been suicide, he admitted that as far as suicides go, a man plunging a knife into his own heart was at least a believable method. But who would bash their own head in against a brick wall? There had to be a thousand less miserable ways to take yourself off this rock.

Besides, Turnblatt wouldn't have committed suicide even by a more conventional method. He entered the priesthood to deal with his guilt, for Christ sake, Hutchens thought. This is all that troublesome nigger's fault! If he had only stayed in his place as most of his kind do, this whole fix would've never happened. But the uppity son of a bitch just couldn't do it.

Now Virgil appeared to be far bolder than even his dead cousin. Instead of figuring that the other darkie had gotten his just desserts for assaulting a police officer, Virgil chose to undertake a revenge spree.

Hutchens had no idea how the nigger had done what he'd done, nor did he spend much time pondering it as he raced toward his adversary's Pennsylvania Avenue row house. Maneuvering the big Model-T through Old West Baltimore, he noticed the occasional side-walk strolling darkie tense up at the sight of the big white star on its' driver's side.

That's right, he thought, resisting the urge to scream it out. I am a Baltimore City police officer, and I'm about to serve justice to one of you baboons.

8

Reckoning

I.

Naomi sat by her bed, clutching a string haired doll that Alma had given her. Alma and Virgil are always so nice to me, she thought. She loved her family. Alma, Virgil, David, Eli- and most especially Nathan. Her son, Nathan.

She felt terrified for Nathan. He was always getting sick and today he seemed to be worse than ever. He was in a deep, deep sleep and couldn't wake up. She hoped that he didn't end up like his father. Naomi remembered what had become of James when he… when that young policeman shot him! It hadn't been the young man's fault really. His bigger, older partner had started it all. The big policeman kept pushing and pushing, she thought, saying the meanest things until James lost his temper and fought him.

Naomi wished that she could have James back. She wished that she wasn't so simple now- like a little girl in a woman's body. She wished that watching James die was not the last memory of how she was before.

Though she had become very much like a small child, Naomi was not innocent enough to believe that those wishes had any chance of coming true. She decided that she could be satisfied if her wish for Nathan's well-being was granted. She was willing to do anything if God would just wake her son up.

II.

Nathan saw it all with his mind's eye. The burly, ham-fisted police officer was a picture of wildness, having grown thick stubble on his chin.

Hutchens careened the police car to a stop at the curb, reaching for his service weapon before jumping out. He's come for Cousin Virgil, Nathan realized.

He thinks Virgil is responsible. The thought sickened Nathan, mortified him.

Nathan tried to bypass the mental barriers that prevented him from warning his unsuspecting family. Desperate, he marshaled all of his strength, straining again and again to send a warning vision. It was useless. He could not send out a signal strong enough to penetrate their minds.

He tried once more, placing every iota of his will into the effort. He did not care if he died or fell into a coma for the rest of his days. Saving his family was all that mattered.

On this latest, Herculean effort, Nathan sensed himself breaching the black wall that had vanquished his previous efforts of psychic communication. The warning he sent was very weak after passing through, like a lantern flickering out. He prayed, hoping that one of his loved one's minds stood uncluttered enough to receive it.

III.

At Nathan's bedside, Virgil and Alma experienced uneasy feelings at the same moment. They looked at the boy. He remained still, excepting his fluttering eyelids and the consistent rise and fall of his breast.

They exchanged a silent glance. Virgil shrugged. Alma did the same. They clasped hands and prayed, as they had countless times since discovering their comatose charge in this condition.

Down the hall, a hush fell over David and Eli at the same time that the uneasy feeling seized their parents. Images flashed through their young minds, images too fleeting to be made out.

In her attic dwelling, a hush fell over Naomi as well. The image that flashed through her mind was crystal clear. The bad police officer who hurt me, she thought. The bad police officer who hurt me is right outside! He wants to kill Virgil!

She lowered the hanging staircase that led to the second floor before bolting down it, leaping the last rung in her sock feet.

"Bad man!" she shrieked. "Bad man!" She streaked downstairs like a stampeding horse, making a sharp right into the kitchen off the landing.

Upstairs, Alma and Virgil eyed each other in shock. "I'll see what's the matter with her," Alma said, flying from Nathan's bedside.

The boys came into the hall, headed toward the commotion. "Don't go down there," Virgil commanded from his seat.

"But Daddy…," David started, looking into Nathan's room.

"I said don't go down there. Your mama has a way wit' Naomi. Let her see what's got her so stirred up. Y'all come in here an' we'll stand watch over Nathan."

Having followed Naomi into the kitchen, Alma gasped at what she saw. Her feeble charge held the largest knife in the house, a gleaming steel cleaver.

IV.

No, Nathan thought. *No, Mama!* Things were not going as he wanted.

Even with power as great as yours, you can't control every outcome. The words of the old woman's departed ghost taunted him. *There are always consequences that even those with the sight can not foresee.*

The ghost was right. Nathan couldn't control every outcome or foresee every consequence of his actions. At the moment, he was unable to breech the recovered strength of the black barrier. He could only watch with his mind's eye, hoping that no one else he loved was harmed.

V.

"What are you doing, Naomi?" Alma asked, speaking with measured calm.

"He's here!" Naomi said. Her eyes were those of a cornered animal. "He's here! The bad man is here!"

"What bad man?" Alma asked.

Just then, the back door crashed in.

VI.

Hutchens expected to catch the Walkers off guard by creeping through their backyard and up their back steps. He'd only come for Virgil. The rest were inconsequential to him.

If he had to hurt anyone else, so be it. But the plan was to kill the stocky nigger and get out of there.

He hurled his large body into the back door, causing it to buckle and crash inward. Nearly falling as the door did, he straightened himself just in time to see James Walker's feeble widow running at him, yielding a cleaver with deadly intent.

V.

Nathan "watched" with bone chilling dread, wishing that there was something he could do, knowing that he would be responsible if any of his loved ones were hurt.

Naomi hurled herself at the vile cop, swinging the cleaver in a downward arc. Without hesitation, he fired his revolver into her abdomen.

She took the shot without breaking stride, plunging her weapon into the hollow at the base of his throat, just above the clavicle.

The big Irishman staggered backward, firing a wild second shot as the cleaver jutted from his wound. Moving at the bent angle from which it had been fired, the bullet came to rest in the highest part of the wall behind Alma- just below the ceiling.

Virgil rushed into the kitchen, brought running by the sound of the back door crashing in. David peeked into the doorway, keeping back in accordance with his father's gruff instructions.

A whistling sound signified the first release of air from the cop's trachea. Blood spurted from the wide wound that the blade had torn, birthing a red fountain that painted his uniform. His eyes registered far greater shock than pain as he made a feeble attempt to dislodge the bloodied cleaver with his free hand.

The fingers of his gun hand unclenched, sending the weapon clattering across the pristine kitchen floor. To the relief of his intended victims, its landing did not cause the trigger to depress.

The big cop crashed to the floor, coming to rest back first alongside the door he'd destroyed. A last spurt of blood sprayed from the fountain wound. He made a gurgling sound as blood poured from his mouth. His eyes glazed over as he passed from the realm of the living.

Father, mother, and eldest son stood in shocked silence. David took action first, running to Naomi's side.

"Cousin Naomi!" he cried, kneeling to haul her into his ever strengthening adolescent arms. His father's arm fell upon him.

"Tend to your brother and your cousin," Virgil instructed, a slight quaver in his voice. "We'll see to her."

David lost no time in obeying, scaling steps with the quicksilver of youth.

As David entered Nathan's room, he saw his younger brother entranced at the sight of their once comatose cousin. Nathan's eyes remained closed, but he tossed and turned as if his bed were the most uncomfortable in the world.

VI.

Please don't let her die, Nathan prayed. Please, God. Not Mama. I already lost one mother at birth and now my father's gone. Please don't take Mama Naomi from me.

He blamed himself for Naomi being shot. If he had not set out for revenge, the cop would never have had reason to want Cousin Virgil dead.

I should have heeded Miss Ruth's warnings, he thought, but- but I'm just a kid! He'd been so angry- wanting to get even. Now at the tender age of eleven, he realized that there was no getting even for some things. Trying to get even was a thousand times worse than accepting misfortune and trying to move on.

He swore right then that if his mother survived and the rest of his family turned out okay, he would never use his powers to harm others again. That applied even to bad men like Hutchens.

He made up his mind to bid his family goodbye and go far, far away once he emerged from his crippled state. I'm a danger to them like this, he confessed to himself. I have all this power but I'm still a kid. I still make dumb mistakes, like kids do.

Nathan thought he might be safer to be around when he grew to be a man. But for now, it was best for him to go off somewhere. Maybe he'd find a nice place in the woods like Miss Ruth had done.

An epiphany blindsided him, breaking off that train of thought. Perhaps it was God answering his prayer, for at that very moment he realized that he could help his mother stay alive.

9

Rejuvenation

I.

Naomi strolled along the path of the most beautiful garden she'd ever seen. All of her favorite flowers stood at fantastic heights. She was surrounded by red roses, daffodils, daisies, white orchards, black eyed Susans, tulips, and violets. The beautiful tableau extended as far as her eyes could see. The path itself was made of cobblestone that alternated all colors of the rainbow. A radiant, golden light bathed her and her surroundings.

Far ahead of Naomi, much farther a distance than her childlike mind had words for, waited the origin of the welcoming light. She made up her mind to head toward it, sensing that it illuminated a place even more wonderful than the path she strolled.

"It's not time to make that trip, yet," A familiar voice spoke from behind her. It was adolescent in pitch, yet full of adult seriousness and wisdom.

She turned in its direction and beheld her son. "Nathan," she squealed, hugging him. " Nathan. My son."

Holding him, she realized that she was now smaller than him, though he had not grown any. Looking at her hands, she realized that they were smaller and less lined than she remembered. They were the hands of a young girl.

"What happened to me?" she shrieked, aborting her embrace. "Why am I like this?"

Nathan smiled, as if to say that all was well. "We're in another realm now, Mama. The realm that people come to when they pass. In this realm, this is how you are."

"A little girl?" Naomi pouted. "I don't want to be a little girl, Nathan. I want to be someone you look up to."

"I do look up to you, Mama. How could I not? You and Papa raised me. You and Papa always took good care of me."

Naomi smiled for a moment; then thought about what he'd just said. "No." She shook her head. "No! You can't look up to me. Not me. You look up to the way I was...before." Tears filled her eyes. She unleashed a wail to rival the howl of a grief stricken hound.

Her tears flowed unrestrained, rushing to meet the mucus that fled her nose. She did not bother to wipe either substance.

Nathan sighed and clutched her to his thin chest. "It's alright, Mama."

Her bawling downgraded to sniffles as she rested her head on his shoulder. "No it ain't. I can't even look after you anymore."

"You don't have to look after me, Mama. We'll look after each other."

She lifted her head as he lowered his to meet her gaze. "I'm a burden to you."

"No, Mama. You're not a burden to me. I need you. I need you so much."

Naomi turned from him, looking toward the source of the golden light. "Maybe I should just go to it. I bet iss real peaceful there."

Nathan's spectral eyes lit up like Christmas bulbs as he looked in the same direction.

"Oh, it is peaceful, Mama," he said. "You'll have no more troubles when you get there. Only thing is..."

"Only thing is what?"

He took gentle hold of her shoulders and turned her around. "Only thing is... it's not your time to go there yet. You must come back and look after me."

Naomi wiped her face with the back of her hand before shaking her head. "I told you I can't look after you. I'm no good any more. More like a little sister to you than a mother."

Nathan's eyes lit up once more. "No, Mama. You will always be my mother and we will look after each other."

He turned his back to the light and strolled away from it. He held one hand out, palm toward her, his desire unmistakable. She cast a long stare in the direction of the light's source before switching her gaze to him.

"I'll be back," she said, smiling as she spoke to no in particular. She skipped and giggled, catching up to her son and grasping his outstretched hand.

As they left the garden together, Naomi noticed something she hadn't known before. This path, this beautiful place, felt freezing cold.

II.

Nathan sat up on his bed, realizing that freedom had returned to his limbs. He felt hazy, as if he were returning to a place that he hadn't been to in a long time.

"David!" he called, knowing that his cousin was heading up the hall.

"Nathan!" David's adolescent voice cracked. The creaking of the floor and closeness of his voice told Nathan that he had hurried bedside. "You're awake! You're awake! Hot damn, this is great!"

"Where's my Mama?" Nathan asked. The sound of David sighing and declining to answer annoyed him. "Where's my Mama?" he growled.

"Nathan... you've been out of it for a long time. Things happened while you were..."

"I know what happened! That policeman came here, wanting to kill Virgil! Now where's my Mama?"

A long silence fell as David processed his cousin's revelation. He still wasn't accustomed to Nathan's clairvoyance and he had not imagined that it could work while his cousin lay in a virtual coma. "How could you know that, Nathan?"

Nathan lunged from bed, slipping and almost crashing to the floor before David's strong hands caught and steadied him.

"Where's my mother, David?"

"She's at the hospital. My folks and Eli rode in the ambulance with her."

Nathan lifted his head onto the bigger boy's shoulder. "Is she…?"

"She got shot, Nathan. That crazy cop shot her. But it looks like she'll be okay. She was talking fine when they loaded her on the ambulance. And she wasn't bleeding much."

Nathan collapsed into violent sobbing, the tears wetting his cousin's shirt. He trembled as if he were standing naked in subzero temperatures. He threw his arms around David. His older cousin hugged him hard, trying to offer comfort.

"She'll be alright, cousin. I swear she'll be alright. I wouldn't lie to you about that."

"Thank God," Nathan managed. "Thank you, Lord."

They held each other for a while, having no concept of the passage of time. They released each other when Nathan grew calm.

A question spread across David's face. "Hey, Nathan?" he asked. "Why don't you open your eyes?"

As soon as the question was asked, Nathan realized the answer. "Because I can't," he sighed. "I just can't."

III.

Good fortune befell the Walkers when Hutchens's attack was investigated. Even in the racial climate of Baltimore, there was no way for the police department to justify one of their own breaking into a law-abiding citizen's house (even a law-abiding Negro citizen) with the intention of gunning him down. They felt no motivation to do so, anyway. Hutchens had already bought public embarrassment and scandal to the department with the first tragic incident involving the Walker family. His precinct captain harbored no secrets about Hutchens paranoid ranting prior to his illegal commandeering of a vehicle for the purpose of seeking and murdering Virgil.

The NAACP rallied to the cause, their lawyers portraying the Walkers as victims of unmitigated hatred by the Baltimore Police Department. They decried the BPD as an organization that targets hard-working, law-abiding Negro citizens without just cause. In the end, the Walkers were awarded $20,000 for their pain and suffering. Their legal fees were deducted from the payout, leaving them with $12,500. As much as they cared about the cause of the common Negro, the NAACP couldn't sustain its operation on peanuts.

The residents of Old West Baltimore celebrated the triumph of their residents in understated fashion. Fear of angering street cops into finding excuses to give out beatings kept them from being more demonstrative. They did not know that even the most racist of policemen felt that Galen Hutchens had met the just fate of one who went off the deep end.

Naomi Walker healed well while the legalities worked themselves out. Hutchens's bullet struck her in the abdomen, but did not damage any vital organs. Doctors removed it without complication.

She returned home after ten days in the hospital. The remaining Walkers welcomed her with great cheer, glad that Hutchens's second assault on her had not proved as disastrous as the first.

IV.

"Mama and I, we're going to go," Nathan spoke in a near whisper. His eyes remained closed, as they had been since bringing Naomi back from the land of the dead.

He sensed Virgil and Alma watching him, wishing that he had consented to allow Dr. Tilden to examine him. He had refused, knowing that the problem couldn't be solved by medicine or surgery.

All of the Walkers congregated at the dinner table. Virgil sat at the head, opposite Alma. David sat to the right of his father, flanked by Eli. Nathan and Naomi sat across from them.

Nathan's announcement halted the festive mood of Sunday dinner. Before he spoke, they had all been enjoying one of Alma's legendary Sunday spreads: fried chicken, okra, corn, mashed potatoes, cornbread, and southern style sweet tea. The wonderful spread was now forgotten.

"What do you mean?" Virgil asked.

Nathan halted his okra-stabbed fork before his mouth, clearing his throat before answering. "Mama and I, we've been talking about it. As soon as we get the money from the city, we're going to go."

"Why do you want to go, boy?"

"I just don't want to bring nothing else on y'all," Nathan sat the fork down. "Lots of times I feel like I can't control it."

They all knew what he meant by "it". In the aftermath of Hutchens's assault, he'd come clean, explaining that he could do a lot more than just see the future. He confessed to affecting the actions of others, starting with his vanquishing of John Turner and ending with murdering Officer Turnblatt. He also told them how he had warned Naomi of Hutchens's murderous intentions.

They surprised him by treating him the same as they had before they knew it all. "Well here's hopin' you've learned not to interfere," Virgil grunted. "Jus' 'cause you kin do somethin' doesn't mean you should."

"I know that now," Nathan said, nodding his agreement as tears spilled from his eyes. "I swear I know that now."

Nathan knew that his cousins had thought their acceptance of his transgressions meant that he would remain with them for some time. The revelation that he was leaving both shocked and disappointed them.

"You jus' got to try hard, boy," Virgil scowled, setting his fork down on his plate. "Ain't no use runnin' off. You jus' got to try hard."

"I do try!" Nathan banged a fist on the table, causing plates to clatter. He didn't need a functioning pair of eyes to know that everyone else's eyes had widened. "I try so hard. But, I feel so many things. I'm not yet twelve years old, you know. Kids my age are already full of emotions. Plus, so much has happened. Sometimes I just get so…tempted."

Virgil folded his hands together and began cracking his knuckles. "Yeah, well…when you feel like that, you got to remember the consequences. An' you got to remember that you swore before God not to use your powers to hurt nobody. You recall that? After you told us about all of it…all of us, this whole family got on our knees an' clasped hands in prayer? You swore you'd never hurt nobody again. An' we swore to be there for you, help you weather this terrible burden."

Nathan sighed. "Yes, I remember. But sometimes I feel like I might end up hurting y'all just by staying here. Sometimes I can't help wanting to interfere."

Virgil cocked his eyebrows. "Interfere with what?"

Nathan cleared his throat. "Like the thing with that man, Thurmont. It's not right. You're the one who should be getting all of the glory for your artwork. Instead, he keeps right on taking the credit. I don't see how you can stand it."

Virgil ceased cracking his knuckles and unfolded his hands. Regarding the faces of his family one by one, he knew that they all shared Nathan's sentiment. It was as if James had passed it to them from the grave.

"Has it ever occurred to you that I don't want the recognition?" Virgil asked. "I've always had enough to care for my family. And if white folks knew a Negro was producin' all that work, they might not want it as much."

"They'd probably like it even more," Nathan said. "The novelty of it." He sighed. "But that's not the point. The point is…whenever I think of Thurmont, I want to interfere, to make things better for you. There are other times I want to interfere, too. Leaving would keep me from doing that."

He turned toward Naomi. "Anyhow, Mama and I agree that we should go off somewhere simple, away from this city life. It's way too much stimulation for us."

Naomi smiled and kissed him on the cheek. "Yes. We'll look after each other. We'll be fine."

"Especially with the money and all," Nathan said, nodding. "That much money can last an awful long time for people living simply."

"What about your schooling?" Alma asked. "Your father would want you to finish your schooling."

Nathan sighed as he turned in Alma's direction. "Come now, Cousin Alma. We all know that I don't really need school."

"Maybe you don't need school," Virgil admitted. "You're smarter than everyone as it is. But still, it's somethin' to do."

Nathan grinned like a Jack-o-Lantern. "I think doing nothing in particular will be a lot better for me. At least for the time being. Doing nothing will do just fine."

Virgil threw up his hands in surrender. "So there's no changin' your mind?"

Nathan shook his head. "Maybe I'll come back when I'm sure I can control myself. Until then, I don't think I should be around so much excitement. I figure when I get to be a man I'll be able to handle things a lot better."

"I do believe you're a man already," Virgil said. "I do believe you're a man already."

Epilogue

The money from the city came early in January of 1914, shortly after Nathan's 12th birthday. He and Alma wanted to split the payout with their cousins, but Virgil and Alma only agreed to take enough to host a big sendoff for them. It seemed like every resident of Pennsylvania Avenue partook in the revelry.

Nathan promised to stay in touch with his cousins, although he didn't divulge exactly where he was going. He couldn't tell them because he didn't know. He expected his sight to guide him to where he needed to be, acting similar to a bat's sonar.

He and Naomi began their trip by boarding a northbound train. All bundled up in a winter coat and wearing glasses to obscure his still shut eyes; Nathan had no idea where they'd get off. Nor did he have any idea if their chosen stop would be their ultimate destination. Nathan didn't mind not knowing. In fact, he enjoyed having no knowledge of the immediate future.

Also Available from Montebello Books:

Dirty Hands

A novel by

T.R. Braxton

Terrell Hawkins, his closest cousin, and his best friend set out to have a good time on a Saturday night. Alcohol, marijuana, and immodest girls who like to partake in both are part of that pursuit. They don't expect the debauchery to end in tragedy, just as they don't expect their horrible response to embroil them in a struggle to avoid the authorities while growing increasingly distrusting of each other. Terrell and the others quickly learn that dirty hands can lead to desperate acts and that the worst of circumstances can cause even the best of friends to become enemies.

Available at Amazon.com, trbraxton.com, and everywhere books are sold.

ebook available at Amazon.com and trbraxton.com